I0673137

The Second

Prudence MacLeod

Published by Prudence MacLeod, 2024.

The Second
by
Prudence MacLeod
(second edition)

Copyright, Prudence MacLeod, December 29 / 2006

THE SECOND

First edition. March 26, 2024.

Copyright © 2024 Prudence MacLeod.

ISBN: 978-1927478790

Written by Prudence MacLeod.

Slave's Tale

"Tell us a tale, Mother," pleaded the boy, as his mother tucked the three siblings into their sleeping blankets. "Tell us the tale of Red Meera."

Their father snorted in derision, but the golden-haired woman smiled and nodded her head. "Alright, but then you must go right to sleep." With a sigh, she settled down beside the children and began the story that she had invented to entertain her babies. "Long ago, before any of you were born, there was a beautiful princess who lived in a land far away. One day some bad men came and took her away to be a slave. The men were cruel, and eventually she managed to escape them. She stole a ship and sailed it into the east.

"The men were very angry, and they chased after her, but they couldn't find her. Soon after that, a ship was seen in a far away land. The captain was now a pirate princess. Her name was Meera and she still sails around the world, and no one will ever catch her.

"There now, go to sleep for tomorrow is a new day, and it will be filled with new things."

As she slipped quietly away from the children, her mate spoke harshly, causing her to cringe. "Porga, why do you tell such lies to them? Red Meera's a pirate, a thief, and a murderer. She will make slaves of us all if she isn't stopped."

"To a slave it matters little which master they answer to."

"You are not a slave."

"You bought me. I dare not leave. What else should I call myself?"

"You are my chosen mate, now shut up and get over here to our bed. I've heard enough from you tonight. Displease me again and it is off to the great wheel for you."

Trying to hide her fear and disgust, she came to him. *"A slave by any other name is still a slave,"* she thought as she removed her poor garment. A few short moments later he grunted and rolled off her. She slept and dreamed of her days as a child at her father's house. Her last days of freedom, of joy.

A Fateful Meeting

It was a cold damp day in a strange land, but the three figures trudging along the remnants of an ancient roadway made no complaint. In truth, they barely made a sound, the thickness of their cloaks muffling the odd creak or rattle from their weapons. They had spent nearly a full season wandering through this region, learning what they could of the people, their language, customs, and beliefs. Much of what they had learned did not impress them.

The trail wound down the hillside and into a broad-leafed forest. As soon as they found a stream the leader and one companion stopped to rest, while the other ran on ahead. "What food is left, Kellan?" The leader spoke softly in a rich feminine voice. She shrugged off her cloak, revealing her well-muscled body that was barely concealed by a vest and short kilt. As the cloak settled to the ground, she sank into a cross-legged position upon it, pulling back her long dark hair and letting it fall down her back as she trained those piercing blue eyes on her companion.

"Little enough, Lady Meera." He sighed as he, too, let his cloak fall and sank onto it. "A little dried meat, nothing more." He rummaged in his pack for a moment, then pulled out a small leather bag which he passed to her. He was lean and hard muscled as well, but he was obviously older than she, with a road map of battle scars on his bare torso.

The woman cut off a small piece then passed back the bag as she popped the meat into her mouth and began to chew thoughtfully. A short while later the third traveler returned. "There's a small walled town up on the next hill, by the edge of a cliff." He grinned as he tossed down his cloak and sank onto it. "There seems to be some sort of gathering. The gates stand open, and no guards are posted." This one was young and, although somewhat brash, still in awe of the woman.

Meera grinned with delight, exposing her slightly canine teeth. "They will be in a festive mood. Perhaps we will do better at trading these strange coins; I could do with some decent food."

"Aye, that's the truth of it, Lady." The old warrior grumbled as he rose easily to his feet. "The land around here still holds traces of the poison, and you can taste it in the meat."

"You're spoiled, Father," laughed the youth. "Tella's cooking has you ruined."

"Sadly, Tallon my son, that's the truth of it."

"Enough, any more rest and you both will be ruined. Let's go see what the good folk of this land are celebrating." She rose gracefully to her feet, sweeping her cloak up around her broad shoulders as she did so. The younger man followed her lead.

As they neared the walled town on the hill, a woman's keening could be heard amid the rest of the babble. "Not a single guard posted," muttered Meera, as she passed through the open gate. "How have these fools managed to survive?"

"More by good luck than by good leadership, I'd wager." Tallon stepped forward as he spoke. A large man was approaching them with a glower on his face.

"Who are you? What do you want here?"

"We're traders from the south." Tallon had more easily mastered the language of this region, and so he usually spoke for them.

"Then where are your wares?"

"We were set upon by robbers some days ago," Tallon lied easily. "All we have left to us is a few coins. We would trade them for food and safe passage on the next ship leaving your fair city."

"You're far too smooth of tongue, boy." The man snarled as he stepped closer to go nose to nose with Tallon. "I think you're a band of pirates from the west. Red Meera's been raiding up and down these coasts for years; I think you're some of her men. Today is a Day of Justice; perhaps we should slay a few pirates as well."

"Hold, Broc," called another man, as he approached from a nearby hut. This man was obviously the one in charge, for all gave way at his approach. "We don't slay travelers without good reason. Bring them here."

Through the entire exchange the woman's moans could be heard. As they rounded one hut, Meera was suddenly confronted by the author of the keening. A woman was tied, naked and face down over a large cask, her legs spread well apart exposing her genitals to the world. She had been beaten, and her head crudely shaved. The bodies of three children and a young man lay piled a few feet in front of her. Their throats had all been cut.

The woman's voice fell silent the moment her eyes met Meera's. Something in those steely blue eyes cut through her pain like a knife. Meera spoke no word, but her eyes went to Tallon's, and he nodded slightly.

"Welcome, travelers." The man in charge approached them with a gesture of greeting. "My name is Born the Strong; I'm chieftain of this clan, and ruler of this city."

"I'm Semon, a trader from the south." A sly grin played at Tallon's lips. "My companions are my parents. Unfortunately they have not managed to learn much of your form of speech. Such things are more difficult for the elderly. Tell me, great chieftain, what has transpired here this day?"

"This day, friend Semon, I have rooted out a serpent from my own household. That thing there, was once a slave. (Here he spat on the helpless woman tied before him.) I freed her and made her my companion, giving her status, and giving her children. I discovered that she has been unfaithful to me all these years, and so I have cast her out and passed judgment upon her.

"Her children I have slain, as I cannot be certain of their parentage. The other is her lover. She has been shaved in shame, and staked out for any man who wants her until the rising of the tide. Broc himself has had her thrice already." He laughed harshly then went on. "When the tide is full she will be bound and thrown from the cliffs into the sea. Perhaps the sea gods will accept the sacrifice and bring us good weather for fishing."

Through all this speech Meera had not spoken a single word, nor had she shown any emotion at all. Kellan grinned as he saw the shift of her shoulders. He, too, eased his weapons beneath his cloak. He had to agree with Meera; this fool surely needed killing. The fact that they were badly outnumbered concerned him, but he did not let it show.

"Come friends and travelers, we go to the sacred hill to await the tide with food and drink." Born waved them on as he turned and led the gathering up the hill toward the cliff edge. He paused to look back, and saw the three strangers still gathered around the tormented woman. A look of concern crossed his face as he called out to them. "Hey there, what are you doing?"

Meera swept her cloak from her shoulders and sat cross-legged upon it near the woman's head. The cloak settled to the ground, covering most of the dead lying before her.

Tallon smiled easily as he responded to the chieftain's concern. "It is the custom of our people to prepare each person bound for Summerland. Our wise woman will sit the death watch with this one."

"Leave her, she is for the use of the men until the tide comes full," growled Broc, as he returned to where they stood. "I think want her again."

Broc stepped behind the helpless woman, unfastening his breeks, but Kellan stepped in his way and swept a knife to the man's throat. "Not pirate," he snarled into the frightened man's face. "Me want her." The terrified Broc backed away as Kellan turned to the stricken woman and stepped close behind her. She gasped as she felt the warmth of his kilt and leggings against her bare body, and then his warm woolen cloak was swept over her, hiding her from view. He began to rock back and forth gently, keeping her warm and covered.

Some of the townsmen began to return, but Tallon swept aside his cloak, allowing his weapons to show. He slid his long sword easily from the scabbard as his cloak settled over the dead children. Tallon grinned as he leaned on the hilt of his sword. "Father is old and will need to take his time. He will probably not finish before the rising of the tide."

At this point the chieftain called out again. "Leave them, Broc, the tide is nearly full anyway. There's no need to shed blood over something as foul as that thing."

The woman sobbed a thank you, as her body began to soak up the warmth of Kellan's cloak. "Why are you not using me, good sir?"

"In another time and place, did you come to him with smiles and a willing heart, perhaps he might, but not this way; it is unworthy." Tallon replied softly to her question as he kept a wary eye on Broc and the others. He then switched back to their own language. "We have little time now, the tide comes swiftly. Lady, what is our course?"

Through all the exchange Meera had not budged from her spot, nor had she stopped crooning softly in a language the woman could not understand. At Tallon's question her eyes snapped back into focus. She reached out to lightly caress the woman's abused scalp, gently touching a remaining tuft of blonde hair. "She's a golden hair, Tallon. Golden hair brings good luck, so we'll take her with us."

"They'll put up a struggle, Lady," Kellan said softly, "there are only three of us, and she has been bound a long time. I doubt she can run or fight."

"I know, Kellan. When they come for her, back away. Return for the ships and sail north. Take the entire fleet to our stronghold at the abandoned place of the ancients. Secure the area and prepare for winter. I will join you later. Tallon, when the time is right you will take my cloak and weapons, and then join Kellan on the trail."

"Lady, what are you going to do?" Tallon asked softly.

"I'll take to the waters with our new friend. Be ready now, Mista comes with the tide."

"What did she say?" the woman asked softly.

Tallon patted her shoulder gently as he replied. "Hush now. Your life is about to change. It will not end this day, but it will change. For good or ill, I cannot say."

"It could not possibly be more ill."

"Then trust and be ready. Hush now for here they come."

Over the Edge

Kellan suddenly withdrew from the woman. She gasped as the warmth of the cloak was withdrawn, and the cold dampness of the sudden fog seemed to envelope her. "Mista has arrived with the tide as you said, Lady. Stay sharp, Tallon my son, and stay close to Lady Meera. When it happens it will happen quickly, and you will need to be swift. You must catch me on the trail, for I cannot wait for you."

"I am the rider of the storms; I'm the dancer on the winds, Father." Tallon grinned wolfishly, his long canine teeth gleaming in the dim light. "I'll catch you, have no fear." Kellan chuckled and seemed to vanish into the thick gathering fog. He had high hopes for his brash young son, but here in this strange land, and so very far from the old empire, opportunities for advancement might be few and far between.

Broc and several men with spears approached. "Enough. Where is that old fool?"

"She has taken the good from him." Tallon slid his sword back into the scabbard and stepped aside. "He has gone to rest, recover his strength, and savor the delights he has tasted."

"Well it will have to last him a lifetime; the tide has come, and her fate with it." Broc spat on the ground as he spoke. The men with spears watched the strangers carefully as Broc cut the woman's bonds then jerked her to her feet. She stumbled and fell, but was hauled roughly back upright. Half dragged, half stumbling, the woman was forced to climb the hill to the waiting Born. Her hands were bound again as were her feet, and then two men grabbed her arms and jerked her to the edge of the cliff.

As the woman was led up the hill to the edge of the cliff, Meera's shoulders squirmed under her cloak. Unseen by the others, her kilt and vest were passed to Tallon who stowed them in a pack inside his own cloak. Soon her two short swords, and the harness that held them, as well as two of her four daggers, came his way and were stowed out of sight. As the prisoner was moved to the edge, Tallon stepped close behind Meera. His heart was racing now, for he could guess what she was going to do.

"Death to all deceivers," roared Born. He gave the signal and the men thrust the hapless woman over the edge.

Even as the words escaped his lips, and the woman screamed, Meera swept the cloak from her shoulders. Tallon caught it easily as Meera sprang past the startled townsfolk to the cliff edge, easily ducking past, and brushing aside, their feeble attempts to stop her. Naked, except for her boots and the dagger clenched between her teeth, she charged past the men with spears. Both men at the edge screamed as her wide-swept arms struck them a hammer blow, carrying them both over the cliff with her. Everyone surged toward the edge of the precipice, and in that moment, Tallon vanished into the mist.

As the bound prisoner fell helplessly toward the dark waters below she did not see the strange woman knock the men off the cliff. They fell as wildly as she, but the warrior woman turned her fall into a graceful dive. Unable to turn in the air with her hands and feet bound, the condemned woman struck the waters with a hammer blow that drove all the air from her lungs. She fought desperately not to inhale as the waters closed over her, and then strong hands seized her waist, thrusting her upwards to the surface where she lay gasping in her rescuer's arms.

"Swim?" Meera asked around the dagger in her mouth.

"Yes."

"Be still." She tried to be still as Meera disappeared beneath the surface. Suddenly her feet were cut free, then her rescuer resurfaced to cut the bonds on her wrists.

"The razor fish..."

"I know. Stay here." Meera vanished again and the former prisoner tried to make as little movement as possible. She could hear Born shouting for his men to find and kill them. The two men in the water were calling for help as well. Suddenly they screamed and then there was a great threshing of the waters as the razor fish feasted.

Meera swam deep beneath the waters, avoiding the razor fish which like to feed at the surface. Coming up beneath the men in the water, she slashed at their legs with her dagger then swam away quickly. The blood would draw the fish.

Meera suddenly reappeared at the woman's side. "Quickly now, follow me." The woman didn't understand the words, but she got the idea. Struggling to keep Meera in sight in the heavy mist and heaving icy cold seas, she forced her exhausted battered body onward.

"There are men on the beach, but we have little choice," breathed Meera as she returned to the woman's side. "Come, I will help you now." The woman had not understood the words, but with strong hands to help buoy her, she made much better time. Soon the roar of the surf was closer, and then the grip of the waves took her ashore. She was hurled onto the gravel beach, but the waters tried to drag her back.

Again Meera's hands caught her and pulled her from the water's deadly grip. "Hush now," whispered Meera, laying her finger along her lips for silence, "the men are near."

They lay behind a log on the beach as six men with spears tromped by. "How are we supposed to see anything in this bloody fog?"

"We heard the screams and the razor fish thrashing about; I say they are all dead. Let's go home to a meal and a warm bed; we can look for whatever's left of the bodies when the sun burns off this accursed fog."

"Agreed," replied the first voice as the men turned back. They climbed into their boat then disappeared into the mist. Meera suddenly realized how hard her companion was shivering. She had to get her warm, and soon.

"Come, quickly but silently now. Mista will hide our passage, but her breath is cold, and we must find shelter." With Meera's help the woman struggled to her feet, and then, despite the pain in her body, followed her rescuer up the beach to the base of the cliff. A short while later Meera found a tree that had fallen from the forest above. A few moments' work with her dagger and she had secured a number of branches. She burrowed into the sand beneath the sheltering tree, made a small bed, then motioned her companion to join her there.

Meera's heart melted at the look of fear in the woman's eyes. "You do not understand a word I say, do you?" She smiled gently. "We need to get warm, and we can do that more easily together. Come to me now."

She smiled as she patted the sand and, shivering violently, the woman lay down tentatively beside her. Meera covered them both with branches then cuddled the woman into her arms. "Sleep now and rest. Tomorrow is a new day, and we must be rested to face it." Suddenly the exhausted woman melted into those friendly arms and began to sob uncontrollably. Meera held her gently, crooning soothing sounds, until the shivering stopped, and the woman cried herself to sleep.

The abused woman awakened in gentle arms to the crippling pain in her own body, and to the sounds of Meera's deep rhythmic breathing. It took a few moments for her to remember all that had happened the day before, but the aches and pains of her injuries brought the memories with them. As her bladder cried out for relief she tried to ease herself from her companion's embrace.

"Leaving me to freeze in the mist?" Meera asked softly, struggling with the woman's language.

"I must relieve myself, Lady," came the soft frightened answer.

"All right, you first. I'll remain here to hold the warmth in. When you've returned I'll go."

The newly freed captive made her way painfully a few paces then squatted to relieve herself. The fog was thick and she was once again shivering violently when she returned. Gratefully she snuggled back into the warm spot in the sand, and into Meera's waiting arms. She was held gently once again until she was warm and the shivering stopped.

"There, that's better. Tell me, what's your name, my new traveling companion?" She grinned ruefully at the woman's confused expression. "Name?"

"Whatever name you give me, Mistress," was the soft tentative reply. "I am your slave now. Whatever name you give me, I will answer to." Meera rose up on one elbow and gazed into her eyes with a puzzled expression. "Your slave," said the woman softly with down cast eyes. "You give me name."

"I am neither so lazy, nor infirm, that I need a slave. I prefer a traveling companion. You can't understand me, I know. Let me try again. Your mother, name you did she? What name?"

"Oona." The woman smiled with delight as understanding hit her. She was to have one of her most precious things returned to her, the name her mother had given her.

"My name is Meera." Meera smiled at her puzzled expression. "Meera," she said as she placed her hand on her breast. "Oona." Meera touched Oona's chest gently. "Meera, Oona, no slaves here. Friends only. Now, Oona, are you warm enough again?"

"Yes, Lady," replied Oona as she got the gist of the question.

"Good, for I must abandon you for a few moments. Do not fear, I will return soon." Meera chuckled, as the realization that the

Red Witch of the Western Isles was her rescuer began to register on Oona's face. It was obvious that Meera's reputation had reached all parts of this huge island.

Meera swiftly returned, snuggling into the warmth of their small shelter. "Now, Oona, tell me of this place. Can we move north along the beach or are there more cliffs?" Meera chuckled at Oona's expression then tried again. By using some sign language and a few words they were able to communicate.

"This beach is small, Lady Meera," Oona replied deferentially. "We can't go far and we can't return. When the sun rises men will come in boats to see what the tide has dropped here. They will find us then and kill us."

"Only by boat can we be reached?"

"Yes, none can climb the cliffs."

"All right. We need food, fire, clothing, weapons, and a boat. Let us begin with what we have now, my boots, and a dagger each."

"A dagger each?"

"This one for you." Meera smiled as she sat up and passed the dagger to Oona hilt first. "And the one in my boot for me. Now, you make a fire while I see about food." Meera pulled a small piece of flint from the top of her boot and passed it to Oona, who nodded that she understood. As graceful as a hunting cat, Meera rose to her feet and disappeared into the mist.

"What harm can it do," sighed Oona, as she began to search for dry tinder. "I may as well be warm while waiting for death to come. I will join my children soon enough."

She had a fire going and was warming up nicely when Meera, dripping wet, returned with a good sized flat fish. Meera cut the fish into four strips then squeezed one over her mouth and drank the water. Oona looked puzzled as Meera passed her a piece, but she tried it. The water was surprisingly refreshing. Meera poked sticks through the remaining pieces of fish and cooked them by the fire.

Soon they were well fed and warm as the sun burned away the fog and mists.

Oona sighed with near contentment as she finished her piece of fish. Meera grinned at her and passed over most of her own fish. "But, Lady, you must eat too."

"You are wounded, Oona; your need is greater. I'll get more food soon, but for now you must eat." Oona smiled shyly as she accepted the fish and the gesture, if not understanding of the words. "Now then, we have our food and our fire. Let's take our ease until the rest arrives."

"The rest?"

"You did say that men would come here."

"Yes."

"Then our clothing, weapons, and boat are on their way. All we can do now is rest and wait."

"Lady Meera, those men will have fishing spears. They will use them to kill us."

Meera smiled reassuringly at her new friend. "I'm not as easy to kill as a fish. Do not fear, rest now."

Oona lay beside the fire, allowing the warmth of the sun on her back and the fire before her, to soothe her aching, bruised, body. Meera smiled as sleep claimed her companion and she dozed fitfully, the pain in her body disturbing her rest.

Meera gently shook Oona awake, and she awakened to the soft snarl of an animal nearby. Oona spun about fearfully, and was startled again to hear that feral growl come from Meera's throat. Following Meera's gaze out onto the waters she saw two small boats, with three men in each, bobbing toward them. There were two spearmen and one rower per boat.

"Arise, Oona, our boat is about to arrive. Go to the base of the cliff now and hide yourself as best you can. You're still wounded, and I am the warrior here. Leave this to me." Oona didn't understand the words, but she understood the gesture, and needed no further urging as she scurried to the base of the cliff and hid behind a large piece of driftwood. She looked back in time to see Meera race down the beach and dive into the cold waters of the sea.

The men had also seen Meera run down the gravel beach, and they rowed quickly toward that spot, readying their spears as they did so. They were startled as she came up beside one boat and hauled a man into the water from behind. The small boat flipped over with his struggles and three men were in the water. Meera was beneath the waves again, and her dagger slashed at the flailing legs beneath the surface. As soon as blood entered the water she dove deep and swam towards shore.

As Meera climbed back onto the beach she could hear the screams of the dying men, and the thrashing of the waters, churned up by the razor fish as they feasted. The men in the other boat didn't try to rescue their friends in the water, for they knew they too would soon be fish food if they did. They rowed swiftly toward shore where Meera was wringing the water from her hair. She waved at them then ran up the beach to the fire where she turned at bay, scooping a stone into each hand.

The cursing men beached their boat, and then charged up the gravel slope toward Meera. The man in the lead hurled his spear with all his might, but she easily danced out of its path. Oona gasped in fright as the next two spears flew toward Meera, but again Meera was able to avoid the deadly missiles. Leaping high into the air, she turned a complete somersault as the spears passed harmlessly beneath her. Meera landed easily on her feet. She grinned wolfishly at the advancing men.

The three men drew their long, sharp, fish knives and charged toward her, spreading out as they did so. Meera grunted with the effort as she hurled one of her stones at the nearest man. He managed to dodge it, but the second stone was deadly. It struck him squarely in the belly, driving the air from his lungs. Grinning, Meera pulled the dagger from her boot and motioned the other men to come on.

As they closed with her, Meera dove to the ground, rolling past them and driving her dagger deep into one man's hamstring. Howling in pain, the crippled man sank to the earth. Leaping to her feet again, Meera hurled her dagger with all her might. The last man gasped, then sank to his knees with the knife protruding from his throat. He slowly fell sideways, dead.

Meera spun back to the one she has crippled, and twisted out of the way of his slashing knife. Scooping up another stone, she hurled it at his face. With a sickening smack it took his life. Meera spun around again to face the first man she had felled; he was already back on his feet. He charged at her, flailing wildly with the knife in his hand, but she danced easily out of harm's way. With a diving roll Meera came back to her feet near the fire. Snatching a burning brand from the fire, she faced him.

Suddenly a stone whizzed past his head, and he ducked involuntarily. Meera was on him then, and they fought for the knife. Using combat techniques unknown in the east, she managed to squirm behind him, then take him down. Gripping his knife hand tightly in both of hers, Meera managed to wrap her powerful legs around his neck and choke the life from him. A moment later he lay dead at her feet. They now had cloaks, knives, spears, and a boat. It was shaping up to be a good day.

Meera swiftly yanked off the last man's tunic and set to work with her knife, motioning for Oona to approach. As Oona drew near, Meera wrapped her handiwork around the woman's waist and tied it there. Oona now had a passable kilt. They gathered the spears and knives, then headed for the boat.

Another surprise was waiting for them in the poorly made craft, some food, and a water skin nearly full. The men's cloaks were there as well, and Meera swept one of the rough woolens around her companion's shoulders, then helped her into the boat. Just as Meera was pushing the craft into the surf there was a shout from the cliffs above, and a spear rattled on the gravel as it narrowly missed them. Meera gave a mighty heave, and then, as the small round boat gained the waters, she leaped aboard and began to row with all her might.

They had barely gained open water when Oona shouted a warning, and pointed back toward the town. There was another boat coming after them. This one was a long boat, much sleeker and faster. It had four men rowing and two spearmen in the bow. Meera snarled and renewed her efforts.

Oona was terrified; she knew they couldn't outrun the larger craft. Suddenly she realized that Meera was chanting. She turned to see Meera chanting in that unknown tongue, her oar strokes matching her song and lending her strength. Meera's eyes were focused on another world, and she seemed oblivious to this one.

The larger boat was gaining, and Oona could hear the shouted threats of the men. Born himself was in the bow with a spear. Suddenly Oona shivered as a cold damp breeze bit through the cloak around her shoulders. She looked up to the sky to see great dark clouds building swiftly above them. Thunder crashed and lightning split the sky as the rain began to fall in torrents. The sky darkened further, and to Oona's horror, Meera turned the small craft and headed straight out to sea. A few strokes of the oars later, Born turned back. He would not risk the open water in a storm like this.

Oona bailed as best she could. She heard Meera's soft growl and chuckle as she turned the boat back toward shore once again. Meera rowed around the headland, then beached the craft near a stream. It was nearly filled with water by this time. Gathering the weapons and the food, Meera urged Oona up the beach and into the trees.

In what seemed like little time at all, Meera had her cloak spread on branches for a shelter and a small fire blazing cheerily. Oona lay beneath the shelter, warming herself by the fire and marveling at her rescuer who was already asleep. Oona put another stick on the fire then snuggled closer to Meera.

Northward Bound

Kellan had traveled swiftly. It would take many days to reach the ships, and weeks more to reach the abandoned city of the ancients. Meera was smart, for she'd known that the docks of the ancients would still be usable, to a degree. Some of the fallen buildings would make fine shelters as well. The new capitol city was growing rapidly as the builders plied their trade with vigor.

The problem would be providing enough food for the entire fleet, as well as the small army of warriors still loyal to Meera. There were all the families of the common folk who had managed to join them to be fed as well. The capitol would also need a name.

With a deep sigh Kellan decided to make an early camp, even though there was still plenty of daylight left, he began to look for a likely spot. It had been days now, and still there was no sign of Tallon. This wasn't good, Tallon should have overtaken him before this.

Kellan worried about his only son. The boy had a wealth of talent, and was a skilled warrior, but here in this strange land, how was he to help Tallon advance? Back in the isles he would have built Tallon a ship of his own by now, but, ah well... Suddenly he smelled the aroma of cooking food on the breeze. Kellan faded into the bushes, then approached the bend in the trail with caution.

"Hungry, Father?" called Tallon, a huge grin on his face.

"What took you so long?" groused Kellan as he entered his son's small camp.

"The hunting was poor. Still, I knew you'd be hungry by now, so I kept at it. It's not much, but you can eat it."

"Not bad," Kellan grunted as he tore off a bite of meat with his fangs. "So, what happened?"

"Lady Meera took to the waters, just as she said she would," replied Tallon. "She took a few with her as well. I could hear them screaming as the razor fish feasted on them."

"And the lass?"

"Still alive and with the Lady, I'd wager, by the size of the hue and cry."

"Hung around to see the fun did you?"

"Just a bit. They were pretty upset at losing their sacrifice."

"Bloody fools. Are they following us?"

"Some are, and they're close. We'd better eat up then get on the road if we want to avoid a battle."

"Aye, well, we'll be on shipboard by nightfall anyway, if we hurry. Kieran should be anchored just beyond that next rise."

"Then let's go, Father. I'll feel a lot better with a deck under me."

They kicked out the fire and set out again. They hadn't gone far when they heard the shouts of their pursuers behind them. Breaking into a run, they made for the next rise and the beach beyond. They were only halfway up the hill when a troop of armed fighters charged down the slope. The men sped past them and straight at their pursuers who turned tail and fled.

"Well met, Kieran!" Kellan seized the huge man's forearm in the warrior's greeting.

"Well met, brother," smiled the big man. "What have you done with our queen?"

"Lady Meera has another errand, Uncle." Tallon grinned as he, too, greeted the big man with a warrior's grip.

"We go north, Kieran, to the city of the ancients. Lady Meera says she will join us along the way."

"You doubt her, Kellan?"

"Nay brother, but she has stirred up a school of razor fish this time. She may have trouble shaking off the hunters."

"You can tell me all on board ship," sighed Kieran. "Come." He led them down to the beach where three long boats with full crew waited. In the harbor was a fleet of sixty ships anchored, each one flying the green flag of Queen Meera of the Western Isles.

"SO THAT'S THE TALE of it," sighed Tallon, as he leaned back against a coil of rope and relaxed.

"We'll need more food and supplies," grunted one of the sixty captains gathered on the deck of Kieran's ship, "if we're to last the winter."

"That we will." Kellan rose to his feet as he spoke. "I know just where to start the gathering."

"Planning to take the hunters off the lady's trail, Father?"

"Indeed I am, Tallon, my son. I don't like the idea of her traveling alone without food or clothing either. That poor lass was pretty beat up, and she may not be able to travel well. Tallon, you take one ship and see if you can locate Lady Meera. The rest of us will begin gathering supplies for the long winter ahead."

"Alright, Father. Which ship shall I take? I'd prefer The Hound if I can choose, she's the smallest and the most nimble inshore."

"The Hound is my ship, young Tallon." A huge misshapen manlike creature, a Trog, rose to his feet as he spoke. As tall as Kellan and twice as thick, the creature looked truly formidable. Trogs were forest dwellers by nature, and savage fighters. They lived in small tribes and seldom had anything to do with other folk. This one was the first to try seafaring. They weren't particularly good at it. "It will be a pleasure to have you aboard as passenger."

Tallon rose easily to his feet as well. "A ship can have only one captain, Master Kreeg. You can have her back when I'm finished with her."

"The Hound is my ship." Kreeg hefted a huge war club and slapped it against his massive hand. "You ride as passenger, boy, or not at all."

"The Hound is Lady Meera's ship, Kreeg," snarled Kieran, as he and the others rose to their feet and drew swords. "You sold the ship to her in exchange for your life. She sails under anyone Lady Meera appoints. In Lady Meera's absence, Kellan speaks for her. Tallon commands the Hound. You will serve here on the Raven."

"Actually, I have another task for Captain Kreeg and his men," Kellan grinned, as he sank back to his seat on the deck. The others followed his lead, and the tension was relieved. They all resumed their seats, and only the Trog remained standing, his great weapon still at the ready.

"What might that be, Kellan?" Kreeg eyed Kellan suspiciously.

"You lads make poor sailors, Kreeg. I'm going to give you a castle in exchange for your ship."

Kreeg slowly lowered his club. "A castle you say? Very well, I'll return to The Hound and ready my crew. The ship is yours, boy." He turned away and climbed over the side to the waiting boat below.

"Bringing the Trog among us was a mistake," grunted one of the other captains, as Kreeg's boat pulled away. "They don't really understand the idea of cooperation, or chain of command. Trogs work toward their own good, nothing more."

"Agreed," sighed Kellan, "but don't let Lady Meera hear you say it."

"You can't trust Kreeg," said another. "Especially now."

"I know, but I have an idea that will make the Trogs work for us, even if they don't know they're doing it. I don't trust his crew either. I'd like Tallon to have a crew of our folk on board that ship."

"Agreed," said Kieran, rising to his feet and addressing the assembled captains. "Each captain here shall give up one trusted man for Tallon's crew. We'll spread the Trogs out among the rest of us, one to a ship. We should be able to keep an eye on them that way, at least until we land them. I'll take Kreeg myself."

"I'm growing bored with all this lying about," said a battle-scarred woman who was standing nearby. "I still have keen eyes, and Tallon will need a mate he can trust."

"Tella, you're a dream come true," laughed Tallon, "but I doubt father will be willing to part with you."

There was a great round of laughter at that, and Kellan shook a threatening finger at Tallon. "Ah well, Tella has the truth of it, Tallon." Kellan grinned as he gripped her arm affectionately. "He will need someone to keep him out of trouble, Tella my love, and there is none better suited for the task than you."

"Settled then," laughed Kieran. "Tallon, will you have Tella as mate on your ship?"

"In a heartbeat," replied Tallon. "There is no other better suited, or capable, of watching my back than Tella of Tragee."

It was thus decided. When Kreeg arose in the early morning, he was startled to find his ship surrounded closely by the fleet. He had actually thought of slipping away in the night, but had decided against it. It was too late now. Muttering under his breath, the big Trog watched sullenly as his crew was dispersed throughout the fleet, and his ship was taken over by an untried boy. Ah well, perhaps Kellan would honor his word. Kreeg would be a lot happier on land anyway.

"What a bloody mess," Tella sighed, as she stood gazing about. "Trogs are definitely not sailors." The new crew was now aboard and waiting for orders as the main fleet moved off north. "This was once a good ship, I'll wager, but just look at her now."

"Ah, she'll be just fine, Tella," laughed Tallon. "We just have to clean her up a bit."

"Shouldn't we be about the business at hand first, Captain?" Tella grinned as he visibly tried to adjust to being called captain.

"Aye mate," replied Tallon. "Make north. Keep out of sight of land until we're past the fleet. Set some of the crew on clean up duty. I don't want to bring the queen aboard a midden heap like this."

"Agreed, Captain."

"Tella?"

"Aye sir?"

"Teach me how to run a ship and be a good captain?"

"It'll be my pleasure, Captain. You've shipped with Lady Meera before. Just do what she would do."

"Sound advice, and I will heed it. Very well then, let's make north."

Tella began to shout commands and soon the oars were manned, the sail was up, and the small ship was on her way. As soon as everyone was busy, Tallon went among them, learning every man's name, and personally thanking him for joining the crew. It was well done, and Meera would have been proud of him.

Night came and went again, and the ship was looking a lot better. The decks were freshly scrubbed, the tangled ropes freshly coiled, and the tattered sails had been mended. A tall sailor approached Tallon and Tella. "Captain Tallon, sir."

"Eggar, isn't it?"

"Aye, sir."

"Eggar, the *sir* thing is starting to get annoying. I'm Tallon, only that and nothing more. I well remember, on that southern raid last season, the day you brained that galoot who was about to skewer me."

"Aye, and well do I recall you standing over my fallen Trudi, keeping the slavers off her," replied the tall man. "I recall the wounds you took, and I want you to know that I begged Captain Rogert for this berth. You've earned the right, and you are Captain Tallon." There was a cheer from the rest of the crew. As young as he was, Tallon was one of the most feared and respected fighters in the western fleet. "Captain, the rest of the crew and I think this is a fine ship and she has a lucky captain. There is only one thing more she needs."

"And what might that be?"

"A lucky name, Captain," replied Eggar, matching Tallon's grin.

"A fine idea that. Any suggestions?"

"We thought Raptor might suit her, Captain."

"I like it," laughed Tallon. "What think you, Tella?"

"It's a good name for a good ship," agreed Tella. "Somebody get over the side with some paint."

THREE DAYS LATER THE folk of Davor, the town where Born held sway, awakened to a strange and terrifying sight. It looked like the entire fleet of the Red Witch of the Western Isles lay off their tiny harbor. The marauders were already ashore and at the gate. One was calling for Born to come out. It was the old man who had been there with the mad woman; the one who had stolen Born's victim from right under his nose. Dear gods, that must have been Red Meera herself.

"He's not here, you old fool," bellowed Broc as he poked his head over the wall. "He's gone hunting for that runaway slave. Go away! Born is not here."

"Open the gate," shouted Kellan.

"I will not. Do I look like a fool?"

"Yes, you do," Kellan bellowed in reply. "Open the damned gate, or we will open it for you. If we have to open it ourselves, none will survive. Open up now, and none will be harmed."

Broc disappeared from the wall. A long moment later the gate opened slowly, and the westermen swarmed inside with drawn swords. The townsfolk were swiftly rounded up in the square and disarmed. Kellan spoke not a single word until all were present. "Well, Kreeg? Is this a fair trade for your ship?"

"What is the bargain, Kellan?" asked the misshapen man suspiciously. He still didn't trust Kellan, for trust does not come easy to a Trog.

"You shall govern this place, and surrounding lands, in the name of Queen Meera. We will take half the stored supplies for the fleet, and leave the rest for you. Each year a tenth portion of harvest will go to supply the fleet. If Meera goes to war, you will go to war as well. If you are attacked, we will come to your aid. With luck you should winter well. We'll contact you again in the spring. Agreed?"

"Agreed," grunted the huge Trog, well pleased with the bargain.

Kellan turned back to Broc and grinned. "This one is Kreeg. Kreeg is chieftain here now. Obey him and live. Defy him at your own peril." He laughed as Broc blanched at that announcement. The huge Trog was a frightening sight indeed.

"Hear me, people," shouted Kellan, raising his voice to reach all the gathered captives. "This fate is of your own making. Had you not mistreated one of your own so badly, we might have passed you by." Again he laughed as he turned away to direct the looting of the storehouses.

Kreeg spoke not a single word until the westermen were all back on shipboard. He grunted then and took the largest hut for himself, assigning his men to many of the rest. Those who were displaced were left to their own devices to find shelter. It wasn't until after the Trogs had confiscated all the weapons, that the townsfolk realized there were only fifty of them. While the westermen put back to sea there had been a chance, but now, without weapons, that chance was gone.

KELLAN SMILED AS THE Raven sped northward. "Lady Meera isn't going to like this," sighed Kieran as he leaned on the rail beside his older brother. "She had other plans for the Trogs."

"I know, but still, I'm well pleased with the way things have turned out."

"Why? Deliberately annoying Lady Meera is no cause to rejoice, brother."

"I'm pleased that my son now has a good ship of his own," grinned Kellan. "Also, we knew we had an enemy at that town. Now we have an ally."

"Aye, an ally that will bear watching."

"I know, Kieran, but we're rid of the Trogs for the winter, and I'm sure that Kreeg will thin out much of the opposition there by the time spring arrives."

"If he survives that long."

"Aye, but if he doesn't, he will deplete their numbers before he goes down, thus weakening them. If he does survive we have our ally in place. Lady Meera will see the sense of it all, I'm sure."

"I hope you're right, Kellan, for I've no desire to be an only child." Kieran grinned and slapped his brother on the back as he returned to the steering oar.

While the fleet sailed north to the place of the ancients, Tallon searched ever bay and cove for Meera. He was a long while finding her.

Healing

M eera awakened with a start as something cold touched her arm. She was on her feet with Oona's neck in her hands before she caught herself. Dropping the terrified woman to the ground, Meera stepped back and shook off the adrenalin rush that gripped her. Oona lay at her feet cringing in fear.

"Oona, sorry, I was startled. Did I hurt you?" Meera's voice was full of contrition. Oona did not understand the words, but the gentle hands that helped her to her feet, and the look of concern on Meera's face, eased her fears. She held out the leaves she had been trying to rub on Meera's scraped arm.

"For healing, Lady, not for harm." Oona spoke softly, her eyes downcast as she gently touched the bruised leaves to Meera's arm again. The annoying sting vanished almost instantly.

"You know the ways of healing?" asked Meera, as she sank to a cross-legged sitting position at Oona's feet, patting the ground beside her.

"Yes, Lady." Oona sat where Meera had indicated.

Meera sighed deeply as she put her arms around the smaller woman's shoulders and hugged her gently. "Oona, forgive me, I'm sorry to have hurt you."

"I'm not hurt, Lady, only frightened. You moved so quickly."

"We folk of the Western Isles are not like other folk, Oona. We see better and we can move faster." She released Oona then looked carefully at her. "They beat you very badly, Oona. We'll remain here a few days, until you're rested and your wounds have healed."

"Thank you, Lady, but Born will find us if we stay here."

Meera rose to her feet and offered her hand to Oona. She smiled wolfishly, exposing her long canines, as she helped the woman to her feet. "Born will be sorry if he comes. Oona, do not fear. I swear I will keep you safe. Can you find things here to help you heal?"

"Yes, Lady. There are many herbs here that I can use."

"Oona find healing herbs," grinned Meera. "Meera find food."

She swept up one of the fishing spears and returned to the beach where she found the boat full of water. With a mighty heave of a heavy stone she broke a large hole in its side. As soon as it was drained she dragged it into the waters and pushed it off to sink, the small round boat would not betray their location. She then returned to the task of fishing.

OONA'S MOVEMENTS WERE painful, but she managed to find several healing herbs near their small camp. She made a pulpy mass of several and was smearing them on her cuts and bruises when Meera returned with a razor fish nearly as big as Oona. "I'm not even going to ask how you managed that," sighed Oona, as she shook her head from side to side in disbelief.

"They are good to eat," grinned Meera. She had not understood Oona's comment, but she could guess. "Besides, you need boots."

"Boots?"

"Razor fish have tough hides." Meera began to expertly skin out the fish. She set the fish cooking over the fire and Oona placed some of her herbs on it. While the fish cooked, Meera scraped the fish hide then spread it out by the fire to dry.

Once the fish was eaten, and Oona warm by the fire again, Meera gently began to explore the woman's injuries. Oona had been badly beaten, worse than Meera had thought. It was a miracle that she had been able to walk at all on those battered feet. "They beat the bottoms of your feet?"

"Yes, with leather straps. It is very painful."

Meera sighed again and continued her exploration. "These will show scars," she said as she lightly touched the rope burns on Oona's wrists and ankles.

"I know. It doesn't matter, Lady."

"Some here as well," mused Meera, as she gently stroked Oona's scalp. "The hair will cover them."

Oona ran her fingers over her head for the first time and burst into tears. "It'll grow back." Meera spoke gently as she gathered the crying woman into her arms. "It will grow back."

"Born killed my children," sobbed Oona, as she fell into Meera's embrace. "They will not grow back."

Meera held her gently until the tears stopped. "Rest now, Oona." Meera lowered Oona back onto the bed of cloak and boughs that she had made for her. They rested for three more days in that small camp, waiting for Oona's body to heal. On the fourth day Oona awaken to see Meera by the fire, working busily with her dagger.

She had stiffened the thickest of the fish hide by the fire while alternately rubbing the softer skin with seaweed then drying it. Meera was now working the leather into shape. Oona watched as Meera pulled several strands of long dark hair from her head, then plaited them into a strong cord which she used to sew up the leather. Oona had never owned anything like the boots that Meera tossed to her.

"Try them."

Oona looked puzzled so Meera helped her put them on. The tall boots were surprisingly soft, and Meera had put moss inside for extra padding. The soles were hard, and as Oona took a few tentative steps, she broke out into a huge grin. These were the finest boots she could have imagined, and they were much like Meera's own.

"Razor fish have many uses," Meera smiled with delight as Oona took a few more dancing steps. "Feel strong enough to travel?"

"Yes, Lady, I could walk all across Mooreland in boots like these. Thank you for the wonderful gift."

"A traveler should always have a dagger in her boot." Meera knelt and placed one of the daggers in Oona's boot, showing her the proper way to do it so the knife would not chafe her leg. "And now for your kilt and cloak." She swept the cloak around Oona's shoulders. "A lady of the court is ready to travel."

"A woman of shame, that's what I am." Oona burst into tears. "As soon as anyone sees me, they will kill us."

"They will not. I won't allow harm to come to you, Oona." Meera gathered the distraught woman into her arms. She hadn't fully understood the words, but got the gist of it. "The shame lies in what was done to you, Oona, not in what you did."

"I did nothing."

"Oona?"

"Broc forced me, then told Born it was Atti. Born believed his brother."

"I'll kill them both one day," Meera growled protectively.

"Lady, you should leave me here. No one will have reason to attack you if I'm not with you."

Meera did not fully understand. "You want me to leave you here?"

Poor Oona had known more kindness from this legendary marauder in the past few days than she had experienced in many long years before. "No, Lady," she sniffed, "but safer for you."

Meera chuckled and gave Oona's shoulders a friendly squeeze. "I like you, Oona, I want keep you. We must travel by land now. We'd be seen too easily on the water." Oona nodded her agreement then stepped out of Meera's arms. They gathered what they wished to carry, then set out for the north.

Meera kept her pace very slow and she stopped often. Oona was healing up nicely, and Meera did not want to interfere with that. The first day they actually covered very little ground. Alone, Meera could have gone farther in an hour. Each day thereafter they increased their distance.

On the fourth day of travel they spotted another small, walled town, much like the one where they had first met. Meera gave it a wide berth, as Oona told her the chieftain here was a friend of Born's. A few days later they came upon a small village, just a few poor huts gathered together near a beach and stream. The place wasn't known to Oona so Meera decided to approach; she pulled Oona's cloak up into a hood and admonished her gently not to speak.

Meera approached a woman tending a cooking fire. She spoke slowly, struggling with the language. "Greetings, good woman."

"Who are you? What do you want here?" demanded the woman, as she straightened up from her task. She seemed frightened of them for some reason.

"We are travelers far from home," replied Meera slowly, stumbling over the words. "We're hungry and in need of food."

"We've heard of two women traveling alone." The voice came from a man who appeared from one of the huts. "We've been told to kill them on sight. They're very dangerous outlaws." Meera didn't understand fully, so Oona whispered in her ear.

"Who told you this?" she asked, once Oona had translated for her.

"A man who is chieftain of a clan to the south of here, came in a boat with many men." It was the woman who spoke first.

"He gave us food and said he would reward us greatly if we could show him we had done this," added the man. "I am sorry, but I must feed my children." He whipped out a long fish knife but it was gone from his hand in a heartbeat, and Meera's dagger was at his throat. She hadn't understood his words, but she understood the gesture.

Before anything more could happen there was a child's shout as a boy came running toward the huts. "Men in boats! Men in boats!" Indeed several men carrying weapons could be seen climbing from two boats. One of the men was Born. He saw Meera and Oona almost as soon as they saw him. Cursing, Meera thrust the man away from her and turned back toward the forest. Oona was already ahead of her.

Even as she ran, Meera heard the telltale grunt of effort behind her, and she turned in flight. Just in time, she easily dodged the fish spear that the man had hurled at her back. To the man's horror she scooped up the spear and took a few running strides toward him. He fell over backward as she hurled the spear with all her might. He needn't have worried; the spear wasn't meant for him.

The slender missile flew high above the frightened man, driving hard with deadly intent toward the men on the beach. There were shouts of alarm as the spear drove deeply into the ground just feet in front of Born. Grinning, Meera turned and followed Oona into the sheltering arms of the forest.

"This way, Oona," Meera called softly, as she turned off the trail and into the trees. Puzzled, Oona joined her. Laying her finger against her lips for silence, Meera led her companion off the path, then hid them behind a fallen log where they could still see the trail. A few moments later Born and his men went racing by. She gave them plenty of time before she sighed deeply and relaxed.

"Meera, why do we hide, should we not run as fast as we can?"

Meera smiled with delight, then replied in a voice so soft Oona could barely hear her. "They think we're afraid, so they think we will keep running."

"What will we do?"

"We rest. They'll return at dusk. Tired men sleep deeply and long. When they awaken we will be far away. Don't worry, Oona, they won't find us. I promised to protect you, Oona, and I will. I won't allow these men to harm you again."

For the first time, Oona asked the one question that burned in her mind. "Lady Meera, why?"

"Why?"

"Why do you risk so much for me? Why do you protect me?" It took a few tries, but Meera finally understood the question.

"Because no one else would, Oona," Meera sighed in reply. "Once I, too, was helpless and abused. No, not in the same way as you, but helpless nonetheless. Someone came to me at great risk, Oona; now I pass that to you. One day you will pass this to another. It is the way of good-hearted people."

Oona nodded thoughtfully as she gained the gist of what Meera had said. After some thought she spoke again. "Meera, where are you taking me?"

"I will take you to a place of safety, Oona. You will go wherever you choose from there."

"I was young, barely a woman, when the slavers came. They killed all the men and older women. They took the young women and children for slaves. I have known no place of safety since that time. There is no safe place for me to go, Lady. Can I not stay with you? My people were healers, and I can be of use to you."

Meera reached over to take Oona's hand in her own for a moment, as she searched the woman's eyes. "If that is your wish, my Lady Healer, then it will be so. I'll keep you with me always, so I can protect you."

Oona snuggled deeper into her cloak then with a tiny bemused smile. "Who could have guessed my fate?"

"Your fate?"

"I, a slave condemned to death, saved from the waters to become healer to the most feared woman in the known world."

"Rest now, my Lady Healer," smiled Meera, as she pulled her own cloak tighter and closed her eyes.

Meera awakened later to hear Oona's whimpers of fear. The woman was still asleep and dreaming. Meera gathered Oona into her arms, crooning soft soothing sounds as she did so, and soon the girl relaxed into a restful sleep once again.

Oona awakened much later, still cradled in Meera's arms. She lay still for a moment, reflecting that she had found a place of safety, for this was the first time she had felt safe in many long years.

"Awake, Oona?"

"Yes, Lady," replied Oona softly as she slowly untangled herself from Meera's embrace.

"Hush now, Born returns." They watched silently from the gathering shadows as the men returned to the beach and their boats. The muttering and complaining were easy to hear, and Meera grinned with delight as they passed.

The men were long out of sight, and darkness had fallen, before Meera stirred. "Wait here for me, Oona, I will soon return."

"Lady, it is dark. Where are you going?"

"We need supplies," Meera whispered in return. "I will return soon, then we can resume our journey."

"Lady, it's dark and you will lose you way. What...?"

Oona's question died on her lips, as the soft moonlight showed her Meera's eyes. They were no longer deep blue; they were now a feral yellow and the pupils were huge. "Do not fear, Oona. I can see quite well in the darkness." With that Meera vanished into the shadows of the forest, leaving Oona to ponder what she had seen. It was a long time before Meera returned.

Meera suddenly reappeared at Oona's side, frightening her half to death. "Come, Oona, we must be away from this place." She led Oona back to the trail, and then, shouldering a huge pack, she set out with Oona close behind. They were well away when dawn came.

"This is a good place to rest, Oona." Meera sighed with fatigue, as she dropped the pack to the ground. She produced some tinder and a fire starter kit from the pack, and soon had a small blaze going. Food, as well, appeared from the pack and was set to cooking on the flames.

"Lady, where did you get all this?" asked Oona, as she adjusted the sticks that held the cooking meat.

"Born is most generous. He has given us food and clothing."

"Lady?"

"As I guessed, Oona, those men slept soundly. I took food from them, another water skin, some leather to make carrying pouches for you to gather herbs into, a tunic that should fit you, and more weapons. I also made a few holes in their boats. They will be too busy making repairs and burying their dead to chase us now. We are well away."

"Burying their dead? Lady?"

"Born was too hard for me to reach, but I left two of his men with their own daggers in their hearts. They won't be in such a hurry to chase us any longer. Born has lost too many men because of this. He's paid too high a price; he'll return home now." Meera underestimated the man's determination, but even if he had wanted to, Born now had no home to go to.

BACK IN WHAT HAD BEEN Born's home, the new chieftain was establishing Trog rules. Trogs may not have the best of social graces, but they know how to fight as a unit, and once they're dug in, nothing short of a cataclysm can root them out.

The first morning in his new castle, Governor Kreeg had ordered every man, child, and woman capable of wielding arms, to begin training under the guidance of his own men. One span of time was allotted for training each day before any other work was done. Those who refused to train soon learned the meaning of Trog discipline. They trained. In fewer days than one might expect, the town was much better fortified, and guards patrolled the walls both day and night. Kreeg had been given a castle, and he meant to keep it.

Reunited

Meera and Oona traveled inland for a number of days. By now Meera had gained a good working knowledge of the local language, and was starting to teach Oona the western speech. They slowly worked their way around a small mountain range, taking their time, but ever moving northward. Meera wasn't concerned; she knew this land was just a big island. She'd already sailed completely around it before setting her plan in motion.

It was a sunny morning with a true nip in the air, when they found the river and wide valley below. Oona gasped and crouched fearfully behind a huge boulder. "I have heard of this place. It's a place of pure evil and sorrow."

Meera was beside her in a heartbeat, alert for whatever danger had frightened Oona. "What is it, Oona? Why do you fear this place?"

Oona replied in hushed tones. "It's the valley of the great wheel."

"The great wheel?"

"When runaway slaves are caught, they're sent here to die at the wheel. Born always threatened to send me here if I didn't please him, or if I tried to run away. See? There it is in the valley below."

Meera gazed at the thing in the distance in bemusement. It was a huge wheel with dozens of half starved people chained to the wooden spokes. As they pushed against the spokes the wheel slowly turned huge stones upon one another. "What is its purpose?"

"It's how the masters grind the grain, Lady. People from far and wide bring their grain here to be milled. The stones turning against each other makes the flour."

"Beasts could turn that wheel much easier," muttered Meera, "as could the waters of that river. What fool built it so far from the waters?"

"It was built as a punishment for slaves, and those who cannot pay their debts. This year Broc had to send his eldest daughter, Morel, here to pay for the grinding of his grain. I can see her from here. There on the right, she's the tall one with the red hair."

Just as Oona spoke a guard took the girl from the wheel and dragged her aside. She was forced to serve him then she was put back on the wheel. "I'll cut out his heart for that," snarled Meera, but Oona gently gripped her arm to hold her back.

"No Lady, there are too many. See there. Those men riding from that castle on the far hill? They control the whole valley, and the wheel belongs to them, as do the slaves. One half of all the grain that is ground they keep for themselves. They're well fed and well armed. We should avoid them. We cannot help Morel now."

Meera sighed deeply and relaxed her posture. "I bow to your greater wisdom, Oona. One day I'll return to this place, and put a stop to that hateful practice. We'll rest here until nightfall, then we'll steal one of those boats and make our way down river to the sea. It should be safe enough for us on the water now, and I'd like to catch up with the fleet before the snows begin to fall."

They sat in silence for a long time, watching the valley below, Oona shuddering at the fate she had so narrowly escaped, and Meera planning how she was going to commandeer a boat. At length Oona spoke again, voicing another question that had been on her mind.

"Lady, you do not like the keeping of slaves, do you?"

"No, Oona, I don't; it is hateful to me."

"But all great chieftains have slaves, don't they? Men judge their wealth, strength, and power, by the number of slaves they own, do they not?"

"Owning slaves makes one neither great nor strong, Oona," sighed Meera. "Slaves make one dependent and weak. Our legends say the elder folk once met a golden-haired people long ago. The golden-haired ones enslaved many of the elder folk, but the westerfolk make poor slaves. They revolted and enslaved the golden-haired ones, but they didn't make docile slaves either. The battles were long and many, and few of either race were left alive at the end. Of those remaining, a number decided to blend their folk together, and agreed that never again would any of them ever keep slaves.

"As the two peoples blended, they created a new people. The new westerfolk had some of the wildness of their elderkin, and some of the more clever ways of the golden-haired people. There are few among us now with brown eyes, and there has not been a child with golden hair in two generations."

"The elder folk were not human, were they, Meera?"

"No, Oona, they were not truly human, although some believe they once had been. Most say we westerfolk are not fully human either."

"I believe that; you are far too honorable to be truly human."

"You haven't fared well at the hands of your fellow humans, Oona. Life among the westermen will be better for you."

"I truly hope it will," Oona replied with down cast eyes.

"Oona, this accursed wheel has you upset. I promise this will not ever be your fate. You're safe with me. I'll always protect you from harm."

"I do feel safe with you, Lady Meera. It's been a long time since I felt safe."

"But?"

"I am a woman shamed and cast out. Are you so sure your people will accept me among them?"

"Oona, you have asked to stay with me, have you not?"

"Yes Lady, that is my wish."

"Then you must trust in me to keep you safe. Believe me, my people will treat you with the respect and honor you deserve, Oona."

"Meera?"

"Hush now and trust."

"Yes Lady, I will trust. Oh dear gods..."

As Oona gasped and covered her mouth with her hand, Meera spun as quickly as a cat to see what had frightened her companion. There was a boat, with six men rowing, making its way up the river. Born was standing in the bow, a spear in his hand. "Does that fool never know when to quit?" Meera muttered under her breath. "He's truly starting to get on my nerves."

"You took me away from him, Lady. He's sworn to see me dead. That man will never stop."

"Oh yes he will," snarled Meera. "I'm growing quite tired of this man. Ah well, let's see what he is about."

They watched intently as a dozen riders left the castle on the hill and charged at Born's boat. Armed men were not allowed in the valley. Stepping ashore, Born laid his weapons on the ground just as the lead rider reached him. The rest of his men cast their weapons on the ground as they were surrounded. There was a lot of talk, then the riders turned their tall lanky horses back toward the castle. Born's men hauled up the boat and began to make camp. Born went to sleep that night, completely unaware that the object of his search was close enough to strike him with a stone.

OONA HUDDLED BESIDE the small boat Meera had cut loose and pushed into the river. Having stored all their gear and supplies in the boat already, Oona was holding it for Meera's return, and she didn't have too long to wait. Like a hunting shadow, Meera appeared from the darkness and helped Oona into the boat.

Stepping in herself, she then pushed off with an oar. Meera relaxed back and let the river current carry them down stream, away from the wheel and the sleeping Born. Oona could see Meera's canine teeth as the moonlight glittered off her wide grin.

"Lady, what did you do?"

Meera chuckled her delight as she answered. "Born has generously donated more food. He has another man to bury as well."

"Lady, it frightens me that you take so many risks."

"Oona?"

"I want you to be safe, too."

"We'll both be safe very soon now, my Lady Healer. The river will take us to the sea, and the sea will return us to our people. I'm tiring of this foolish game. Rest now, my Oona, all is well."

Oona slept fitfully, and awakened several times in the night as the boat bumped along. She awakened fully as she heard Meera's growling snarl, and opened her eyes to see Meera at the oars. She was rowing hard, but the pursuing boat, with Born in the bow, was gaining swiftly. Meera's growl changed into her chant and, before they could be overtaken, the small boat reached the sea and was engulfed in a dense fog bank. Meera rowed straight into the fog and didn't stop.

Eventually Meera had to rest, and she stopped rowing and chanting. She leaned heavily against the rail, her breathing labored from her exertions. As her chant died on the air, the sun began to burn away the fog. Suddenly Oona screamed as she saw Born's boat appear out of the fading mist. He was almost upon them.

Meera screamed her challenge as she leaped to her feet and whipped out her daggers. Her battle cry changed to a laugh of pure delight, as a small war ship flying her colors, the green sea dragon, burst from the fog and bore down on Born and his men like a harbinger of death. The tide had turned now, and Born was shouting orders while his crew rowed like madmen.

Oona recognized the young captain of the ship, as the Raptor swept alongside their small boat. Meera fairly tossed her into the waiting arms of the men above. Oona was set easily on the deck as Meera swarmed over the side of the ship, bawling orders as she came. Oona cowered beside the rail as the sailors leaped to obey Meera's commands. As graceful as the bird she was named for, the ship turned and bore down on Born's fleeing boat. Meera stood at the bow of the ship, clutching a long spear.

Meera's revenge was not to be however, as Born knew these waters too well. His small boat slipped across a shallow reef and the Raptor dared not follow. Meera was cursing vilely as the men reversed oars and the Raptor came to a halt. Born was out of reach and he knew it.

Born's gloating laughter was short-lived as Meera leaped to the rail and called his name. "Born, you son of a sniveling bag of snot, hear me and hear me well. I am Meera of the House of Lothar of the Western Isles, and I have claimed my prize. Oona is now the Healer Queen of the westerfolk, and before I am finished with you, you will bend the knee and face her justice. Do you hear me, Born? Oona is my Second, and she will sit in judgment on you before I'm through."

Muttering to herself, Meera hopped back to the deck. "Hard about, full oars and sail, I want to rejoin the fleet as quickly as possible."

"Aye Lady, it shall be as you require," grinned Tallon as the men set to obey her orders with a will.

As the nimble ship turned and sailed away, Meera noticed Oona, still cringing on the deck. Still gazing out to sea, Meera offered her hand and helped Oona to her feet as Tallon translated for the crew the words she had shouted.

Oona was somewhat in shock at what she had heard Meera say to Born. She had no idea what Meera had meant, and she was frightened as well as confused. Before she could ask a single question, the young captain approached and dropped to one knee before her.

"My Lady Meera, Lady Oona, if no other has already spoken, I claim right of champion."

"Nay, Captain Tallon," laughed a battle-scarred warrior woman as she laid her hand on his shoulder, "you are ship's captain now. I'll claim right of champion until Lady Oona has time to choose someone."

Meera laughed and lightly slapped the woman on the shoulder. "Be careful, Tella, Oona may not ever let you go."

"Lady, what is going on?" Oona asked softly. "What did you mean by the things you said to Born?"

Meera smiled as she turned to give Oona her full attention. "I meant exactly what I said, Oona. You asked to stay with me forever, and I asked to keep you near me. Among our people there are always two monarchs, Oona, but I've been alone for years. It will be good to have a companion again."

"Lady, I don't understand..."

"Oona, trust me now. I'll explain all when we're camped for the night."

"Yes Lady, I will trust."

"This one is Tella, she'll be your guardian and champion for now. At a future time you may choose another if you wish to do so."

"Lady?"

"Trust me, Oona, I'll keep you near, and keep you safe as I've promised. Tella's service to you is another part of fulfilling that promise. All right?"

"Yes Lady, please forgive my fears. I will trust you to keep me safe." Oona was still very puzzled, but Meera was busy with the ship and her captain now. Oona settled herself in where Tella suggested, and bided her time, trying to make sense of all that had happened. One thing was certain in her mind, Born would not try to follow such a ship with so many hardened warriors. Oona could not know that she was on the smallest ship of a vast fleet.

Understanding

As the Raptor sped northward, Oona gazed out over the passing waters. She was seeing the land from the sea for the very first time, and it was exciting. "Is this your first time on a ship, Lady?" Tella asked softly, as she noticed the smile of delight that crossed Oona's face.

"What? Oh, yes. Forgive me, Lady, I forgot myself." Oona swiftly pulled her hood up to hide her hair. She lowered her eyes from the scarred woman's face. Meera saw and rose swiftly, but Tella shook her head gently, and Meera resumed her conversation with Tallon. Tella would sort this out better than she could.

"I'm Tella, Lady Oona. Just Tella." She reached out and gently tipped Oona's chin up so their eyes met again. Tella smiled and went on softly so no other ears could hear. "Among our people, the title of Lady belongs only to the queen, or in this case, queens. Lady, you are Lady Meera's chosen Second. By her own words she's declared it, and it's now the way of things. Tallon has related the tale of your meeting, and I can easily guess your lot among those people, but that's now in the past. You are among the westerfolk now, and you are our queen, as is Lady Meera."

"What are you trying to tell me?"

"You must call no one Lady except Lady Meera, and only you can call her Meera without the title of Lady before the name. You must never lower your eyes from anyone except Lady Meera."

Oona sighed deeply, then turned back to the view from the rail. At length, she spoke again. "Tella?"

"Yes, Lady?"

"I was barely a woman when the slavers took me. I was tortured then sold to the man who was pursuing us. I don't know how to be a queen. Will you teach me the ways of the westerfolk?"

"I'll do all in my power to assist you, Lady."

"Can you truly accept a slave among you so easily? A shamed woman at that?"

"There are no slaves among us, Lady Oona, and the shame lies in what was done to you, not in you. All are free folk here, and yes, the folk will accept you."

"Why?"

"Because you are the embodiment of our greatest hope, Lady."

Oona smiled in bemusement as she turned back to give the warrior woman her full attention. "In what way, Tella?"

"Lady Meera said you are a healer. There has been no one of the healing talent or a golden hair among us for two generations. You bring great hope to us, Lady Oona. Lady Meera has the power of sight and song, and you have the healing touch. Surely now, the people will prosper and grow strong again."

"I hope you're right, Tella," sighed Oona, as she returned to watching the shore go by.

Tella grinned as she leaned on the rail beside Oona. "I am, as you will soon see, Lady."

"How can you be so sure?"

"Has Lady Meera told you the history of our people?"

"She told me some. It is why you don't keep slaves."

"Slaves make you weak and dependent."

"Meera said that. Tella, your eyes are brown and..."

"My skin is darker with more hair than the rest of the folk? Yes, Lady. Sometimes one will be born to us who more closely resembles one of the elder races. All are considered lucky, but for the luck to hold true there must be signs of both elder races. There are three like me among us, but there was none with the golden hair until now."

"Yes, but how can you be so sure that the luck will hold true, since I was not born to the Westerfolk?"

"The elderkin had a certain way of knowing that most folk do not. That ability is within me as it is in Lady Meera. When first she saw you, she knew."

"Is that why she saved me?"

"Nay Lady, she saved you because of what was done to you."

"But she has protected me because of the luck?"

"Nay Lady, but her reasons are her own, and hers for the telling."

"Forgive me, Tella. I know I ask too many questions."

"Ask what you will, Lady. I am yours to command."

"No, Tella," sighed Oona, "I keep no slaves either. I place no bonds upon you except those of your own choosing."

"I am your champion, Lady, that's the task I appointed myself. I serve you by my own choosing, not by the bonds of terror or might."

"I would prefer by the bonds of friendship."

"Accepted, Lady, with great honor, for those are the strongest bonds of all. Rest here now, and I will bring some food to you."

Tella soon returned with food, and Oona set to with a will. "Tella, can you tell me more of the history of your people?" she asked, around a morsel of food.

"Gladly, Lady. Our history began so very long ago, as is true for all folk. At that long past time, it is said that the humans ruled the entire world. They built great empires and mighty weapons to defend them, but one fateful day they turned against each other.

"Panic was everywhere as people cried out in horror and disbelief, many praying to their various gods, but all to no avail. Great kings strove for dominance, but none would succeed. The time of Ragnarok, world's end, had come. Death rained from the heavens as madmen turned their mighty weapons against each other, in vain attempts to gain power.

"The great cities were swept from the face of the world. The very foundations of the world were disturbed, and lands sank into a boiling sea as others rose to take their place. The explosions threw poisons into the air that choked the people and blocked the sun. Thick clouds hovered in the skies and, without the warmth of the sun, the world grew cold. It took nearly a generation for the vast populations of humans to die off, but die off they did. Well, most of them did.

"In the years that followed those days of madness, most of those who were left turned against each other. They fought for food, medicines, and power; but all too soon the food and medicines were gone, and political power was useless without them. The remnants of mankind fell back into barbarism, starvation, disease, and madness.

"Still, there had been remote places where the ancient wisdom of small subsistence farming survived. Also, the changed weather patterns left a few places with breathable air, and it was there our ancestors managed to survive. Thousands of generations passed before the Great Mother Earth slowly renewed herself, and the world became livable once again.

"In this time of renewal, the species that managed to survive the days of disaster evolved, changed, until many became quite different from the time before the fall. This includes some who were once human, and those who might someday become so. The remaining humans, and near humans, were few and widely scattered.

"In the ninth age of Terra Renew, a sub species of man was discovered by a band of golden-haired explorers. Many were captured and enslaved, but they made poor slaves. In the months that followed they revolted and tried to enslave their masters, but they failed. Both sides fought until few were left alive in either camp.

"It became apparent to those who remained that they needed each other, if any were going to survive at all. Intermarriage became common until an entirely new people emerged, many of whom had abilities as unique as their ancestry. In the generations that followed, they used the knowledge of shipbuilding, combined with the ferocity of their feral ancestors, to build an empire that spanned most of the western isles.

"As all empires do, the western isles flourished for many generations, but eventually fell into decay and rotted from within. It is Lady Meera's hope to build a new empire here in the east."

For the rest of the day Oona continued to ply Tella with questions, and Tella did her best to respond. A bond of friendship was growing swiftly between them, and Meera smiled her approval as she glanced their way from time to time. In the days to come Oona would need a friend as fierce and loyal as Tella of Tragee.

At length, the light of day dimmed and Tallon dropped anchor near a sandy beach with a small stream. Some men set to work on making camp, several more scouted the area to be certain of its safety, and still more replenished the water casks on the ship. As darkness fell, guards were posted, and everyone settled down to eat and rest. Oona was sitting quietly between Meera and Tella when a tall man approached, stopping a respectful distance away.

"Eggar, isn't it?" asked Meera, as the man paused before them.

"Yes, Lady, I'm Eggar." He was looking straight at Oona, and she pulled her hood up to hide her hair again.

Meera saw where his gaze fell. Unsure of the man's intent, she questioned him further. "What is on your mind, Eggar?"

Eggar did not take his eyes off Oona, but his voice was soft and his manner deferential as he responded to her query. "Lady, I have taken an injury this day. The oar behind me broke and struck me a mighty blow."

"So...?"

"I hoped perhaps the Lady Oona, being a healer and all, well..."

"Oona, can you help this man?" Meera asked gently.

Oona looked up and met his eyes at last. She saw the pain and pleading there. "I'll try. Lie down here," she said, as she patted the ground before her. "Face down now. The injury was to your back, was it not?"

"Aye, Lady," he grunted, as he eased himself to the ground before her.

Oona's eyes almost glazed over as her delicate fingers began to explore his lower back. One or two spots elicited a grunt of pain from him before she stopped. "Lie still now." Oona placed her hands, palms down, on his injury then sang a high sweet note that seemed to linger on the air long after she stopped singing. Eggar was asleep at her feet before the note faded away.

Meera was quite impressed, as were the others. It was easy to see on their faces. "Oona?"

"He is more badly injured than he will admit, Lady Meera. He has taken great hurt inside his body. If there is time in the morning, I might be able to find herbs to help him, but he should not pull at the oar for many days, or the injury will surely kill him."

Tallon was sitting nearby and had watched the whole thing intently. An idea suddenly occurred to him and he spoke softly. "What of the steering oar, Lady Oona?"

"Does it require one to exert great strength against it?"

"No, Lady, in fair weather a child could easily manage it."

"That should be alright, if the weather is fair. If he can take his ease for half a moon cycle, he should be fine."

"Then I'll pull his oar, and he'll work the steering of the course."

Eggar awakened a few moments later, and Tallon explained his fate. "But I feel fine now," he protested, as he rose easily to his feet. "Lady Oona has healed my wound, and I'm good as new."

Tallon rose to his feet and went nose to nose with Eggar, a twinkle in his eye. "I'm your captain, and you will obey my orders.

I've decided to pull an oar, and it's your oar that I mean to pull. You'll be the steersman for the next half moon cycle."

Eggar grinned and nodded his head. "Aye captain, it shall be as you command. Lady Oona, you've restored me. What thanks or service can I offer?"

"You pulled the oars that saved our lives this day, Eggar, no thanks are necessary. Rest and grow strong again, for your captain has need of strong oarsmen."

"That was well done, Oona," Meera said, as Eggar smiled and backed away, "I'm quite proud of you." Oona blushed under Meera's praise and lowered her eyes.

Before anything further could be said, another of Tallon's crew approached. She was a tall woman with broad shoulders and a mass of dark hair falling around them. Her leather armor had seen much use over the years, and it was obvious that she was a warrior to be reckoned with. Oddly, she had shears in her hand as she approached, and the merriment dancing in her clear blue eyes was easy to read.

"Dalla, it was good to pull an oar with you again," grinned Meera, as the woman approached.

"Aye, Lady, truly it was. If I may, I've come to ask a favor of the Lady Oona's champion."

Tella shook her head and laughed. "What are you up to now, Dalla?"

"Well," began Dalla, as she spread her arms wide and gave an impish grin, "as you all know, I have ever been a slave to the latest fashions of the royal court." There was a great round of laughter at this, for nothing could have been further from the truth.

"Of course Dalla, that's well known throughout the isles. So, what's on your mind?"

"Well, seeing as how the Lady Oona is obviously the new royal trend setter, I thought I'd be the first to get the new hairstyle. You know, before everyone else does it. It's fun to be among the first once in a while." She tossed the shears to Tella then plopped down onto the ground before her. "Cut it as short as Lady Oona's girl, it's just in the way anyhow."

"Alright," laughed Tella, as she used the shear to cut off a huge handful of Dalla's hair, "but I'm next."

Oona just stared in disbelief as the woman's great mane of hair was quickly shorn from her head leaving only about half an inch all over. "Gods that feels better," Dalla laughed as she ran her hand over her head. Seizing up the shears she set to work on Tella, who was soon shorn, and then, to Oona's horror, Meera too asked to have her hair cut off.

"No, Lady, no. Please, I can't bear to see this happen to you," breathed Oona, as a tear ran down her cheek.

"Now, now, Oona, you're not allowed to be the only one with the new fashion you know." Meera laughed merrily as her long hair was cut short.

"Why are you all doing this?"

"The growing of hair is a long and difficult task, Lady Oona," grinned Dalla. "We thought it would be easier if we helped you. Now, with all of us growing hair at once, it won't take long at all. Actually, I might just keep mine this way. I think I like it. The last battle I was in, that gobber got me by the hair, and I had a demon's own time getting loose again."

"You people are all quite mad," sniffed Oona, "and I love you all for it." She knew they had done this so she wouldn't stand out as a shamed woman. Short hair had just become the fashion for the women of the Westerfolk. Oona would be the same as all others. Once they rejoined the fleet the word would spread quickly, and within a day there would be not a single woman left with long hair.

Soon after the haircutting, Meera made her bed then patted the ground beside her. Oona swiftly snuggled into her accustomed place and cuddled into Meera's arms. "Lady, does no one object to us lying together like this?"

"Of course not, Oona. Why should they?"

"It is forbidden for women to lie beside each other."

"Pure foolishness, Oona," sighed Meera, as she gently tightened her arms around Oona's shoulders. "You're my chosen companion. Who else should lie beside me."

"The ways of Westerfolk are very different from what I've known before. Please forgive me if I make mistakes. I thought you would have a man as companion, and that I would be given to another man."

"Nonsense," chuckled Meera. "I like you, Oona. I plan to keep you."

"Meera, did you truly make me a queen?"

"Yes, I did."

"Why?"

"Many reasons."

"May I know them?"

"Yes, my curious one." Meera sighed as she squirmed a bit to get more comfortable. "You may know them. Listen now, and I'll tell you my tale. I've spoken to you of how my people came to be. Now I'll speak of how I came to be where we met, and why I chose you for my companion.

"Among our people, the royal bloodline is kept pure. It's believed that this is how we came to be strong, and it is done to keep us that way."

"Keep the bloodline pure? How Meera?"

"There are always two monarchs, Oona; usually a brother and a sister. Their children mate and eventually their children as well. If no brother or sister is born then an uncle or aunt may mate with a royal, but that is rare. When a man chooses another man as companion, or a woman chooses a woman, then another member of the bloodline must give them children or bear the children for them. In this way it is thought the bloodline will be kept pure. It's ever been the way of our people, as it was with the elder race. Once the two elder races combined, the royal bloodline came from one of each."

"So, because you have chosen me as companion, you will need an uncle to give you children?" Oona asked thoughtfully as she absorbed this new information.

"He will mount me only when my body is dead and long cold," snarled Meera, with pure hate in her voice. Oona shrank away from her, trying to stammer an apology.

"Oona, sorry, sorry, come back here now," soothed Meera, as she gathered Oona back into her arms. "Listen now to my story. My mother brought forth only two children strong enough to live, my brother and me. His name was Garnor, and I loved him dearly. He was so sweet and gentle, Oona. One could not help but love him.

"When my mother died of the ague, I took her place at my aging father's side as Second. Father was too old and feeble to lead the fleet into battle, and so I sailed with Kieran and Kellan to fight the half men of the southwest who were trying to invade our empire. I was gone several years, but I was victorious. I sailed home with hope in my heart.

"I fully expected to find Garnor on the throne by then, and I was ablaze with desire to bear his children. Ah, Oona, I loved my poor brother so very deeply. My life fell apart when I arrived back at the capitol. I was arrested and brought before my uncle, Drado, who had taken father's throne and imprisoned poor Garnor. Held in chains, I was forced to watch as Garnor was put to death."

"Oh gods, Meera, how terrible for you." Oona snuggled closer to Meera and made soothing sounds.

"Yes, Oona, I was forced to watch as my beloved was killed, leaving Drado as the only living male relative close enough to give me children. He had wanted me since I was a child, and now he meant to have me, but I refused him."

"Oh, Meera, what happened?"

"Under the ancient law, I could leave my throne and set out to sea in a small boat, as sacrifice to the waters. Drado would then be able to take another woman of the royal line to sit beside him, but there was no other close enough in line. I chose to take to the waters just to kill his bloodline, as he killed my darling Garnor.

"I was left in heavy chains and put into a small boat as the moon rose. I sang up the mists, and rowed into them. I rowed for as long as my body could pull the oars, and then I slept. For three long days I rowed, and when I awakened on the fourth day, I was in the middle of the great fleet. Drado had sent three ships to find and kill me, but my loyal fleet had slipped away in the night and followed them. They sank Drado's ships and joined me on the high seas.

"Many more ships came to us over the following few months as Drado put a distant cousin on the throne beside him. You are now companion to the Queen of the Wandering Folk of the Western Seas. We've been raiding all over these lands for the past five years as we searched for a new homeland."

"A new homeland?"

"Yes, Oona, a new homeland, that's why I was in your town that fateful day. I was scouting out the defenses. When the snows have gone we'll take this huge island for our own. Those who wish to join us will be welcome. Those who don't will be exiled or killed."

"Meera, even if you have a new homeland, do you not need a man of your bloodline to give you children?"

"There are none, Oona." Meera sighed as she gave Oona's shoulders a gentle squeeze. "My line dies with me. Another bloodline will have to be established, but first we must secure the homeland."

Oona was thoughtful for several moments before she spoke again. "So that is why you chose me as companion. You want your uncle's line to vanish, and I can't give you children. Also, because of what was done to me, you believe I wouldn't want another man to touch me. Therefore I would be content as companion to a woman."

"That was a part of my reasoning, yes. Oona, I won't hold you to this if you would choose ..."

"No, Lady, no. You promised I could stay near you, and that's what I want to do. I don't care about being queen, I just want to stay near you."

"Then it shall be so, my Oona. We'll secure a homeland for the people, and then they'll have to establish a new bloodline. Ah well, first things first. We must return to the fleet before we can put any further grand plans into action."

"Meera?"

"Yes, Oona?"

"Your brother sounds like a beautiful man, and I've come to know your heart and courage well. I think the loss of your line will be a great loss indeed for the people."

"Thank you, Oona, but there's nothing to be done about that now." Meera's voice trailed off as sleep began to claim her.

"Perhaps, perhaps not," Oona mused to herself. A moment later she spoke again, but so softly Meera could barely hear her.

"Lady Meera?"

"Yes, my Oona?" Meera pushed back the sleep that was trying to take her, giving Oona her attention once more.

"If I am to be your chosen companion, am I expected to...serve your needs?"

"Oona...?"

"I don't know how to do this, but I'll try to please you..."

"Hush, Oona, go to sleep now." Meera smiled as she cuddled Oona closer.

"But..."

"Hush."

"But you didn't answer my question."

"Nor will I this night. Hush now and sleep."

"Lady?"

"Oona, have mercy," laughed Meera. "Hush now and let me sleep."

"Yes, Lady." Oona snuggled back down beside Meera and allowed the fatigue to claim her.

WHILE OONA SLEPT IN safety, Kreeg continued to drill his troops in nighttime combat. Led by Broc, several men had fled from the Trogs, but the rest had stayed to protect their families. These men were now becoming fearsome defensive fighters. Kreeg nodded his approval as he watched. His new castle would be well defended.

The men who had stayed to defend their women soon realized that the Trogs had no interest in human women at all. Some speculated that the Trogs were a completely different species, and indeed they were, for their ancestors were neither human or simian, but a rather nasty minded burrowing creature called a badger.

Trogs make poor sailors, indifferent farmers, and worse herdsmen, but they're natural foragers, and if you allow them to dig into a defensive position, the gods themselves would have trouble rooting them out. Born was in for a nasty surprise when he arrived home a week later.

A Victory on Two Fronts

"Born, you're a bloody fool," snarled one of the men, as they dragged their boat up the beach and watched the Raptor swing north and disappear into the distance.

Born spat in the direction of the vanishing Raptor. "Ha, I'm not finished yet. I'll see the both of them as fish food before I'm done. This isn't over, not by half."

"Are you mad, or just foolish? For the love of all the gods man, that's Red Meera you're chasing. She's killed nearly a dozen of us already, and we've not yet laid a hand on her. Did you see that crew of hers? There had to be over forty warriors on that ship, and she has a hundred more ships larger than that. Leave off, for pity's sake, let's go home to our families before winter catches us out in the open."

Born continued to stare defiantly at the disappearing Raptor for a long moment before he allowed his shoulders to sag. With a sigh he turned away. "Alright, we go home. It'll take me most of the winter to raise an army anyway."

"Raise an army?" exclaimed another man. "Look Born, if you're planning to make war against Red Meera, you do it without me. I want to live to see my children grown." There were grumblings of agreement all round. Born just sat and snarled as he turned towards the north again.

The next morning they set out for home, but it was days later when they arrived. It wasn't a warm welcome they received. After beaching their boat, and shouldering their gear, they marched wearily up to the walled town on the hill. It looked different somehow, stronger, and more forbidding. They found the gate closed, and armed men at the wall.

Born heaved against the gate, but it didn't budge. Cupping his hands around his mouth, he called out to the people inside the walls. "Open the damned gate."

"Who goes there?" growled a rasping voice as a misshapen manlike creature leaned over the wall.

"I'm Born the Strong, chieftain of these people, and ruler of this town;" snarled Born, "now open the damned gate."

"Kreeg is chieftain here, not you. What do you want?"

"I want that damned gate open, that's what I want."

"I will not. You have no business here. Go away." With that the creature vanished from the wall. Born waited a few moments, but there was no sign of the gate being opened. Furious, he took his axe and began to chop at the offending obstacle. This time it opened.

As the gate swung wide, a wall of spears drove through the opening, forcing Born and his crew back. The spearmen fanned out, and in a heartbeat Born and his men were surrounded by hard-faced warriors. Some he knew, others he didn't. "Drop all weapons," barked a commanding voice. Born and his men obeyed.

The circle of spears opened and a huge manlike creature, carrying a massive club, stepped right up to Born. "I am Kreeg. This is my castle. These are my people. I rule in Lady Meera's name. Leave and live, stay and die. Choose now."

Greatly outnumbered, and somewhat cowed by the well-drilled troops he faced, Born backed away and retreated to his boat. He wouldn't return until spring, if at all, yet he had all winter to nurse his growing hatred of Red Meera. Many of the spearmen who had driven him away were once his friends. Born would spend his winter imagining all the ways he would avenge himself on Meera and the slave she had stolen from him. Kreeg would spend his winter improving his defenses and drilling his troops.

"Where are we supposed to go now?" asked one of the men, as they put back to sea.

Born grunted as he heaved against an oar. "Back to the great wheel. Hammiel owes me; he can feed us this winter."

THE NEXT MORNING OONA was up early and gathering herbs. She made a strong tea which she poured into a waterskin and then gave to Eggar. "Sip it slowly through the day," she smiled, as she passed it to him. "When it's gone, return to me and I'll make more." She patted his arm as she left to seek out Meera.

For the following number of days the swift Raptor sped northward, seeking the rest of the fleet. On the fifteenth day they found them leaving the harbor of the ancients. The Raptor swung alongside the much larger Raven, and Meera tossed Oona up to Kellan who helped her aboard. Tella was right behind her, then Meera swarmed over the side and seized Kellan in a bear hug.

"It's about time you returned to us, Lady Meera." Kellan grinned broadly as he released Tella and embraced Meera. "I see you've brought us some company."

"Indeed I have, Kellan." Meera laughed and pounded him affectionately on the back. "Hear me one and all," she shouted, and the ship fell silent instantly. "This woman is Lady Oona, healing woman, and my Second. As my chosen companion she will expect the same loyalty and respect you show to me. Are there any objections?" There was only a round of cheers.

Kellan dropped to one knee before Oona and bowed his head slightly. "A golden-hair with the healing touch, my Lady Oona, you are most welcome indeed." There were wild cheers of agreement at that, as everyone on board dropped to one knee.

"Please rise, all of you." Oona blushed at being the center of attention. She took Kellan's hand and helped him to stand. "Good sir, you warmed me and showed me kindness when the entire world sought to harm me, or worse. I am forever in your debt for that. I hope that I may someday find a way to repay your gift."

"Lady, your presence among us is a gift beyond measure. Again I say, on behalf of one and all, welcome, Lady Oona." Kellan smiled as he rose to his feet.

"Enough of this," laughed Meera. "Kieran, why in the nine hells are you leaving the harbor I sent you to?"

"Another fleet approaches from the west, Lady." A large man, who was obviously related to Kellan, replied to her query. "We think it may be from Drado, and I would prefer to meet them on open water instead of penned up like a fish in a weir."

"Agreed." Meera was all business now. "What time do we have?"

"Little or none, Lady. We should see their sails at any moment."

"Damn," snarled Meera. "The Raven and twenty more pull back into the harbor. The rest run out behind that island then circle behind them. Let's find out what these folk are all about."

Signals were made and the fleet parted with alarming speed. Oona was amazed at how everybody leaped to obey Meera's every command. She commented on it to Tella who grinned her reply. "All too often, Lady, it's been swift obedience to Lady Meera's commands that has kept us alive on the high seas."

A short time later the Raven and twenty others were all that were left in the harbor, and then came the call from high atop the mast. "Sails west."

"Colors?" bawled Kieran.

"They're flying the gold," called the watchman. "They're coming in."

Oona watched fearfully as nearly sixty ships rose from the horizon and sailed into the harbor. With the largest ship in the lead, they approached, and when they were close, Kieran cupped his hands about his mouth and bellowed across the waters. She was surprised at how well his voice carried.

"Come no closer," he roared. Oona watched as every ship in the oncoming fleet backed their oars until they were still. Only then did a voice reply to Kieran's challenge.

"Will you confer on terms, or will you fight?"

"Lower your small boat and come to us," replied Kieran.

"Name yourself, and your house, first."

"Kieran, of the house of Kellar. This ship is the Raven, Lady Meera's flagship. You're safe to confer with us, but first, name yourself and your house."

"I am Borad of Kellar. I feared you long dead, cousin."

A few short moments later a small boat came alongside the Raven, and a tall man swung easily over the side. With a broad smile, he landed on the deck right in front of Meera. "Lady Meera, it is good to find you alive and well, but may I ask what's happened to your hair?"

"We women of Easterlund wear our hair this way, at least for this season." Meera matched his smile, but Oona could see this man could not be trusted. "Why have you come here, Borad?"

"We've come to seek you out, Lady, and to beg you to return home. You're sorely needed, as King Drado has succumbed to madness." Suddenly he turned, and with a swift step, was almost in Oona's face. "And who is this?" he asked as he moved, but the words were choked off by Tella's daggers. Even as he had moved, so had she. As he entered Oona's personal space, Tella had both her daggers at his throat.

"This woman is Lady Oona, my chosen companion as well as my Second," grinned Meera. "Show her disrespect again, and her champion will surely take offense."

Borad gulped as he tried to back away. "Forgive me, Lady, I've been too long at sea, and have forgotten my manners. May I compliment you on your choice of champion? Few in their right mind would face a member of the elder race in single combat, and fewer still would face Tella of Tragee."

Oona was startled at the sight of Tella. Gone was the ready smile, replaced with a savage snarl that showed her extra long canines. Her eyes were no longer brown, but a feral yellow with narrow slits for pupils. Tella's daggers didn't flinch as she spoke through gritted teeth. "Your flattery won't save your life, boy, only shorten it. Step within reach of Lady Oona again, and it'll be your last step."

Borad swiftly retreated from Oona who hadn't spoken a single word. He was quite familiar with Tella's reputation as a warrior, as well as her skill with weapons. "My Lady."

Meera glanced out to sea for a moment then turned her attention back to Borad, allowing her impatience and mistrust to show. "Enough of this, why are you really here Borad?"

"As I said, Lady, we've come to seek you out, and beg you to return home."

Kellan raised an eyebrow as he spoke. "You needed sixty ships for that?"

"I had no idea where to find you, cousin."

"Then I would expect to see your fleet much more spread out along the coast," put in Kieran.

"I was indeed about to give that order when my lookout espied the Raven. It grieves me that so few of you have survived."

"Fortunes of war," sighed Kellan, winking at Oona, who suddenly realized they didn't trust this man. She could see through him with ease, but wasn't sure the others could.

"I can understand that, for we've suffered a similar fate. The half men have nearly destroyed what is left of our fleet. I managed to drive them off last season, but what you see is all that is left to me."

Meera smiled as she pointed out to sea. "Indeed, Borad? Then I do wonder what that might be burning in the distance."

They all turned to see a large plume of smoke rising on the horizon. "You have more ships," snarled Borad as he spun around to face Meera.

"As did you, now you pay for your treachery. Watch and learn the true ways of a warrior." Meera's gaze was cold as she watched the fate of Borad's ships.

Even as he turned to see where she pointed, he knew he had lost. There came Meera's warships over the horizon, one hundred ships or more, all flying her green sea dragon. The great oars rose and fell with deadly precision as the warships sped toward the harbor, the deep boom of the drums sounding the knell of his doom. As well as oarsmen, each ship had a full compliment of fighting men.

Two of Borad's smaller vessels swiftly raised the flag of surrender. Oona covered her mouth with her hand as the great warships plowed through the smaller fleet like a scythe through grain. The battle came to an abrupt halt as Borad's flagship began to run up the flag of surrender.

One of Meera's ships moved alongside the Raven. Her captain leaped nimbly aboard. "Did you get them all, Doral?"

"Aye, Lady Meera. We sank a dozen or more, but there are at least sixteen we can salvage. The rest of the fleet is already at the task."

"Take what men you need and finish it. Order the prisoners to drop anchor, then row ashore to that island and await me there." As captain Doral set about his business, Meera turned to Borad who had gone deathly pale. "Don't worry, Borad, I won't hang you from your own yardarm, even though I believe that's what I should do. No, I have a worse fate in mind for you."

"Lady?" Borad gulped nervously as his eyes darted about, seeking any advantage at all, any friendly face or sign of a possible ally.

"I shall send you back to Drado. You'll have your own ship, and as many men as wish to go with you. The rest can join with us, or stay on that island. I care not which."

Borad blanched at that. His fate would be far worse than hanging if he returned to Drado like that. He had left with nearly ninety ships, the bulk of the remaining fleet. He dare not return with just one. Meera had now crippled Drado, for all intents and purposes.

The old empire was ripe for picking now, and the half men would not be long in taking advantage. Borad had only one chance left and he took it.

"Lady, under the ancient law, I, as prisoner of war from a noble house, am entitled to be ransomed by the head of my household."

Oona was paying close attention, as she was very much afraid this man meant to harm Meera. His very energy screamed malice toward her, and he was close enough to strike. Had Oona been more familiar with these folk, she would have known that Kellan was still Meera's champion, and he was close enough to thwart any attack.

"You are absolutely right, Borad," agreed Meera.

"I can send messages with my fleet captain." Borad smiled smugly. "I am content to enjoy the hospitality of your court, until my father has time to pay my fee."

"Why, whatever does your father have to do with this affair?" Meera smiled sweetly as she spoke.

"He's the chieftain of our house, Lady Meera," Borad replied, a note of suspicion in his voice.

"No, that isn't so, Borad. That traitor Drado may have declared him so, but I haven't. Drado stole my father's throne, which should have gone to my beloved Garnor, whom he murdered. Oona is now my Second, so that throne is hers.

"No Borad, Drado had no right to make such a proclamation. Therefore Kellan of the House of Kellar, is chieftain of his house, as he has been these past thirteen years. It's Kellan who will ransom you, or not, as he chooses. It is Kellan's justice you must face if he does. Kellan, will you ransom your kinsman?"

"I will. What is the price of his ransom, Lady?" Kellan asked, a hard note in his voice.

"Your kinsman came with a fleet of ships. His intent was to make war upon me, Kellan. We have defeated him and captured his fleet. I return that fleet to you, for you're a loyal man of the empire. The price for Borad is his flagship, and your son to captain her. I think my Lady Oona needs a flagship of her own. The ship shall be renamed the Raptor, and completely outfitted as befits the flagship of a queen. Do you accept these terms?"

"I do, Lady Meera."

"Then it's done. Your kinsman is yours to deal with."

"Thank you, Lady Meera," Kellan said sadly as he turned face Borad. "Seize him," he barked, and several men at arms grabbed Borad and held him fast. "Borad, you've committed high treason against the Crown of the Isles. Worse yet, you sought the death of Lady Meera. My one regret is that I can't lay my hands on your father. Could I do so, I would him hang with you."

The condemned man began to struggle. "No Kellan, no; you can't do this. I'm a member of your house."

"A traitor has no house," sighed Kellan. "Hang him."

"Wait, please, just for a moment." It was Oona's voice, and it brought a hushed silence.

Meera stepped to Oona's side and put an arm about her shoulders. "The head of his house has spoken Oona. Even you or I cannot gainsay this."

"No, Lady, I don't seek to interfere; his fate is of his own making. I only want to offer this." She held out a small ball of crushed herbs to Borad. "Chew and swallow slowly. The herb will rob you of your senses, and ease the pain of your passing."

A man released Borad's arm and allowed him to reach for the herbs, but Borad suddenly grabbed Oona's wrist. He had no time to do more as Tella's dagger was buried in his heart up to the hilt. "I gave you fair warning," snarled Tella as Borad sank lifeless to the deck.

"Hang that body from the yardarm," bawled Kieran. It was swiftly done. A short while later the Raven, with her new adornment, sat rocking gently in the waves just off the island where all the prisoners were now standing.

"I say we maroon the lot of them."

Kellan agreed with his brother, but Oona protested. "They'll all die in the coming winter. Please tell me the westerfolk are not so cruel as that."

"We won't maroon them, my Lady Healer." Meera smiled as she reassured Oona. "Don't let the brothers of blood frighten you. We will give these folk a choice and a chance. Kieran, be my crier will you?"

"Aye, Lady." Kieran grinned as he stepped to the rail beside her, and cupped his hands about his mouth. "Hear me well, I speak the words of Lady Meera," he bawled. His voice carried easily to the men on the shore. "Your traitorous leader has been dealt with." Borad's body dangling from the yardarm testified to his words.

"The Ladies Meera and Oona give you all a choice. You can join with us, and prove to be good men and true, or you can sail back to the Isles. One ship will be given to you for the return journey. Those who would prove true stay where you are. Those of you who would return, take the small boats to the ship flying the gold standard."

One of the larger of the captured ships was raising the gold flag, and several small boats went to her. Barely half of the men needed to sail her boarded that ship, and slowly she put out to sea. The remaining men were taken to the rest of Meera's fleet. Only a few men were put onto each ship. Meera's fleet had grown by a full fifty-five ships.

Healer Queen

The sun was low in the sky by the time the new sailors had been dispersed throughout the fleet, and new crews had been chosen for the new ships. Oona had spoken very little all day. She just watched the hustle and bustle, almost mesmerized by it all. "Are you alright, Oona?" asked Meera, as she finally took a break from her council and sought her companion.

"Yes, Lady, I'm fine. I'm just trying to understand all that's happened this day."

"It's been an exciting day for you, my Lady Healer." Meera smiled gently as she took Oona into her arms. "I'm sorry about Borad, but I caution you not to take unnecessary chances like that again."

"I took no chances, Lady."

"Oona?"

"The herbs I offered would not have helped him, Meera."

"Oona, then why?"

"I knew he would attack me, and I knew Tella would kill him."

"You knew?"

"I could see it in him."

"Oona? What have you not told me, my Lady Healer?"

"Perhaps it takes a healer's eye, Lady, but I could easily see his intent to harm you, and I knew he would attack me."

"So, just as I can see in the darkness, you can tell when someone has ill intent."

"Yes, it's been a curse through much of my life, for I was forced to live among people who meant me harm."

"I can believe that, Oona. The life of a slave is no life worth living at all. Oona, if you knew he would attack you, why did you give him the chance?"

"I have seen Born hang people before," Oona replied from Meera's shoulder. "He always made me watch, and said if I did not please him... well, that could easily be my end. I wanted to spare that man such a fate. At least Tella's blade was swift."

"There's more to you than we have yet seen, my Lady Healer." Meera smiled as she released Oona from her embrace. "Tell me now, are you ready to meet the people of whom you are queen?"

"Lady?"

"Oona, all you have encountered so far, are our fighters. Many more of the people came with us to the new lands, and more come each season. Kieran tells me they've already built many new shelters to keep the winter cold at bay."

"Where are these people, Lady?"

"We can't see them from here, we have to dock and go ashore. It seems that they like this place. They've begun to build us a proper capitol city. We'll spend the night aboard the Raven, then we go ashore to meet them. Kieran's already sent messengers ahead to let them know we're coming."

Much to her own surprise, Oona slept the night away. Morning arrived, and with it the tide. Oona said nothing as Meera called to Kieran to get under way. The great fleet then rowed deeper into the harbor.

Oona was amazed to see all the ancient docks as the Raven rounded a small headland. Beyond that maze of docks, hundreds of small halls, houses, and shelters could be seen amid the ruins of an ancient city. Upon a small rise a large hall was under construction, and she could see people busy working on it. In fact, Oona could see people everywhere. She could never have imagined that the world held so many people, let alone expect to find them all together in one place.

"Well, my Lady Healer, what do you think?" grinned Meera, as she saw the look of wonder on Oona's face.

"Lady, truly, I know not what to think. One thing is for certain, Born would never dare to come here."

"That he would not, my Oona. Look now, they've seen us coming." Indeed they had, for Oona could see that everyone had dropped what they were doing. Everyone was rushing to the docks to greet them.

As the Raven tied up at the dock, Kieran leaped ashore. "Make way," he bawled at the crowd, "make way for the Ladies Meera and Oona. Make way, I say." The gathering throng duly parted to allow them safe passage through. A party of armed men suddenly appeared and surrounded the two queens, then led them through the crowd toward the large hall on the hill.

Oona clung tightly to Meera's arm as, half frightened, yet filled with wonder, she was led through the throng. Every woman she saw had very short hair, and all displayed it proudly as she passed. Suddenly, Oona spotted a young girl with her head shorn of hair, and she stopped to approach the child. The guards instantly stopped as well, as did a smiling Meera.

"Sweet child, who has done this to you?" Oona asked gently as she lightly stroked the girl's shorn head.

The child smiled shyly with downcast eyes. "My mother, Lady."

"Why would she do that to one so young?"

"Because I asked her to, Lady," the child responded. "Please don't be angry with Mother."

Oona smiled gently and patted her shoulder. "I'm not angry, little one, I'm just puzzled. Why would you want your hair cut off?"

"Everyone wants it, Lady."

"Why child?"

"We have all heard of Lady Oona, the healer queen with golden hair, and of how she wears her hair very short. It seems strange to me, but everybody wants to try the new fashion. We all want to make you feel welcome, Lady. Mother says you have returned the luck to the people, and I know that is true."

"Oh?" Oona smiled broadly in spite of herself. "How do you know that?"

"Lady, my father's ship went to battle this day past, and she has returned without losing a single man. That is how I know the luck will be true."

Oona smiled with delight. "How can you know that, girl? The Raven was the first ship to dock, was it not?"

"See there, Lady." The girl smiled, delighted to show her knowledge to the new Queen. "His ship returns with only the green and white flags flying."

"You can read the flag signals?"

"Yes, Lady, can't you?"

A woman beside the girl tried to hush her, but Oona just laughed. "No, I can't. Perhaps one day soon you might teach me this new skill."

"Yes, Lady, I would be pleased to teach you the flags," replied the girl solemnly.

"Come, Oona, you are holding up the parade."

Oona blushed and returned swiftly to Meera's side. "Forgive me, Lady..."

"Hush, my Oona, it was well done indeed. Come now. Let's see what the good people of the Isles have built for us, for that hall was not there when last I saw this place."

They followed their guide right up to the great hall where they were greeted by a large number of people, all of whom were richly dressed. To Oona's eyes they appeared to be great chieftains, yet they all dropped to one knee and lowered their eyes as she and Meera passed.

There were long tables along both sides of the hall, and at one end there was a raised platform with two huge seats which were covered with fine furs. Meera took Oona's hand and led her to the high seats. There she sat Oona in one, and then she sat in the other herself. Oona shrank into her seat with a puzzled expression. "Might as well get comfortable, Lady Oona." Tella had taken up her station right beside Oona's chair. Oona noticed that Kellan was beside Meera's seat as well.

"Tella?"

"You'll be spending a lot of time in that seat before the winter has run her course."

Oona admonished Tella in a loud whisper. "You didn't tell me about this."

"I didn't want to frighten you, and make you run away," chuckled Tella. "Lady Meera would have skinned me alive if I let that happen."

Meera had squirmed a few times in her seat to test its comfort and she smiled with delight. "Who built these seats and this fine hall?" An old man shuffled forward, a delighted smile on his weathered face. "Bellar? You found your way here?"

"Aye, Lady," grinned the old fellow, "the royal household left the isles in such a hurry, they somehow forgot to bring me along. I had the demon's own time getting to this place."

"How did you manage to get here, old friend?"

"Lady, I was imprisoned for some years. I refused to make a new throne for the usurper king. He didn't take the refusal well. This past spring I managed to dig my way out and find a few folk willing to share an oar with an old man. In our travels we encountered the captain of the Inge. He told us how to find your new harbor."

"Bellar, I am truly glad to see you well and whole. These high seats and hall are magnificent. I was about to say they are as good as

Bellar himself could make, but I should've known. Thank you, my old friend."

"It is my pleasure to serve," beamed the old fellow, as he backed away.

Smiling, Meera rose to her feet and spoke loud enough for all to hear. "Now then, I am ravenous, and poor Oona has grown weak from hunger. Any and all other business can wait until we have been fed."

At that announcement there was a great flurry of activity. The tables were brought to the middle of the hall, and then laden with a variety of foods. Benches were brought up, and the folk lined up behind them. Oona looked completely bewildered as Meera took her hand and led her to the table, where she presented her to her new people.

"Good folk and true, hear me," Meera said, in a voice that was meant to carry throughout the hall. "This is Lady Oona, my companion and my Second. Oona is a healer of great talent, and she will bless the realm with her presence. I pray you will honor her, as you do me, in all things."

"Lady Oona, we welcome you," came a chorus of voices, as one and all bowed to Oona.

Blushing to her roots, she thanked them and bade them to rise. Meera seated Oona at the table then took her own place. Only then did the others sit. Tella and Kellan stood behind their chairs. Oona looked distressed as she saw them standing there so stiffly and Meera smiled as she took pity on her.

Meera shouted over the din. "Hear me, good people." The room went silent. "This is a new land, and we have a new queen with us. Oona brings many new things to the people, and we should all embrace and enjoy them. As you can see, Oona has already set the trend for hairstyles, and now, I believe, she wishes to start another."

Here she looked meaningfully at Oona who blushed deeply as she spoke.

"I'm afraid my manners aren't what you good people are accustomed to," Oona began hesitantly. "I beg you to forgive me, but I'd prefer to have my champion sit near at hand and share food with us, instead of taking root behind me. Please, Tella, sit with us. Surely it's safe here among such good-hearted folk. I can see them all clearly and all are true. None mean to bring any harm here."

"Oona has the gift of knowing a man's heart," spoke up Meera. "She can see when someone is lying, or intends harm, and when they're true. Sit with us, Tella, you too Kellan. From this day forward the queen's champion will sit by her side at table."

Oona leaned over to whisper in Meera's ear. "Thank you, Lady. I'm sorry to make such a fuss and disrupt things."

"Be at peace, my Oona. I would prefer a more informal court, and I believe you will help me achieve that."

As the feasting went on, Oona soon found herself unable to eat any more. She sighed deeply as she rested her elbows on the table, the great platter of food before her still half full. A thin man who had been hovering nearby, overseeing the serving of the table, approached hesitantly. "Is the food not to your liking, Lady?"

Oona smiled as she turned and gave him her full attention. "It's all quite wonderful. I've not eaten so much at one time since I was a small child in my father's house. At the times of the great feasts of the year, the table would be laden heavy, and I'd eat until I fell asleep. This must be a very special feast day for the folk, but I'm not familiar with the occasion. Can you tell me what we are celebrating?"

"We are celebrating your arrival, Lady," he said, lowering his eyes. "The coming of a healer queen with golden hair is a great day indeed."

"Thank you, good sir. Tell me, did you cook all this food?"

"No, Lady, I am not the chief cook. She is still in the kitchens. Do you wish to speak with her?"

"Another time for certain, but for now, please tell her I'm stuffed to the gills, and amazed at the taste and quality of her food."

He smiled as he backed away. "I'll tell her at once, my Lady."

"That was well done, my Lady Healer," whispered Meera.

Oona observed that Meera kept nibbling until she was sure that everyone was satisfied and well fed. As soon as Meera stopped eating everyone else stopped and rose to their feet. Meera rose, took Oona by the hand, and led her away. They were soon in a private chamber, where Meera sighed deeply and lay back onto a pile of furs. Kellan and Tella sank easily to benches as well, but Oona remained standing.

"I know that look," laughed Tella. "Come, Lady, I too, hear the call."

She led Oona to a private place where they could relieve themselves. They washed in a bowl of water before they returned to the chamber. Meera took a turn, then they all sat and chatted until Meera was sure there had been enough time for everyone to rest and relieve themselves. She sighed as she rose to her feet. "I guess we should be getting back. Brace yourself, Oona. You are in for a long day."

"Lady?"

"All the chieftains of the noble houses will want to present a gift to you, and to declare their loyalty. I'm sorry, Oona, after today life won't hold so much pomp and ceremony, but the folk truly do want to welcome you, and I confess, I want to show you off a bit. Will you do this for me?"

"I'll do anything you ask of me, Lady," replied Oona as she gazed deeply into Meera's blue eyes. "It will be very strange for me to receive gifts, instead of making them for someone else. Just tell me what I'm supposed to do."

"Try to make every person feel their gift is special, Oona. It'll be easy for you, as I've seen that you have a natural way with people. Come now, to battle we go." Oona giggled a bit as Meera led her back to the great hall.

By the time they entered the hall again the tables had been pulled back, and the folk were now standing in two long lines, through which they had to pass to reach their high seats. Once they were seated, a man near the dais called out a name.

One of the folk stepped forward and bowed before speaking. He named himself as well as his house, and then signaled. A woman came forward to present Oona with a cloak of the finest furs she had ever seen. Oona rose and stepped down so the woman could place it on her shoulders. After snuggling inside for a moment Oona took off the cloak and passed it to Tella. She then turned to the woman and gave her a gentle hug. "That is truly a royal gift," she said, smiling at the blushing woman. "I'll cherish it always. Thank you. May your house be blessed with good fortune." Beaming their delight, the man and woman withdrew.

Oona resumed her seat, and the next house was called. In all her life Oona could not have imagined such wealth. To comprehend that it was being given to her freely, was more than her mind could encompass. She did her best to complement each gift, and the folk who presented it to her. Meera sat smiling her approval through it all. The procession of houses took a long time, but at length there was only one left.

Kieran rose to answer for his house. "Lady Oona, I am Kieran of the House of Kellar," he said formally as she smiled at him. "Since my older brother, who is head of our house, has lost his tongue, it falls to me to present our gift to welcome you." He got no further as there was a sudden ruckus at the door and Tallon hurried in, slightly out of breath.

"Forgive me, Ladies, Uncle. I beg permission to present the gift of Kellar to Lady Oona."

"As you wish." A somewhat perplexed Kieran waved back a man holding a finely jeweled dagger. Kieran stepped aside to allow Tallon the center of the floor.

"Lady Oona," grinned Tallon as he knelt before her.

Oona smiled with delight at the twinkle in his eye. "Please rise, Captain Tallon. I can easily see that you're well pleased with yourself. Tell me, what have you done?"

"Lady, your flagship, the Raptor, is now ready and well-manned, waiting only for your banner to be raised on her mast. I've been overseeing the work, Lady, but have hurried here to present the gift of Kellar on behalf of my entire house.

"Lady, earlier this day past, Lady Meera acquired a small fleet of fine ships which she then gave to my father, chieftain of the House of Kellar. Father, being a man who has always spoiled his son, then gave that fleet of ships to me to do with as I choose. I now present that fleet to you as the gift of Kellar. Lady Oona, the Raptor lies ready to lead your fleet wherever you wish to go. They are yours to command." There was a buzz of voices throughout the room at that. This was a mighty gift indeed.

"There is now another matter for you to consider, Lady Oona."

"Oh? What is that?"

"My former ship, once called the Raptor, is now among your fleet, Lady. She will need a new name and a new captain. Your men await your decision."

Oona's sweet laughter floated on the air like a song of joy, and Meera smiled broadly to hear it. In their time together she had heard it little enough. There'd been too much danger, too much need for stealth, and too little to laugh about. Oona rose, and shaking her head, stepped down to look Tallon in the eye.

"Good people, hear me well. Since first I met the folk of the House of Kellar, I have been blessed by their kindness, their ferocity, their loyalty, and their generosity. I'm sure I won't live long enough to repay them for all they have done for me. However, I believe that Tallon, as all young men often do, is trying to slide some of his responsibilities off his own shoulders, and onto those of another."

The room fell completely silent at this, and a look of concern crossed Kellan's face as well as Meera's.

"I am sorry, Tallon," Oona went on with a bright smile, "but you'll have to do your own work yourself."

Tallon was somewhat perplexed, and unsure of how he should respond. "Lady Oona? I don't understand."

"You are as quick with your words as you are with your swords and ships, Captain Tallon, but I can see right through you. You are captain of my flagship, are you not?"

"Aye, Lady," he replied, still perplexed, "by your grace, I am that."

"Well then, as captain of my flagship, it is only fitting that you should be commander-in-chief of my whole fleet. As fleet commander, it is you who must choose which man or woman will captain which of my ships, and it is you who must choose what name those ships will bear. I won't do your work for you, Commander Tallon."

"My Lady," choked out Tallon. He actually had tears in his eyes.

"Well do I remember the kindness of the House of Kellar, Tallon my friend," Oona replied softly. "Will you not command my ships for me?"

"I will be honored beyond measure to do so, Lady Oona."

Oona laughed as she turned away and resumed her high seat. "Then get out of here and name that ship, sir." When she faced the room again Tallon was still there.

"With your permission, Lady Oona, that ship will bear the name Lucky Lady." She smiled as he turned on his heel and strode from the great hall. Kellan sighed with delight, well pleased with this turn of events. His bold, brash, son had found his place. Now he would have to prove himself worthy of it.

Prepare to Sail

Meera sighed deeply with contentment as she lay back on the sleeping furs. She cuddled Oona closer and lightly kissed her hair. It had been a long, but very successful, day. Oona had been royally welcomed, and Meera now knew for certain that she had broken the back of Drado's fleet. They had nothing more to fear from that direction. As she mused over that, she felt Oona's trepidation. "What troubles you, my Oona?"

"Lady, you are disturbed, was my behavior not to your liking this day? Have I done something to offend...?"

"Oona, no, hush now. I'm so very pleased with you. I have no words to express the depths of my pleasure. It's an old matter that held my thoughts, a matter that matters no longer. Oona, I'm so very pleased with you."

Oona sighed and snuggled deeper into the furs with Meera. "Thank you, Lady. Lady Meera, what am I to do with all those things the people have given to me?"

"We will store them here in this room, if you wish. You can do with them as you will, Oona. I do caution you, Sweet Oona, be careful of everything you do, or say. For the folk will be watching your every move, listening to your every word, seeking to gain your favor, and through you, mine. You'll have to be careful."

"I have seen this behavior in people before, trying to gain Born's favor. Is that why you ate so very slowly at table?"

"Yes, I watch carefully, and don't appear to finish eating until everyone else has had their fill."

"How do you manage that?"

"I taste everything, but actually eat very little. When I'm on ship I can eat my fill with the sailors, but in court it is very different."

"Then I will follow your example, Lady."

"You'll do fine, my Oona," sighed Meera, as she floated on the edge of sleep.

"Lady Meera?"

"Yes, my Oona?"

"How are we going to fit a whole fleet of ships into this room?"

Meera chuckled and returned slightly from sleep. "Perhaps we should leave the ships on the waters, Oona. So tell me, how does it feel to have a fleet of ships?"

"Lady, when you found me, I was a slave and could have nothing, not even a name of my own. I have no idea what I should do with a fleet of ships."

"What would you like to do with them?"

"I have no idea at all, Lady."

"Perhaps it will come to you in dreams," sighed Meera. "Sleep now, my Lady Healer."

Oona snuggled down for a moment then... "Lady?"

"Yes, my Lady Healer?" Meera was nearly asleep now.

"Lady, are you certain I am not supposed to..., you know..., serve your needs?"

"Oona, for the love of the gods," laughed Meera, "will you please let me sleep before I perish from fatigue."

"Forgive me, Lady," whispered Oona, as she settled down again, "I just wanted to be sure, you know, that ..."

"Go to sleep, my Lady Mischief," Meera chuckled, as she kissed the top of Oona's head. "It's bad manners to tease the helpless, so let me rest."

Oona giggled softly, then relaxed deeper into Meera's arms. As she drifted off to sleep, she marveled once again at how loving, and gentle, the dreaded Red Meera truly was. Her last waking thought was how lucky she was to have been found by the pirate queen.

OONA WAS AWAKE EARLY and already in the kitchen, deep in conversation with the chief cook when Tella found her. "Lady Oona!" Tella's voice cut through the soft hum of voices like a knife through butter. Oona spun around to face a stern looking Tella. She had to fight herself to keep from cringing away.

"Yes, Tella?"

"How, in the name of all the Isles, am I supposed to protect you if you go running about all over the place without me?"

"But, Tella, you were sleeping," Oona smiled sweetly.

"Yes, I was. Now tell me how you managed to leave without waking me? No man or beast has slipped past me in living memory."

Oona fairly giggled as Tella wagged a finger at her. "You did awaken, but I used healing touch to put you to back to sleep. Tella, Kellan is not always with Lady Meera, why must you always be at my side?"

"Lady Meera needs no protection, and well you know it, Lady Oona. She's the most fearsome fighter in the realm. You however, are another matter. What would you do if a man came at you with a spear?"

"I would scream, then run and hide behind my champion," laughed Oona. "Cook, it's easy to see that Tella is grouchy before she's eaten. I suggest we feed her before she starts gnawing on my arm."

"Yes, Lady Oona." The cook grinned as she swiftly prepared a platter for Tella.

"Have you eaten, Lady?" Tella asked, as she accepted the platter.

"Not yet, but..."

"Eat, now there's an idea I can embrace," said Meera, as she appeared in the kitchen as well. "How about it, Cora, is there enough left for a starving sailor?"

"There is, Lady Meera. Lady Oona has taken a hand in this, and it smells delightful."

"Then gather a platter for yourself and join us," smiled Meera, as she sat at the long table and motioned the others to join her.

"You seem quite at home here in the kitchen, Lady." Oona grinned impishly as she took a morsel from Meera's platter.

"I am, my Lady Healer. I always break my fast in Cora's kitchen, whenever I can. You appear to have made yourself at home here as well. I can taste those herbs of yours in this pottage."

"You said you liked them."

"I do."

Suddenly Oona noticed that Tella was looking a bit uncomfortable. Her eyes met Meera's then went back to Tella. Meera grinned and nodded. "Tella, this kitchen is a ship of the line, and Cora is her captain. We use ship's etiquette here."

Tella nodded her thanks and tucked into her food. "Aye, Lady, and thank you both. So, Lady Oona, what do you think of the westerfolk so far?"

"Tella, my friend, I can't believe how lucky I am to have fallen in with such a generous and fierce people. I wonder what is in store for me today?"

"Well, I thought we might inspect that new fleet of yours," suggested Meera. "Have you given any further thought to what you want to do with it?"

"Lady, you once told me that I am to pass the kindness of your rescue on to another, when the time comes that I am able to do so."

Meera sat back and pushed away her empty food dish. "So you believe that time is now? What's on your mind, my Lady Healer?"

"I would like to take my fleet to the valley of the great wheel. I'd like to find a way to free my friend Morel from that awful place. She won't survive the winter there."

"Oona, tell me more about this place," said Meera, her full attention on Oona now.

"You've seen it for yourself, Lady. What more can I tell you?"

"You say they keep half the grain for themselves?"

"Yes, Lady. The year is late now, and most of the grain has been ground. Their store houses must be very full by this time."

"Indeed so." Meera was thoughtful for a moment. "We still need more supplies. The contents of those storehouses would be welcome here. I think it's now time for Lady Oona to be about acquiring her gift to the people. Tella, go to Oona's fleet and call a council of captains. Lady Oona, I beg permission to join you on this adventure."

"Oh Meera, will you truly come with me? I have no idea at all how to go about accomplishing that which I desire."

"I'll be delighted to join you, my Oona. You do have a council of captains to advise you as well, you know."

"It's your advice I desire most, Lady." Oona lowered her eyes and spoke softly.

Meera smiled as she tipped up Oona's chin with her finger tips. "Oona, do not fear. We will do this together, as we'll do all else. I've sworn to keep you near me, and I will do just that."

"Lady, if you don't want us to do this, I will..."

"Nay, Oona, I think it's a wonderful idea, but we must move swiftly. The days are growing darker as we speak. Our time is short." She rose and offered Oona her hand. "Come, my Lady Companion. We have work to do, and it's time to be about it."

Oona soon found herself marching alongside Meera as they approached the docks again. She was wearing as many of her gifts as she could. Dressed in new boots of the finest leather, soft woolen kilt and tunic, finely tooled leather belts, gold and silver jewelry, plus her new cloak of furs, Oona truly felt like a queen as she strode along amid her honor guard.

As they reached the docks, Tella was waiting to guide them to the newly named Raptor. Tallon was on the deck, with a large group of men and women. Kellan was there with him. They all dropped to one knee as Meera helped Oona onto the ship.

"Please rise, good people," said Oona, as she helped Kellan to stand. "From this moment on, I will ask that no one try to kneel on board one of my ships. Please find another way to show respect."

Everyone looked to Meera, but she just grinned and nodded. "What would please you, Lady Oona?" asked Tallon.

Oona laughed with delight. "A smile of greeting would be a good start, Commander Tallon. I don't know, devise something among yourselves, then bring it to me. Now, we have things to discuss. Lady Meera will join us on this adventure, and she's agreed to lead for me, as she is a warrior and I'm not."

"Here is the tale of it," said Meera, as she leaned back against the railing. "There is a valley near where Tallon first found Oona and me. In that valley is a great wheel that is used to grind the grain for most of the farmers in this land. Half the grain ground is kept in the castle above the wheel. That wheel is turned by slaves as a means of punishment. We're going to free those slaves, break that wheel, and sack that castle. We need the supplies for winter, and those slaves need to be set free.

"Now, here's what we'll do. We'll sail with Lady Oona's fleet, carrying as many fighting men as we can. Three empty supply ships will accompany us to bring back the grain. The river is too difficult for most of the warships, but the Lucky Lady should have no trouble navigating up to the wheel.

"The Lucky Lady will take as many men as possible up river at night where they'll hide themselves near the castle. She'll then go back for more. It should take only three days to transport us all.

Once all the fighting men are in position, Lady Oona, her champion, myself, and a few others, will attack the wheel in the night, freeing the slaves.

"At dawn the following morning, the Lucky Lady, full of armed men, will show herself to the castle. When the gates are opened to allow the knights to attack the Lucky Lady, our hidden forces will storm and sack the castle. Remember, you must wait until the castle gates are opened and it is empty of fighters. Once we're inside, those who remain will be easily defeated. Are there any questions?"

"Only one," grinned Tallon. "When do we sail?"

"As soon as you gather the fighters and supply the ships."

"As you desire, so shall it be, Lady. Lady Oona, there is another matter for you to..."

"Now what, Tallon?" laughed Oona.

"Why, your banner, Lady. We will need your colors to fly when we sail."

"Well now," smiled Meera, "He's got you there, Oona. Have you given any thought to what you want for your colors?"

Oona smiled and reached into one of the herb pouches that were tied to her belt. "You have the green of your house, Lady, and the sea dragon set upon it. Since I have no house of my own, might I also have the green of your house?"

"Oona, my Lady Healer," Meera said gently, "the very moment you agreed to be my companion you became a member of the House of Lothar. The green is indeed your color."

"Then my flag shall be the green of my house with this flower upon it," smiled Oona, as she held up a crimson blossom from her herb pouch.

"What plant is that, Oona?"

"It is a plant with great healing properties," smiled Oona. "It is the first to bloom in spring and the last to die before winter. In the language of my mother's people it is called a red meera." Meera had a tear in her eye as she smiled her delight at Oona.

The Taking of the Great Wheel

The next morning Oona stepped outside to see a fleet of ships in the harbor. They were all flying her colors, the red meera. Someone must have worked through the night to make the flags. Only the Raptor was still tied up at the dock. "Come, Lady Oona," grinned Tella, "Lady Meera is already aboard the Raptor. Do you have everything you wanted?"

"Yes, I think I have enough." Oona reached for a large pack sack, but before her hand touched it, one of the silent guards seized it up and threw it over his shoulder. Her second pack was taken by the other guard who never spoke, then they all marched down to the docks. A throng of well wishers had gathered there to see them off.

As soon as Oona stepped on board, everyone stood up straight and placed their right hand upon their left shoulder. "Hail, Lady Oona," they shouted, and she beamed her delight as she responded in kind. The line was soon cast off, and the Raptor put to sea. The rest of the fleet waited at anchor, and then, as the Raptor passed, they followed her from the harbor.

"What is our course, Lady?" sang Tallon, as he leaped up onto the higher deck toward Oona.

"Return to where you found us, Captain Tallon." He well knew where they were bound, and the steersman already had the course. This was just formality, and she knew it.

Meera was gazing out to sea at the rail and Oona joined her there, linking her arm through Meera's. "Well, my Lady Healer, we're on our way. Tell me, what have you got in those huge packs?"

"That healing woman you sent for was most generous, Lady Meera. I have plenty of healing herbs, some light foods, and warm blankets, for the slaves that we're about to set free."

"Yes, Nora is generous and a skilled healer, but she doesn't have the touch as you do, Oona. Nora's skills are learned, not born with her."

"Still, she knows so very much about herbs, Lady. I can learn a great deal from her. I've asked her to teach me during the long cold days of winter."

"What else have you done, my Oona? You seem quite pleased with yourself."

"I have asked Bellar to make a room attached to the great hall."

"A room?"

"A healing room, Lady. Nora and I will store our herbs there, and see to the ills and hurts of the people."

"This is how you would spend your winter, Oona?"

"Lady, if you have something else for me to do, I ca..."

"Nay, Oona, not so. It thrills me that you will do this. I'm the warrior, and must spend my time preparing our defenses, as well as planning how we'll take this land for our own. I've so little time to tend to the rest of my folk. My time is taken up with the warriors and nobles. It pleases me that you'll do this for the folk."

"Thank you, Lady Meera. I understand that I'll have to spend a deal of my days in the great hall, with you and the others. But I'm a healer, or I was once, and want to practice my skills, too."

"And so you shall, my pet, so you shall," Meera said softly, as she put her arm around Oona's shoulders and gave her a friendly squeeze. Oona snuggled closer, and thus they passed much of the next few days, until they reached the mouth of the river at the Valley of the Wheel.

"Lady Oona, Lady Meera," grinned Tallon, as he bounded toward them, "we've arrived."

Meera began barking orders and the Lucky Lady was soon alongside the Raptor taking on more fighting men. Her new captain smiled and waved at Oona's greeting. Tallon had offered the ship to Eggar, but he asked to serve as mate on the Raptor. Dalla was then given the Lucky Lady.

Just before the Lucky Lady set out, Oona stood and addressed the fighters. Tallon sent the signals to the rest of the ships. "Hear me well, good people," shouted Oona. "You are about to face my enemies. When you face these men in battle, show them no mercy, for they will show none to you." She little knew the doom her words carried, but, even as the words were spoken, a guardsman shivered with unease atop a wall high above the great wheel.

As darkness fell, the Lucky Lady headed upstream with her cargo of fighters. Meera and Oona were on board as well. It took a goodly amount of time, but they finally beached near the last bend in the river before the wheel. Meera led the fighters ashore, Oona's hand tightly clasped in her own. Oona didn't see so well as a westerman in the dark.

As Meera led her troops into the forest, the Lucky Lady sped back downstream to the sea. With luck, she could drop another load of fighters before dawn. Meera found a good hiding spot, then left Oona with Tella and the rest. She hurried back to the landing place to guide the next group of fighters.

Once the second group was settled into hiding, Meera sank down to rest beneath a tall pine tree. "Just like the old days, eh Oona?" she chuckled, as she snuggled Oona closer.

"Yes, but it is different as well."

"Different, how so?"

"We were alone and naked then. Lady, are you..."

"Oona, don't even start with me tonight," chuckled Meera. "Hush, if you make me laugh we'll be discovered. Sleep now. Ah, ah, ah; sleep now." Oona giggled as she snuggled closer and closed her eyes. There was nothing to fear this night, she had Red Meera, and an army of fighters, at her side. Oona almost wished that Born would show up. Little did she know that he was well within her reach.

For the next two nights the Lucky Lady transported troops up the river to Meera. During the busy part of the season they surely would have been discovered, but at this late date, there were none to see or warn the castle.

Just before dawn on the fourth day, they set out. The men knew well what they were to do, and they swiftly approached the castle. By dawn the castle would be surrounded by unseen warriors.

JUST AS MEERA'S TROOPS silently surrounded the castle, the guards began to feed the slaves at the wheel. "Be careful with that, for you'll get no more until tomorrow. That has to keep you going all day," snarled the burly guardsman. He slapped a scoop of gruel into each slave's bowl as they were led past in chains. "Remember, if you fall off the wheel, your throat'll be cut and you'll be fed to the crows. We'll not keep lazy slaves here." Both the guards and the slaves were completely unaware as sixteen shadows approached and slipped inside the wheel's keep.

Morel offered her food to the young man chained beside her. He was a strange looking fellow with long canine teeth, and eyes that turned yellow in the darkness. "Eat this as well," she sighed. "I won't be able to rise to the wheel this day. My life force is spent."

"No, Morel, you must eat mine." He spoke softly as he poured his portion into her bowl, and then pushed the food back toward her. "Too often you've given your food to others to keep them standing. Now it's your turn. Eat, Morel, you must eat."

"Konnor, if you don't eat you'll fall and be killed," she sighed in reply. "I'm finished. If you eat both portions you'll be able to last a few more days."

"I'm stronger than I look, Morel. You eat the food, and we both will survive a few more days. That's all we need, Morel, just a few more days. The grain will be finished for the season then. They'll take us into the castle, keep us warm and fed until the next year comes. Once our strength returns, we'll find a path to freedom. Eat, we just need a few more days."

"I can't, Konnor." Morel sighed deeply as she slumped further against the cold stone wall. Suddenly she felt him stiffen, and his eyes fairly glowed yellow. She heard him growl softly like an animal, and then he grinned, showing his long canine teeth.

"Eat and rejoice, my dear Morel," he whispered softly, pushing the food at her. "There will be no need to rise to the wheel this day, or any other ever again. They have come."

"What???" Morel tried to struggle upwards again. "What are you saying, Konnor? Who has come?"

"Hush now, make no alarm. Lady Meera the Red is here, and so are the westermen."

"Red Meera? Here? Have you lost your senses, Konnor?"

"Lady Meera the Red herself stands there in the shadows, Morel. Can you not see her bracelet of gold, which my own father made for her many years ago?"

"No, Konnor. I can see no one."

"Nor can the guardsmen, but I can. Eat, my dear friend. This will be a day of rejoicing. Look, here they come even now."

Even as Konnor spoke, shadows moved away from the wall and made their way towards Morel and Konnor, making little effort to hide themselves. Morel gasped to see the woman with short golden hair in the fur cloak. She looked like a goddess from the old tales, and Morel knew her face. Morel's eyes misted over as the golden one knelt at her side, and brought a skin of sweet water to her lips.

A dark shadow dropped a bundle at Morel's feet, then stepped to Konnor and gave him food. Morel heard him speak to the dark one in that strange unknown tongue he sometimes used.

"Release me, or kill me, but don't leave me in these accursed chains," he said.

"The keys to your chains will soon be here," replied a woman's voice. "I am Tella of Tragee. Name yourself and your house."

"I am Konnor, the last of Tradoon. We left the west two years ago to seek Lady Meera's people. The last of our house hoped to find and join with them. Our ships were swamped in a storm. Only a few of us managed to reach the shore, where we were put in chains and sent here to push the wheel."

"Where are the rest?"

"Dead," he replied softly. She just nodded and turned back to Oona and Morel.

Oona was crooning softly as she cradled the girl in her arms. She was so frail and weak. Tears welled up in Oona's eyes as she fed the girl who once had been her only friend. "Porga, can this truly be you, or are you a spirit here to take me to the land of the dead?"

"Hush, Morel, you're safe now. You're not dead. Yes, you do know me, and one day soon I'll tell you my tale. My name is now Oona, as it was when I was a child in my father's house. You must always call me Lady Oona now. It is the way of these folk."

"Lady?" asked the young man chained to Morel. He had understood much of what had been said. "Has Lady Meera chosen a Second then?"

"She has," replied the dark woman. "This woman is Lady Oona. She has the gift of healing touch, as well as the golden hair. Lady Oona, this one is Konnor of the House of Tradoon."

Konnor spoke softly as he struggled to rise to one knee. "Lady, I am deeply honored to meet you."

"Hush now and be still," admonished Oona, gently patting his arm. "There'll be time enough for kneeling once you're strong again. Tella, are we ready?"

"All is ready, Lady."

"Then let us be about this business." Oona rose to her feet and called out to the guard.

"Guard, guard, are you deaf or just stupid, guard!"

"What the blazes is going on there?" shouted a surprised male voice, as a huge guardsman hurried toward Oona.

"The slaves are free," Oona replied loudly. "Come, see for yourself."

There was a sudden rush and clatter as all ten guardsmen hurried toward the voice and the moving shadows. They drew their swords as they came, but suddenly Meera was among them, several of her hand-chosen fighters at her side. The snarls and barking growls of the westermen sent chills of fear up Morel's spine, but Konnor laughed with delight.

"Dear gods, there's a song I thought never to hear again." Konnor watched as a guardsman rushed at them with drawn sword. The guardsman was dumbfounded by the speed with which Tella moved, and then he felt the pain of the dagger in his breast. Slowly, he sank to the ground at her feet. "There were only ten. You've got them all," grinned Konnor, as Meera felled the last one.

Meera swept up the keys from a fallen guardsman and tossed them to Tella. She swiftly set about freeing the chained slaves. "Are you pleased, my Lady Healer?" Meera asked, as she reached Oona.

"I am well pleased indeed, Lady. Lady Meera, this young woman was once my only friend. Many times she managed to protect me from bad men."

"I did try, but was not successful nearly as often as I would have liked Por..., I mean Oona."

"That's Lady Oona," smiled the tall warrior woman, as she knelt at Morel's side. "You must remember to call her Lady now. You are Morel. I'm pleased to find you still alive, Morel, for we feared the worst. Forgive us, I beg you. We should have been here much sooner."

She rose and patted Oona's shoulder. "Stay here and work your magic, my Oona. I go to join the men at the walls." She trotted away with all but three men following close behind, the rest remained with Oona.

"Go with her, Tella. Keep her safe and bring her back to me."

Tella didn't move a muscle, so Oona rose up and pushed her in the direction Meera had gone. "Go, I'm safe here and she'll need you. Go."

Still Tella did not move. One of the men nearby stepped forward. "I've taken a gash that will prevent me from running to the walls. I can still fight, so I'll stay here. I'm Dor of Kellar. With permission, I and my brothers, will champion the Lady Oona until Tella of Tragee returns."

The man was gazing into Tella's eyes and she was glaring back. "If a hair of her head is harmed, you'll die on my blade before Lady Meera can strike me down," snarled Tella. He nodded his head and she sprinted away.

"Don't worry, Dor," smiled Oona, as she inspected the wound on his thigh, "Tella's always grouchy before she has eaten her morning meal."

"Thank you, Lady," he grinned in reply, "that is most comforting to know." He grunted as she began to sew up the wound on his leg. Soon Oona had all the freed slaves gathered together. She was feeding them while Dor and his two silent companions stood guard.

MEERA REACHED THE MEN near the wall just in time, Tella at her side. "She made me do it," Tella said defensively, as Meera gave her a hard look. "I've left three of our best fighters with her. She made me do it, Lady."

"Alright, Tella, alright. I just want this to be finished, and to get her back to the hall where I know she'll be safe. What are you grinning about?"

"It appears that Lady Oona has managed to gain some of your courage, Lady, and she's managed to pass to you a bit of her natural caution as well. This bodes well for the empire."

"Shut up, Tella," Meera sighed, as she leaned back against a tree. "Who's with her?"

"Dor and his two brothers, Lady."

"Dor and the twins of terror stayed behind?"

"Aye, Lady, that they did."

"I guess Oona is safe enough, then. The gods may have robbed the twins of their power of speech, but they've given them a ferocity unequaled to make up the difference. Now where the blazes is the Lucky Lady?" Even as she spoke Meera heard the blast of a western war horn. The Lucky Lady was just rounding the bend in the river, bristling with armed men.

The great horn sounded again as the Lady beached and warriors poured over the sides. There was a great creaking as the huge castle gates swung open. A large number of armed men mounted on sturdy horses rode out toward the ship. Meera waited until the knights were midway to the landing site, and then she gave the signal. Suddenly several riders turned aside and fled into the forest. Impatience burned in Meera's heart, for she'd recognized one of those riders.

As silently as a sighing wind, hundreds of fighters arose from the shadows beneath the walls, and poured through the open gates of the castle. The men still inside fought hard but were soon defeated.

When they realized there was to be no quarter given they tried to flee, but all to no avail. They were overtaken and slain.

With the castle taken, Meera leaped to the walls to see Tallon and his men engaged in a fierce battle of their own. Even though the knights were mounted, they weren't going to survive, and they knew it. They fought with the desperation of the condemned. Several of them actually managed to slip away into the forest.

The westermen were as wild and feral as beasts, and they leaped onto the backs of the mounts with ease, dragging both horse and rider to the ground. The numbers were about even, but before Meera could lead her men to the shore, Tallon had triumphed.

Several of the mounted men tried to flee, but only a few escaped into the forest to follow the original deserters. Even there they found no sanctuary, for, led by Meera herself, the westermen pursued them. No more than five managed to escape the carnage and flee into the hinterland.

Once the castle had been taken, a troop of warriors sped away from the castle and straight toward the wheel. Oona grinned as Tella led her men into the circle of the wheel, taking up a defensive position around her and the folk she was helping.

"Tella, I'm so very happy to see you," grinned Dor. "My brothers and I are exhausted from fighting off all Lady Oona's attackers."

"Lady Oona?"

"Yes, Tella, I'm well and unharmed."

"Please tell me Dor hurt your feelings."

"Not at all Tella, Dor is a perfect gentleman."

"Then tell me he cried like a baby when you sewed him up."

"I am sworn to secrecy," Oona replied impishly.

"Lady Oona," protested Dor.

Tella laughed heartily then, and clapped Dor on his shoulder. "Dor, thank you, I owe you."

"Do not. Come on boys, we have to take old Konnor here to the ship and feed him some more. Come on, Konnor, we'll lean against each other, that should keep us both standing."

A Queen Takes Charge

Men soon arrived to carry those who couldn't walk back to the landing site. The Lucky Lady was already gone, carrying news of the victory back to the fleet. The wheel slaves were placed beside the wounded, and Oona set to work. It was much later when she paused from the healing.

"Tella, where is Lady Meera?"

"Gone into the forest, Lady. Tracking those who escaped."

"I see. Tella, are there any wounded in the castle?"

"All have been brought out here for you, Lady."

Oona nodded and thought for a moment. "Captain Tallon," she called.

Tallon was instantly at her side. "Yes, Lady?"

"Where is the Lucky Lady?"

"I sent her back to inform the fleet of our victory, and to guide the supply ships back to this place."

"Good, all is well then." Just then she noticed a woman looking at her, but trying not to appear as though she was looking. Oona knew all too well what that was about.

"What's on your mind, good woman?"

"Lady, are you truly Red Meera?" blurted the woman. She instantly regretted her words and shrank away from Oona, as did several others.

"No," smiled Oona, "I'm not Meera. I'm Oona, Meera's Second and her companion. Now tell me, what's your name?"

"Whatever name you give me, Lady," the woman replied with downcast eyes.

"Hear me well, all of you." Oona spoke in a loud voice so all could hear. "We are the folk of the western isles, and we do not keep slaves."

"Are we to be killed then, or will we be sold?" the woman asked fearfully.

"You will not be sold. Neither will you be killed. You're free now. You may go where you will, do as you please to do. Your life is your own to choose."

At this point Konnor stepped forward and knelt to Oona. "Lady, if I may speak."

"Please stand, Konnor, and yes, you may speak."

Smiling, he rose to his feet. "Lady, most of these folk have known nothing but slavery. Many were born in this very castle. Lady, they don't know where to go or what to do."

Oona sighed and allowed her shoulders to slump. "I see. This is going to be more difficult than I imagined it would be."

"There is another problem for you to consider, Lady," grinned Tallon.

"Tallon, I swear, if you start this again..." Oona shook a threatening finger at him. "Alright, what is it?"

"Lady, what are you going to do with the castle?"

"Me?"

"Lady, you saw, we came, we conquered. We're your people, Lady Oona. It's now your castle. You must decide what is to be done with it."

"Ooooh, my head hurts," sighed Oona, as she sank to the ground in a cross legged position and rested her head in her hands. "Wait, I have advisers. Tallon, Tella, sit with me and advise me. You too, Konnor."

"Me Lady?"

"You've been in that castle before, have you not?"

"I spent a full winter there, Lady."

"Then you too can offer advice. What can you tell me about this place?"

"Well, Lady, it is easy to defend as long as you stay inside. A small garrison could hold off an army with the gates barred. By now the store houses will be full to the bursting. There are six and any one of them holds enough for a winter's supplies."

"Why do they hoard so much?"

"They sell it to the slavers from the south, Lady Oona. They're paid in gold and slaves for the wheel."

"That wheel will be turned by beasts in future," declared Oona. "Now, what do you suggest I do with the castle? Tella?"

"Lady, Konnor has already said it, the castle should be garrisoned. If we're going to take this land for ourselves, we'll need bases to govern from. This castle is perfect for that purpose."

"Tallon?"

"Tella has the right of it, Lady Oona. The people of this land are accustomed to coming here. If we're in control here, and if we ask less in payment for the grain..."

"Good point," mused Oona. "Konnor, have you anything to add?"

"Well, Lady, concerning the former slaves, they know well the running of the castle. I believe most would be content to stay and help us."

"Are you sure they would not think they had been sold to a new master?"

"I'll make it very plain to them, Lady Oona."

"You?"

"Yes, Lady, I'll stay with them. If I'm here, since I was one of them, they'll understand that they're free to come and go as they please."

"Alright, that just leaves one thing to figure out."

"What is that, Lady Oona?" asked Tallon.

"Where are we to get a garrison?"

"Lady, you have brought more than enough troops with you," smiled Tella. "Just give the command."

Oona sighed deeply and gazed toward the forest where Meera had disappeared. How she wished Meera was here to make these decisions. Oona had always had to do as she was told, never making any decisions at all for fear of reprisals. "Perhaps I should wait for Meera to return."

Tella nodded her understanding. She knew this was taxing Oona, but if Oona were to become a true queen, she had to stretch herself. There would be many occasions when she'd be called upon for direction. It was best for her to start now. "Forgive me, Lady Oona. It may take Lady Meera days to complete her task, and we need to be ready to leave as soon as she returns. The season grows late, and the gales will soon be upon us."

With a sigh of resignation Oona rose to her feet. "Very well then, if I must, I guess I must. Tallon, arrange for a garrison please. Bring the one who is to command it to me. I also need you to arrange to load what supplies we can onto the supply ships when they arrive. Leave the garrison enough for their needs, but take as much of the rest as possible.

"Tella, you saw Meera's direction, take the twins and go to her. Assist her, then bring her back to me as soon as you can."

"Lady..."

"Just do it, Tella," sighed Oona. "Meera has greater need of you than I do right now. I'm safe enough here and well you know it." Tella looked at Dor who nodded then she trotted into the forest, the silent twins right at her heels.

As Tella disappeared into the forest, Oona turned back to Konnor. "Bring all the former slaves to me here."

"Aye, Lady, but most are right here now. It'll take but a moment." He was good as his word, for they soon had gathered around Oona, who now had Dor right at her shoulder. Oona addressed them in their own language.

"Good people, hear me well. You are now free to go where you will." This brought a murmur from the gathered people. The signs of abuse were evident on all of them, and it broke her heart to see. "Let me tell you this. We're going to garrison this castle. You have knowledge that we lack, and we would appreciate your help. Any who wish to stay will be welcomed among us. Those who wish to leave may do so."

"Lady Oona?" Morel asked softly, her eyes downcast.

"Morel, dear friend, tell me what is on your mind."

"Lady, can you tell us what is happening? Why have you come, and what does it mean for us? Can any of us come with you when you leave?"

"You're as full of questions as ever, Morel," laughed Oona, as she gently hugged the girl. "I'll do my best to explain. We're the people of Lady Meera of the House of Lothar. Lady Meera has claimed all these lands for her own, and we've come to govern these lands for her. The laws of Meera forbid the use of slaves, and so we came to set you free.

"We also came to take the extra supplies from the castle to feed our people. We control the wheel now, and in future it will be turned by beasts, not slaves. All of you are welcome among us if you so desire. If you'd rather not live under Red Meera's rule, then you have until this year's snow melts to abandon these lands.

"We're placing a garrison here to protect our interests. We'd like your help and advice, but we won't compel you. Konnor, a man who is known to you, will stay to help you learn the ways of the westerfolk."

"Konnor, you're staying?" The surprise was clear in Morel's voice as she turned to face him.

"I am, Morel. I'm the last of my house. I have nowhere to go now that all my kin are dead. If I stay in the service of Lady Oona, I may find a house who will adopt me."

"If Konnor stays, then I'll stay as well," said Morel. "As will I," chimed in many of the others until it was agreed that most would stay.

"Morel, have you another reason to stay?" Oona had mischief in her voice as Morel blushed to her roots.

"Lady Oona, Konnor has kept me, and many others, alive when all hope seemed lost."

"Is that the only reason?"

"Ah, no, Lady," grinned Konnor. "A few days ago, Morel agreed to be my life companion, if I could find a way to free us of the chains of slavery. I believe she thought she was safe. Morel, my beloved, I won't hold you to that bargain if you..."

Morel turned to face him, her hands on her hips and a twinkle in her eye. "Forget that, Konnor, a deal is a deal." Just at that moment Tallon returned.

Dor winked at Konnor then spoke to Tallon. "Captain Tallon, old Konnor here says he's looking for a house to adopt him, since he lost his kinfolk to the waters and the wheel. Kellar can always use good folk. What do you think?"

"Well, he survived two years at that accursed wheel, so I guess he's tough enough. He'll need someone to speak for him, Dor."

"Aye, well, I guess I could do that, but he has a companion. She'll need someone to speak for her as well."

"I will speak for, Morel," declared Oona as she stepped up beside her friend. "I'll speak to Kellan myself, as soon as we return to the great hall."

"Very well then, I'll speak to father myself on Konnor's behalf."

Konnor had a tear in his eye as he gazed at Tallon. "I..."

"Quiet you," grinned Tallon. "The garrison is ready to leave for the castle. You go with them and advise Gerrit here. Lady Oona, this man is Gerrit. He'll command the garrison here at Castle Oona."

"Castle Oona?"

"It has a certain ring to it."

"What are your commands, Lady Oona," Gerrit asked deferentially.

"Keep yourselves alive and well, Gerrit. We'll leave the Lucky Lady here with a small crew, in case you have need to send messages or to escape. We'll return in the spring with many more troops, for this place is the key to controlling these lands. Learn what these people can teach you, and teach them the ways of our folk."

"It will be as you desire, Lady. I believe I should feed them up a bit at first, do you think?"

"Gerrit, that is a splendid idea," laughed Oona.

"Then, with your permission, Lady Oona, I'll be about the business." He smiled as he backed away. He turned and addressed the former slaves. "Right, who's coming with us?" They all struggled to their feet, and a man-at-arms appeared beside each one to help them along. The procession set out at a very gentle pace for the castle.

Oona sat brooding at the silent forest, as she chewed thoughtfully on the food that Dor had brought to her. Finally he broke into her reverie. "Lady Oona..."

"Hmmm?"

"The ships are here, Lady. It is time to be about the business again."

"You do it, Dor. I proclaim you king for a day."

"Respectfully declined, Lady. I fear I'm too weak from my wound."

"It was worth a try," she sighed, as she grabbed his arm and rose to her feet. "Alright, I can do it. Let's go." She set out to meet the first ship with Dor right at her heel.

MEERA SPED THROUGH the forest like a hunting wolf, a number of her troops close at her heels. It took a while, but they ran down one of the fleeing men. Meera ignored him and sped right past. One of her men leaped onto the tired animal's back and dragged the rider down to his doom. Meera ran on.

They ran down several more, but eventually had to admit defeat and turn back. Cursing like a madwoman, Meera turned toward the valley of the wheel. They hadn't gone far when three more riders burst into the clearing where they had stopped to drink from the stream. Only one rider managed to escape that encounter. Unfortunately for him, as he turned back, he ran straight into Tella and her companions, with predictable results. Meera found them a moment later.

It was late in the day when Meera, still cursing, reappeared at the landing site. "Tallon," she bawled, "get those ships up here and post a garrison to that castle. I want..." She stopped as she saw the group of people smiling at her. "Alright, what's going on?" It was Tallon who replied to her question.

"Forgive me, Lady Merra, but the ships are already loaded and on their way back downstream. The garrison is in Castle Oona as we speak."

"Lady Oona must have been busy," grinned Tella.

"Oona has done this?"

"Aye, Lady."

"What else has she done?"

"Well, Lady, Lady Oona is at the castle finalizing the preparations. Perhaps she could better..." Tallon was already speaking to Meera's back. She was on her way to the castle.

As Meera reached the castle gate, a man-at-arms stepped aside to permit her entry. He bowed his head and gave her the hand to shoulder salute as she passed. "Meera!" Oona hurled herself into Meera's arms. "Oh Lady, I am so sorry. Please forgive me. I..." Oona was blushing furiously as she lowered her eyes and tried to stammer an apology.

"Oona, my Oona, relax. I'm not offended by your greeting. I am, in point of fact, very pleased by it. I'm sad to report though, that Born escaped me again."

"Born? He was here?"

"He was. I saw him ride out with those men, but he turned tail and fled. I tried to catch him, but that man is as hard to catch as a sand eel. Now, my delight, I've made my report. It is time for yours."

"My report?"

"Yes, my Oona, what all have you done here?"

"Lady, I'm so sorry, but you weren't here and..."

"Oona, stop now, my Lady Healer. I'm not angry, but I am interested in what you have done. Please tell me."

"Yes, Lady. Well, we garrisoned the castle, and loaded most of the supplies onto the ships. There's enough here for the garrison, and the Lucky Lady will remain in case they have need. The former slaves have agreed to remain, and teach our folk the ways and means of this castle. All is in readiness here. The Lucky Lady is ready to take us to the Raptor so we can return to the north before the winter gales come."

"What of the wheel, Oona, what have you done about that?"

"I have left it whole, Lady, but instructed that it be turned by beasts from now on."

"Why keep it whole?"

"Most people of this land are accustomed to coming here for the grinding of their grain, Lady. If we're in control of the wheel, and if we demand less for the grinding..."

"The easier it will be for them to accept our rule, and all the more supplies for us. Oona, I'm delighted with what you've accomplished.

This is wonderful. Now, before we go, there is one more thing I would like to do."

"What is that, Lady?"

"There was a young westerman chained to that wheel. I would know his fate and hear his story. Bring him to me if possible."

"I am here, Lady Meera." Konnor knelt before Meera. "I'm Konnor, last of the house of Tradoon."

"Tell me, Konnor," said Meera, kindly as she took his arm and helped him to rise.

"We were a small house from Okran, one of the outer isles, Lady, workers in metals as your bracelet will attest. We sought to escape the heavy hand of Mad Drado by sailing east to join your people. Our folk always did well under the House of Lothar until..."

"I know, Konnor, please continue."

"There is not much more to tell, Lady. We were swamped in a bad storm and both ships went down. I and a few others managed to make shore, but we were captured by humans and brought to this place. That was two years past. We tried to escape, and nearly made it, but luck did not favor us that day. We were then chained to the wheel where the rest gradually succumbed to their wounds.

"I was more fortunate. I managed to survive the first year. We slaves were brought into the castle and fed for the winter. I alone was kept in chains within a small cell. When the snows were gone, we were again chained to the wheel. I would not have survived another year without Morel, none of us would. She's learned healing skills, and all too often shared them as well as her food. She kept us all alive."

"Where is Morel?"

"Here, Lady," the girl responded shyly, as she stepped forward and bowed.

"I greet you, friend of Lady Oona," smiled Meera. "I am Meera of the House of Lothar. Do you wish to come with us to be near your friend?"

"Forgive me, Lady, but I must stay here with my companion, Konnor."

"Truly? Well then, has Konnor been adopted already?"

"Lady?"

"A man without a house is a poor companion to choose, Morel. He has no allies to help defend you."

"Lady, if I may." Konnor interrupted softly. "Captain Tallon and Dor of Kellar have agreed to speak for me to Kellan. Lady Oona herself has promised to speak for Morel."

"Kellan is far from here, Konnor, and the winters here are long." Meera had a twinkle in her eye. "My own house was depleted of good men by my mad uncle. If you would consider it, the House of Lothar will have you."

"Lady, I could not hope to rise so high..." stammered Konnor.

"Nonsense. You survived two years on that damned wheel. You've proven your worth, Konnor. Dor, will you speak for Konnor?"

"Aye, Lady," grinned Dor. "I think he's made of good stuff all right."

"Oona, my delight, will you speak for Morel?"

"Yes, Lady, Morel is a good woman and true."

"Then, as Chieftain of the House of Lothar, I welcome you, my new kinfolk," smiled Meera, as she stepped between them and gave them a gentle hug. "Now then, Konnor of Lothar, I charge you to remain here and do what you can to ease our new folk into our society. Teach them our language and our ways. If possible, help them find houses to adopt them, if that is their desire. Will you accept this charge?"

"With extreme pleasure, Lady," replied Konnor, beaming his delight.

"Gerrit, are you commanding here?"

"Aye, Lady Meera, if that is your desire."

"It is. Lady Oona's chosen well. Alright, good people, we leave you to your business. The sun is setting, and I would be northbound on the Raptor before she rises again. Live well."

"Fare hale and well," they called in response, as Meera took Oona's hand and led her back to the Lucky Lady.

"I WAS SO AFRAID I WOULD make a mistake," Oona breathed softly, as she snuggled against Meera's side aboard the Raptor.

"Oona, this was your expedition. The decisions were yours to make. Castle Oona is yours to defend, and those are your troops defending her. These were your decisions to make. However, I must say that I fully approve of your choices. May I ask how you arrived at certain decisions?"

"I asked Tella and Tallon for advice. Then I asked the others for advice as well."

"The others?"

"Yes, we agreed to garrison the castle, so I asked Tallon to do it. I then asked Gerrit for his advice about what he would need, and then...well, you can see..."

"Yes, I can, my Oona." Meera smiled as she kissed the top of Oona's head. "Well done, my Lady Companion. I have truly chosen well." She stroked Oona's hair thoughtfully for a moment. "It's growing back nicely."

"Yes, but I believe I may just keep it a bit short. I think I like it this way."

"Then you should do so, my Lady Healer."

"Meera..."

"Oona, behave, I am too tired to play this game."

"Lady..."

"Yes, my Oona?"

"Sleep well." Oona received another light kiss on her head then Meera's breathing shifted and she was asleep. Oona smiled with delight, then allowed sleep to claim her as well.

WHILE MEERA WAS SETTLING down on the Raptor with Oona in her arms, Born was staring into a small fire and swearing softly to himself. Broc and one other were his only companions.

"So, now where do we go?" grumbled Broc.

"Go where you will," sighed Born, "I care not."

"There's nowhere left to go. That damned western witch's cut us off completely. And she's killed most of our friends to boot."

"Hmmm, I know. I'll kill her slowly for that."

"So, what do you plan to do?"

"I'll spend my winter traveling across this land, and raising an army to rise up against her."

"How? What would make reasonable men do that?" asked the other man.

"She's stolen the great wheel. Without that, everyone will have no way to grind their grain. Many will starve or be taken as Meera's slave. No, I'll raise an army, and take the wheel back for myself, for us all. Every damned one of those savages will be killed, or chained to that wheel. Meera and Porga will be staked out in the sun for the men, until they die."

"Meera will put a dagger through your heart, more like," sighed the other man as he settled down to sleep. Born just grunted and continued to stare at the dancing flames.

Far away, Kreeg continued to strengthen his defenses and drill his troops.

Two Against the Storm

It was the second day aboard ship. Oona awakened to a feeling of nausea, and the heaving deck. She fought the sickness and tried to gain her feet. She managed just in time to lose her battle against nausea, and her last meal over the rail. Oona could vaguely hear Meera shouting in the distance, but she could not see her.

"Down sails and hard oars," bellowed Meera. "Tallon, find us a harbor, and soon, this is going to be a bad one."

"There is no harbor we can make in time, Lady," Tallon shouted over the rising wind. "There's too many reefs. We dare not approach the land."

"Head into the winds then, I'll do what I can," shouted Meera, as she made her way to the bow of the great ship.

Clinging to the rail, Oona felt Tella's hand steady her. "Are you all right, Lady Oona?"

"No dammit, I'm not alright." Oona shouted over the winds. "Can't you see I'm dying here?"

Tella did not respond to Oona's weak attempt at humor. Her eyes were trying to pierce the storm clouds that had come upon them so swiftly. Following Tella's gaze, Oona saw the rest of the fleet trying to force themselves into the teeth of the gale. Perhaps the big warships might survive this, but the supply ships were too heavily laden, and wallowing badly. The precious supplies were not going to arrive at the new capitol unless this storm abated soon, and it didn't look like there was any chance of that happening.

Suddenly Oona's searching gaze found Meera at the bow, leaning into the wind with the waves breaking over her. She had tied herself to the rail. It was a good thing she had, for she would have been lost otherwise. Oona screamed as a wave washed over Meera, submerging her completely.

Tella gripped Oona tightly to keep her from trying to get to Meera. With a defiant scream of challenge, Meera rose from the wave and renewed her chant. Oona held her breath for what seemed like a lifetime, but no other wave came to claim Meera. Slowly, grudgingly, the storm began to abate.

"What is it, Tella?" Oona asked, as she saw the look of deep concern of her champion's face. "What's wrong?"

"The storm is too strong to be natural, Lady Oona. Lady Meera should have been able to conquer it by now, but she has had little success. I suspect an evil hand at work here."

"An evil hand? Whose?"

"Drado."

"How could he make such a storm? Does he truly have such power?"

"No, Lady, he has not the power to create such a storm, but he does have the power to strengthen it. Lady Meera could stop it easily, if someone wasn't working against her. Drado is the only one I know of who would do this."

"How did he know where to send the winds?"

"He didn't. He will be sitting alone on his throne, chanting away, sending as many storms toward the east as he can, hoping for the best. This time he got lucky, and found a natural storm to enhance. Now it is a contest to see whose strength will last the longest, but he has the advantage, for the storm's natural desire is in his favor."

Even as Tella spoke, Oona could see Meera struggling in the bow. Oona had to help her if she could. She started forward as the winds began to rise again, but Tella restrained her. "Lady, it is too dangerous," she shouted.

"I can help her, Tella, but I must reach her first. You'll have to steady me once we get there, for I'll not be able to do so myself. Come."

Tella didn't approve, but she complied with her queen's wishes. Steadying Oona as best she could, she helped her make her way forward. It took some time, but at last they reached Meera. Oona could hear the fatigue in Meera's voice as the chant faltered and the winds seemed to renew their attack on the fleet.

Anchoring herself as best she could, Oona placed her hands on Meera's shoulders and began to sing a healing song. Meera's voice steadied as a surge of warm, loving, energy coursed through her, renewing her strength. Meera's voice rose strong and true with Oona's clear sweet tones singing a counterpoint harmony. Their voices blended and the winds began to abate.

Tella shook her head in wonder and steadied Oona as she sang. The two queens of the westerfolk sang more strongly now, and the winds died as swiftly as they had arisen. The fleet was suddenly becalmed, bobbing on a quiet sea. Meera leaned heavily on the rail, drinking in great heaving breaths of air. Oona fainted away into Tella's arms, completely drained. Tella carried her back to the forward cabin and laid her gently on the sleeping mat there. Meera followed, then sank gratefully down beside her.

"How many were lost, Tella," Meera asked softly.

"I'll find out, Lady," replied Tella, as she stood and turned away.

Tallon approached shortly, dropping to one knee as he arrived. "Captain Tallon, what news of the fleet? How many did we lose?"

"Twelve men in total were lost, Lady Meera, no ships."

"Tallon, truly you are Kellan's son. You've chosen your captains wisely, even as my Oona has chosen her fleet commander well." Tallon beamed his delight at her praise. "How many are still sea worthy, and how fare the supply ships?"

"We'll need a day to tidy up, Lady, but the fleet has survived remarkably well. The supply ships took on a bit of water, but the watertight holds weren't broken. All should be well. I'll investigate myself, if you desire."

"Do it, Tallon my friend. Get us under way as soon as you can, but don't disturb Oona's slumber if you can help it."

"Aye, Lady," he grinned as he turned on his heel. As he sped away to do her bidding, Meera snuggled down beside Oona and allowed the fatigue to claim her. It had been early dawn when the storm had awakened her. It was now dark once again. Meera had battled the forces of nature for a full day. She was completely exhausted.

The sun was well up in the sky again when Meera awakened. She listened carefully, but all she could hear was the soft lapping of the waves on the hull, and the creak of the great oars. She arose swiftly and stepped from the cabin. A wild cheer greeted her arrival on deck. She grinned and waved to the oarsmen before joining Oona at the rail. Tallon and Tella were there as well. Oona stepped into Meera's arms and gave her a gentle squeeze. "I thought I'd lost you yesterday."

"I'm not as easily gotten rid of as that, my Lady Healer." Meera smiled as she lightly kissed the top of Oona's head. "I see that you're well recovered."

"I have certain herbs with me." Oona leaned back against the rail. "They've restored me, even as you've restored sanity to the wild seas."

"That was the worst storm I have ever faced," sighed Meera.

"Tella thinks that Drado was behind it."

"It is possible, but I doubt he could have done it alone. I expect he's found another storm singer somewhere. We'd better be on the lookout for another gale, Tallon. It's the time of year for them."

"Yes, ma'am," grinned Tallon. "I heard that loud and clear."

"When did we get under way?"

"Just before dawn, Lady Meera."

"When did you last rest, Tallon?" asked Oona.

"Before the storm, Lady Oona." He was exhausted. It was easy for Oona to see.

"Then off you go." Oona pointed to the cabin.

"Aye, Lady, and thank you."

"You seem to be getting the hang of this command thing," grinned Meera, as Tallon slipped inside the cabin and vanished from sight. "So tell me now, what was that you did to me?"

"Lady, it's a healing thing that I learned from my mother. Often, when she was performing a difficult healing, I would place my hands on her shoulders and give my strength to her. I believed that it would help you as well."

"It certainly did, Oona. Without you I would have failed, and the fleet would be at the bottom of the sea right now. We all owe our lives to you, my Lady Healer."

"Thank you, Lady," Oona smiled softly. They stood gazing out at the waters for a while before Oona spoke again. "Lady, tell me of the western isles."

"What would you like to know, my Oona?" Meera asked, with a delighted smile curving her lips.

"How many are there? What are the lands like? What do the people do there?"

"Hold, hold," laughed Meera. "Now, let me see if I can do this right. There are eighty-seven isles in all. They're strung out along a great reef, like a string of jewels around a young woman's neck. It's thought that it once was part of a great land mass that sank into the seas. A warm current of water comes up from the south and flows past, so the winters are often milder than they are here, but they can be very wet. Personally, I like the snows better.

"Most of the isles are small, and the people make their living catching fish and building ships. They also run beasts of wool in the hills, for meat and clothing. Small gardens they tend as well. Some of the isles have minerals in them, and there the folk delve into the ground for the ores and gems. These folk work the metals, swords for the warriors, and plows for the farmers. Konnor's clan, Tradoon, was one such house.

"Sixteen of the larger isles are exceptionally good for farming, so the people there grow food and raise beasts. They trade with the fisher folk and all prosper thereby, or at least they once did."

"No longer?"

"Most of the forests are long gone from the isles, so the ship builders have to go to the poisoned lands for timber. That was where we first encountered the half men. The half men soon learned to build ships, and they began to attack the isles. We've fought them off for generations, but now, with the fleet gone, I fear they will overrun my beloved isles."

"Who are the half men?"

"Just as the westerfolk are descended from the elder race, we believe the half men are as well, or at least in part. Where we blended with the golden haired folk and grew stronger of mind, the ancestors of the half men were driven to the poisoned lands, and there they faltered. They were once men, it is believed, but they blended with some unknown creature there, and so are human no longer. They are as much beast now as men, without much language as we know it."

"What made them that way, do you know?"

"No one knows for certain, but we believe that it was the poison that lingers in the great land that did it to them. Perhaps that's why they try so hard to drive us from the isles. Perhaps they want to be men again."

"Meera, tell me of Drado."

"Whatever for, my Oona?" Meera asked, somewhat perplexed.

"Something Born used to say all the time. Know your enemy. Drado has tried to kill us, and he must face justice for that."

"Oona?" Meera was truly surprised at Oona now. This was a side of her companion she had not seen before.

"Lady, I was raised to believe that folk should be fair to one another. When the slavers came, I learned that it was not always so, hardly ever in fact. Even though I was unable to ever do anything about the world, I vowed that if I ever got the chance..."

"I understand, my Oona." Meera put her arm around the smaller woman's shoulders. "You want justice, and I will help you get it."

"Lady, I want justice for you."

"But not for you?"

"I want revenge for myself," said Oona, her voice going cold and hard. "Now that I have the power to do so, there are three men I will see dead, or die in the attempt."

"Which three are they, Oona? Tell me and I'll kill them myself."

"Born, Broc, and Drado," replied Oona. "Broc hurt me and lied to Born. Born believed his younger brother. Because of that, Born killed my children."

"And Drado?"

"His evil nearly robbed me of you, my beloved Meera," sighed Oona, as she laid her head on Meera's shoulder. "I can't risk that ever happening again. The folk need you, and I need you. I'll find a way to finish that man, if it is the last thing I ever do."

Meera smiled broadly with delight as she lightly kissed the top of Oona's head. This had been the first time Oona had spoken to her as an equal. It was the first time she had used terms of endearment. Meera was delighted that the years of slavery hadn't completely destroyed the spirit in Oona. It was beginning to surface again. Until now she had expressed only her deep need for a place of safety. Now Oona had shown concern and affection for Meera, as well as expressing a desire for revenge. Yes indeed, a balance in all things. Meera had chosen her companion wisely.

A storm arose late in the day, but Oona followed Meera to the bow. The weather was under control in short order. With Oona channeling the energy to her, Meera was much stronger. The storm, which had no unnatural strength added to it, abated easily.

Day after day the fleet made steady progress under oars. The wind always in their face, but due to Meera and Oona, never getting out of hand. They were able to handle it, but it was taxing their strength. One day they were both sleeping late, and Tella was leaning against the rail beside Tallon.

"How much longer do you think, Tella?"

"How much longer what? How much longer before we reach port, or how much longer can those two survive?"

"Both," he grunted. "The damned storms just keep coming, and it's killing them to hold them at bay. The Ladies need rest, and so do the men. Many more days like this, and we won't have a man left able to pull an oar."

"That goes for you too, Captain Tallon."

"Me?"

"You've spelled off every man on this ship once each day. How long do you think you can keep this up?"

"Until I drop, Tella. I won't ask a man to pull an oar I won't pull with him." Suddenly his head snapped up and he sniffed the air.

"Yes," exulted Tella, as she too felt the errand breeze. "Quickly now, Captain, save your fleet."

"Full sail, lively now, full sail," bawled Tallon as he leaped to the steering oar. "Signal the fleet. Full sail." As he looked all about, he saw that many of his more experienced captains already were hauling sail.

"What's going on?" demanded Meera, as she burst from the cabin, Oona right at her heels. "Is it another storm?"

"Aye, Lady," laughed Tallon, "out of the south she comes."

Meera laughed with delight as she felt the rising breeze. She began to sing softly and the breeze turned to a strong wind. "Ship oars," bawled Tallon and a grateful crew obeyed. The wind could drive the ships for a while, and the oarsmen could rest.

The wind was steady for most of the day, and Tallon was content to let his men take it easy. The next day, just about high sun, they sighted a ship coming out of the north. It was the Raven.

"Ho there, Uncle," called Tallon, as the Raven came alongside the Raptor, "what are you doing so far from home?"

"Looking for you," came the answer, "and who do you think is far from home? You'll sight the harbor within the turning of a glass." There was a wild cheer throughout the fleet at this news.

"Kieran," shouted Meera. "We're all tired and battle weary. Go on ahead, and let the folk know that Lady Oona returns with a gift of three ships full of grain and supplies. This will be a joyful Night of Candles this year."

"Aye, Lady, consider it done." The Raven, with her fresh crew, pulled away and swiftly left the tired fleet behind. A short while later the fleet sighted the harbor. The sun was just setting as the Raptor tied up to the dock.

A Time For Rest

The welcoming celebrations went on well into the night. Meera was nearly asleep on her feet before she could gracefully call an end to it. Oona was already collapsed on the sleeping furs as Meera sank to her place beside her.

"Lady Meera?" murmured Oona, as Meera settled down beside her.

"Yes, my Oona?"

"Do you need me to…?"

"Yes, my Lady Healer, I think I do. Tonight is the night you will serve my needs for me."

Startled awake again, Oona sat up, wide-eyed. "Yes, Lady," she breathed softly, "whatever you need of me, you shall have." The fear was clear in her voice, and Meera instantly felt bad for teasing her, but she continued anyway.

"Come to me, my Oona," Meera purred softly as she reached for Oona. Trembling, Oona closed her eyes and allowed Meera to pull her closer. She felt Meera's gentle breath as their lips neared each other, but the expected kiss did not happen. Instead, there were soft words whispered in her ear.

"I need you to let me sleep, and to stop teasing me when I'm too tired to tease back."

Oona sat away from Meera, her mouth making a perfect "O" at Meera's rich laughter. Meera tried to make a contrite face, but failed and burst out laughing again. "Meera, stop laughing at me," demanded Oona as she lightly poked Meera in the ribs. Meera instantly flinched away. A look of wicked delight lit up Oona's face at that reaction. "You're ticklish."

"I am not," denied Meera, but Oona pounced on her and tickled her savagely.

Meera shrieked her protests, but could not escape without hurting Oona, and that she would not do. Finally Oona relented and plopped down beside Meera who cuddled her closer. "Please forgive me, Lady, I didn't mean to offend..."

"Oona, I'm not offended by your playfulness," smiled Meera, as she squirmed a bit to get more comfortable. "I'm thrilled that you're no longer so afraid of me; that I'm safe to tease you back."

"Lady?"

"My poor Oona, at first you were so afraid of me, I was terrified I might frighten you to death. As time went by you became more comfortable with me, but still you had fear. I'm happy to see that it's passing, and that you feel safe to be playful."

Oona sighed and snuggled closer. After a moment she lifted her lips to whisper in Meera's ear. "Lady, if you truly need..."

"Oona, for the love of all the gods, stop," laughed Meera. "I swear I'll perish of exhaustion if you do not relent."

"But..."

"Hush."

"Lady..."

"Hush, that's an order."

"Yes, Lady, I hear and obey." Oona might have carried the game on a bit longer, but Meera's breathing shifted, and, smiling softly, Oona closed her eyes and allowed the fatigue to claim her as well.

The next few days were busy with affairs of state. Oona paid close attention to Meera, the way she conducted herself, the way she carefully listened to her advisers, and to the types of decisions she made. The Valley of the Wheel had been a good lesson for Oona. In truth, having to make all those decisions was almost as frightening as the battle had been. However, it had made her feel powerful for the first time in her life, and the feeling had been intoxicating.

Finally the supply ships were emptied and the supplies distributed, all small disputes adjudged, ships readied for winter, and now Oona had some time to herself. "What is on your mind, my Lady Healer?" asked Meera, as they shared breakfast in the kitchens.

"I thought I might see how that healing room is coming along. I know that it's been built, but I have not yet seen inside it. Can we do that today?"

"Of course we can." Meera pushed away her platter and smiled. "Let's go have a look at it."

Meera took Oona by the hand and led her out a small side door of the great hall. They didn't even have to go fully outside to access the healing room. As they stepped through the opening, they saw that there were several people lying on beds within a long room. There was a fire near each end of the room, so the warmth was quite well distributed. Nora was there attending to a child on one of the beds.

As the two queens entered everyone tried to reach a kneeling position. "Be as you were." Meera spoke gently as she caught one man by the arm, and eased him back down. "No one is required to rise or kneel in this room. Here we are all as one."

"Thank you, Lady," whispered Oona. "Nora, what do you think of this?"

"Lady, this is most wonderful."

"I do hope it pleases you, Lady Oona," said a soft voice behind her. "I followed your description as best I could. Nora helped with a few suggestions. These cupboards down here are to store the herbs in."

Oona smiled her delight at the old fellow. "It's beyond my greatest expectations. Truly you're a master of your craft, Bellar."

The man beamed his pleasure and backed out of the room. Oona smiled and turned back to her inspection of the room, but a small voice calling her name caught her attention. "Lady Oona, Lady

Oona, have you come to learn of the flags now?" Sure enough, there was Oona's small friend on one of the beds, her mother trying hush her.

"So there you are," smiled Oona. "I was beginning to wonder what had happened to you. I thought you might be there to greet my ship when we returned."

"I wanted to be, Lady Oona," the girl replied solemnly, "but I fell and hurt my leg. Nora says I have to stay here until it heals."

"I shall leave you to this, my Lady Healer." Meera smiled and patted Oona's shoulder. "Seek for me in the great hall when you're ready." She lightly kissed the top of Oona's head then turned and left the healing room.

"What's happened to my teacher, Nora?"

"She's broken her leg, Lady Oona," sighed Nora, as she approached them. "I set the leg back in place, and strapped it with sticks, but it doesn't want to heal."

"Well, we can't have that, can we?" Oona smiled as she sank to a cross legged position beside the girl's bed. "May I help it heal for you?"

Wide eyed, the girl nodded her head. "Yes please."

The mother sat very still at her side, avoiding Oona's eyes. Sitting above the queen would surely get her in deep trouble, but Lady Oona did not seem to mind. "It's alright," smiled Oona, as she patted the woman's knee, "there are no queens in this room, only folk. Don't worry."

"Thank you, Lady, I..."

"Hush now. I need you to help me with this."

"How can I help, Lady Oona?"

"Hold her gently and remember her as strong and full of life." Oona then turned her attention to the child. "Now you, you must help as well."

"What must I do, Lady Oona?"

"Do you remember a warm summer's day when you ran through the fields chasing small birds or insects?"

"Last summer I chased a young dollot. I nearly caught him too, but he flew too high."

"Good. Now, hold that memory in your mind while I fix your leg." The child furrowed her brow, and Oona closed her eyes, placed her hands lightly on the broken leg, and then sang a high sweet note that lingered on the air long after she had stopped. The girl giggled once or twice as the energy flowed into her leg and up through her body. Once Oona stopped the girl tried to stand, but Oona held her back gently.

"Not so fast," said Oona. "Let me see now, how did we do?" She gently felt all over the affected leg then smiled brightly. "I think we did quite well, but it'll take a few more sessions. I'll come back to you once each day, six more times, and then you should be as good as new. For now, you must rest. As soon as we get you going again we'll walk down by the docks so you can teach me about the flags."

"Lady Oona, how can I ever thank you for this? What service can I offer?" the mother asked softly.

"There is a gift I would have."

"Name it, Lady, and it is yours."

"Friendship, good woman, from both you and my teacher here."

"Lady?"

"Do you know my tale?"

"Some, Lady. It is said that you were held slave, and that Lady Meera set you free."

"That is the truth of it. On the day Lady Meera came to me, my children were slain before my eyes. Little Tona was of an age with this one."

"Oh Lady, I am so sorry..."

"I beg you, let us be friends. Allow me to spend time with my teacher once in a while."

"Oh Lady, of course. We are both deeply honored. I'm Toole and this one is Bekka."

"Thank you, Toole. I'm the one who is honored. Tell me, that necklace of yours, did you make it?"

"Yes, Lady," replied the woman, smiling as she removed it from her neck. "Please, accept it as a gift."

"It is very beautiful, Toole," said Oona, as she inspected it closely then passed it back to Toole, "but I don't want to rob you. I want you to teach me how to do that, so I can make one for Meera."

"Of course, Lady Oona. I'll bring the necessary things with me tomorrow, if you like."

"Wonderful." Oona smiled as she rose to go. "First we'll heal Bekka's leg, and then we'll string beads." She smiled again as she turned and left the healing room to go in search of Meera. It would soon be the time for the Night of Candles. Oona would have a gift ready for Meera, one of her own making.

THE NIGHT OF CANDLES eventually arrived, and Oona thrilled to the new and exciting things the westerfolk did to celebrate the time of darkness and the returning of the light. The first day there was a great deal of decorating the halls and houses. This was followed by a day of feasting in the great hall for the royals and their chieftains. The next day the chieftains feasted the folk of their own houses. Meera and Oona fed as many of the House of Lothar as they could fit into their hall. The rest were sent sweetmeats, bread, and sweet water to their homes or camps, and Oona followed Meera as she paid a short visit to each of them.

The day that followed the feasting was the shortest day of the year, the Night of Candles. All day the queens and court were entertained by groups of tumblers, jugglers, etc. Through it all there was music, drums, flutes, something with strings that Oona had never seen before, a type of bagpipe, and the voices, oh those rich sweet voices. How Oona did enjoy the singing.

The highlight of the show was a weapons demonstration, followed by several hand-to-hand combat demonstrations, and finally a challenge battle of the royal champions. Oona gasped fearfully as this last was announced, but Meera hastened to reassure her that it was all well rehearsed. That neither Tella, nor Kellan, would come to any harm. Still somewhat unsure, Oona sat back to watch. What she saw amazed her. It was clear to her now why everyone thought Tella was the right choice for her champion.

Kellan and Tella faced each other with sword and dagger. Suddenly Tella feinted to the right then darted left. Kellan had read the move, and was ready with one of his own. The battle was on. Faster and faster, and with more and more deadly attacks, they fought, until it was nearly impossible to follow their movements. Oona was terrified, but everyone else seemed to enjoy the spectacle.

Suddenly Meera stood up and raised her hands. "Hold," she commanded, and both Kellan and Tella froze in place, her dagger an inch from his heart, and his sword blade almost touching her neck. "I declare this contest of champions a draw."

There was a great round of cheering then, as Tella fell into Kellan's arms, laughing. "I'm getting too damned old for this," gasped Kellan.

"You're out of shape," laughed Tella. "You need more practice."

"I need more of something, that's for sure," he grinned in return, as he pinched her bottom, causing her to shriek and dance out of his arms.

Once the contest of champions was over, they prepared for the parade of light. Torches were brought, as were many candles, which were set out on the great table. When all was ready, a tall woman in a long flowing robe approached, and knelt to the queens. "Ladies, it is time," she announced in a rich contralto voice.

"You may proceed, Priestess," smiled Meera.

The woman nodded, then rose and faced the gathered folk, raising her arms high. "Great Lady of Light," she sang in a powerful voice so all could hear, "hear the call of your people. We know you need rest, but we are failing without the life giving light. We beg you to return to us, and bring the great Light of Life with you. We will keep these small lights burning for you this night, so you will know where to find your people."

As she finished her sing song call, the priestess took a brand from the fire and lit one large candle on the table. "Who will tend this light through the long dark of night?" Three young girls stepped forward at her call. "It is well done, daughters of the light. Keep the flame burning until the sun rises again. Do not let it falter." The three girls stepped closer to the candle, shielding it from drafts with their bodies. "Come, good folk of the Isles, it is time to spread the light." The priestess lit a torch from the first candle as she spoke.

She led them all outside, where there were hundreds of people huddled against the falling snows and piercing winds. Meera stepped forward and began her chant. Oona placed her hands on Meera's shoulders and the chant increased. It was not long before the winds died, and only the gentle falling of the snow was left.

Smiling her thanks to Meera, the priestess began to light as many of the torches held out to her by the folk, as she could. Others took their now lit torches and shared the fire with the rest, until all the torches were lit. The priestess then led them slowly through the makeshift streets, lighting torches for folks as they went. The procession eventually wound down to the docks where there was a sailor by each ship, waiting for his torch to be lit. Eventually the parade of light found its way back to the great hall, where the torches were cast onto the fires.

All the candles from the table were then lit from the first candle the woman had set alight, the three girls doing the honors. When all were glowing merrily there was a singing of songs special to the occasion. Oona truly enjoyed the singing, and vowed to learn the songs before the next year rolled around.

Once the singing was finished everyone left the hall, except for the royals and the priestess. "Priestess of the Lady of Light," said Meera, continuing with the ritual, "the day has passed, and the light has been shared with all the folk. Do you wish assistance guarding the candles?"

"Thank you, gracious Lady, but the three are daughters of great chieftains. They are strong, and well suited to their task. You may go to your rest, and trust that all will be well."

"Then so be it."

Meera took Oona by the hand. She led her out of the great room and to the sleeping chamber. "It's been a long and exciting day my, Lady Healer. Are you ready for your rest?"

Oona smiled as she stepped closer to Meera. "Indeed I am, Lady, but first..."

"Oona, have mercy, I beg you," sighed Meera, as she allowed her head to drop and her shoulders to slump. "I haven't the strength left to be teased tonight."

"So who's teasing?"

"Oona!"

"Forgive me, Lady," giggled Oona, as she pressed something into Meera's hand, "but I couldn't help myself."

"Oona, what's this?" Meera held up the necklace Oona had made for her.

"It is the custom among my father's people, to give a small gift made by your own hand, to the one you love most. The day of the gift is the day called Yuletide, your Night of Candles."

"Oona, you made this for me?" Meera's voice caught as she held up the jewelry. "This is skillfully made indeed, and quite beautiful as well."

"Toole taught me the way of the making. Do you like it?"

"Oona, I love it, it's the finest gift I've ever been given. Oona this is strung on hair, but everyone has cut their hair. Where did you get...?"

"My old boots. The ones you made for me when you pulled me from the waters. They were all worn out, but I took them apart and saved the hairs you used to sew them up with."

"You did? Why?"

"So I would always have you near me," replied Oona softly, her eyes downcast.

"Oona, you amaze me," sighed Meera, as she gathered Oona into her arms and held her gently. "I'm thrilled with the gift, Oona, but I have none to give to you."

"Well, you could..."

Meera laughed as she gave Oona a gentle squeeze. "Oona, have mercy..."

"Lady, you have given me the gift of life, and the gift of freedom, as well as the name my mother gave me. Lady, you have given me gifts beyond measure."

"But still, I..."

"Well, you could..."

"Oona, you are a relentless tease," laughed Meera, as she released the girl and sank down onto the sleeping furs. "I'm going to sleep now. I've been abused enough for one day." She patted the bedding beside her, and a smiling Oona cuddled into her usual place.

"Lady, there is one thing you..." Meera began to protest again, but Oona laid her finger gently on Meera's lips to silence her. "Lady, just promise to keep me near you. That's the only gift I want."

Meera kissed the finger against her lips then pulled Oona closer. "It shall be as you require, my Lady Healer." She breathed softly into Oona's hair as she whispered. "I swear it." She kissed the top of Oona's head then allowed sleep to claim her.

A Winter of Schemes

As winter swept over the land, people everywhere hid themselves inside, huddling away from the cold. In the new city of the Westermen, winter was considerably easier than it had been over the past few years. Lady Oona's gift made it unnecessary to risk men and ships at raiding, and the fishing was easy. There were fish aplenty in the great harbor, and no need to look further. This was a winter of ease where the folk spent their time in mending gear and ships; that, and scheming.

As Oona walked along by the docks with Toole and Bekka, Tella ever present at her side, she became uneasy. Stealing glances all about without seeming as though she was watching, a skill every slave learns well, Oona saw what she feared most. The man's glance at her was filled with hate and malice.

"Bekka, my teacher, will you do a small favor for me?" Oona asked softly, so only her companions could hear.

"Of course, Lady Oona."

"Find the eldest of the court runners for me, would you, dear?" The child was away like a shot.

"What is it, Lady?" Tella gave no outward sign of alarm, but her senses were on full alert.

Oona continued her stroll as though nothing were wrong. When she spoke, her voice was so soft Tella struggled to hear it. "I need Dor and the twins. I have a very important task for them. I also need you to remain close to me for a while."

"Lady Oona, what is it? Have you sensed danger?" Toole's sudden unease was about to give the game away. It was time to change the setting. Oona needed a private place so she could confide in her companions. "Come, dear friends. My teacher has the right of it. It's far too cold to be about today. Let us seek out the warmth of the great hall." She turned and marched off with a watchful Tella close behind, and Toole hurrying to catch up.

As soon as they neared the hall, Oona detoured to the small entryway of the healing room. The room was empty, and so Toole asked the burning question. "Lady Oona, what has happened? What has caused you so much fear?"

Before she could answer Bekka found them. She had one of the runners in tow. The royal runners were teenagers who were chosen to spend at least a year at court running errands for the royals and chieftains. The boy with Bekka was the eldest of them all. "Here he is, Lady Oona," chirped up Bekka as they approached Oona and company.

"Excellent work, Bekka. You, young sir, I have seen you about often, but we have not yet spoken." Oona smiled as she raised him from the kneeling position he had instantly dropped into. "Tell me, what is your name?"

"It is an unlucky name, Lady Oona." He spoke softly, looking at the floor the whole time. "Everyone just calls me Runner."

"An unlucky name? Whatever could be so bad as that?"

"My name is Drado, Lady Oona." The boy was still studying his boots. "It was my father's father's name. My mother gave it to me at birth."

"Have you ever thought of changing it?"

"He cannot, Lady," Toole put in softly. "A mother names her child at birth, and that is the name he has for life."

"Very well then," sighed Oona. "Young Drado, my friend, you have a difficult task before you. It has fallen to you to restore that name to the honor it formerly held. From this day forth, whenever I speak the name Drado, it will be in reference to you. That other one who sits on a stolen throne to the west, will be known only as the Usurper." Tella nodded her approval as did Toole. "Now then, Drado, which is your house?"

"I am of the House of Sabine, Lady," he replied with a bemused smile on his face. "Our house is known for their skill at leather work. Our gift to you was..."

Oona smiled with delight. "The very boots I am wearing. I do prize them greatly. Drado, I've been told that you've remained at court as a runner two years past your duty time. I've watched you carefully, and I see no treachery in you at all, but I don't understand why you're still here. Should you not be aboard a ship by now? I understand that all young men serve at least one year aboard ship, before fully joining the men of their house."

There was a slight catch in his voice, and he could not meet her eyes. "None will take me, Lady, and I can't apprentice to my father until I've served one year."

"Excuse me?"

"Lady Oona," sighed Tella, "we're a superstitious folk, as you well know. No captain will want a man with such an unlucky name."

"I see, well then, Drado of Sabine, I've a task for you this winter. If you serve me well, I'll see you aboard one of my ships in the spring."

"My Lady Oona," gasped the boy, almost completely dumbfounded by this change in his luck. "Command me, Lady. I swear I won't fail you."

"Send Dor and the twins to me, but be sure that no one sees you do this, and be sure they come in stealth. As soon as you've spoken to Dor, do the same with Tallon, then return to me." The words were barely past her lips when he disappeared through the door.

"Toole, I would like it very much if you and Bekka could remain here in the great hall with me for the winter, since your companion is garrisoned at Castle Oona."

"Lady?"

"There is great danger about, isn't there, Lady Oona?" Tella's eyes swept all around, searching for even a hint of danger.

"There is Tella, and I won't allow Toole, or Bekka, to be harmed because they're my friends. Born slew my children just to hurt me more. I will not allow such a thing to happen again."

"Lady Oona," gasped Toole, "surely here in the new capitol we are safe."

"Even as Meera can sing up the storms or calm the winds, I can see into the heart of a man. Today I saw a man who intends to kill me. I've noticed him for some time now, but as time passes his hatred grows, and so does the number of men who follow him."

"Name him, Lady, and I will put a stop to his career of intrigue."

"Not yet, Tella, not yet. First we need to know his plans, as well as the names, and full number of his companions. This is not the time to hurry. It's the time for stealth."

"Will you not tell Lady Meera?"

"She is conferring with her advisors now, but as soon as Drado returns, I'll send him to her. We surely do need Lady Meera and Kellan now."

Oona had barely finished speaking when Drado returned, all out of breath. He skidded to a halt then gave her the hand to shoulder salute. "Drado, I did ask for stealth."

"Yes, Lady Oona, but the sight of a runner taking his time would surely draw suspicion. I ran as though on a normal errand. Dor and the twins of terror are on their way, and Commander Tallon will be here shortly."

"Very good, Drado, I'm well pleased with you. Now, off you go to Lady Meera. Tell her I sense grave danger, and tell her what I've done. Ask her to join us in our chamber as soon as she can, without arousing suspicions." Drado saluted again and slipped away toward the great hall.

MEERA WAS NEARLY BORED to tears, as the men around the board continued to haggle over which street should be named what, and which area should house the greater halls. It had been going on and on for hours. Desperately, Meera glanced about for something, anything, to distract her, and she found it. One of the court runners was trying to get her attention.

With a smile of delight, Meera motioned him forward. He approached, knelt, and then rose to whisper in her ear. Her smile remained on her face, but the pleasure had left her eyes as she listened. "Very well, tell Lady Oona that I'll be there shortly. Kellan, Oona is cooking up another of her secret recipes. She needs two volunteer tasters, and we are the chosen."

She rose lazily from her bench, then smiled at the gathered men. "Good men, I have full faith that you'll be able to come to a reasonable solution. Once you have agreed upon a plan of action, I'll be delighted to hear it. I thank you for your time, and patience. We now leave you to it. Come, Kellan, destiny awaits." The men were still arguing around the table as she followed Drado out of the great room.

Tallon was already there by the time Meera and Kellan arrived, as were Dor and the twins. "All clear, Lady Oona," declared Dor, as he checked to see if Meera had been followed.

"Good. Drado, keep an eye out for unwanted ears, would you?" He gave her the salute and vanished outside the door of the private royal chamber.

"Oona, what is going on?" Meera asked softly, the concern plain in her voice.

Oona sighed as she sank to a cross legged position on the floor. The others followed her example, ready and eager to hear her story.

"I'll explain. On the Night of Candles, while we were parading about the city, sharing the light, I saw a man who clearly meant us harm."

"Oona?"

"Yes, Lady, I said nothing as you and Tella were close, and he made no move towards me, but his malice was easy to read, and it was aimed at us both. I've seen him again many times since, and each time he comes closer. At first he was alone, but then there were others; more and more as time goes on. Today his energy was easy to read. They will act soon; their intent is to kill us both."

"You are certain, my Lady Healer?"

"Yes, Lady Meera, I'm quite certain. That's why I called everyone together. What should we do?"

"Point him out to me," hissed Tella. "Kellan and I will..."

"Hold, my bloodthirsty champion. We need to know what he is about, how many follow him, and what they intend. Lady Meera, what should we do now?"

Meera's grin was one of pure delight. "You seem to have something in mind, my Oona, what do you suggest? What was your idea?"

"I thought Dor and the boys might find out what he is planning. Men are often too outspoken when those who cannot speak are near." The twins just grinned at that and gave her a swift hand signal, which she responded to.

"You've been practicing, Lady," chuckled Dor.

"Yes I have," grinned Oona. "Once we're aware of what they're up to, and how many there are, we can plan how to deal with them."

Meera smiled as she encouraged Oona. "How would you like to deal with them?"

"Lady, that is entirely up to you. I hadn't thought much past finding out their scheme."

"I like your plan, Oona. We'll use it. What does this man look like?"

"He is tall with curly dark hair, a jagged scar over his right eye, and no thumb on his left hand."

"I know that fellow," sighed Dor. "He's a bit of a malcontent, but I've always just ignored his constant complaining. All right lads, let's go see what this geezer is about." He stood and all three saluted as they left the room.

"What else have you done, Oona?" asked Meera.

"Lady?"

"You gathered around you those you trust. I assume that you've taken other steps as well."

"Yes, Lady, it's true. I've asked Toole and Bekka to stay at the hall until this is over. I don't want them to be harmed because they're close to me. If they're here we can protect them."

"Very wise, my delight. What else?"

"Well, there is a certain matter..."

"And that is?"

"The young fellow I sent to find you is Drado of the House of Sabine. He's still here as a runner because he has an unlucky name."

"Unlucky?"

"That name is not spoken with kindness in this place, Lady. Poor Drado can't apprentice to his father until he has served a season on a ship of the line. None will take him."

"I see. So, what steps have you taken to remedy that situation for him?"

"I've promised to call that other one by the name of Usurper. When I speak the name Drado, I'll be referring to Drado of Sabine. I also promised to get him a berth on one of our ships in the spring."

"He'll be welcome on the Raptor, Lady," smiled Tallon.

"That was pretty quick, Tallon. No hesitation at all?"

"Lady Oona, since I first met you my luck has improved beyond measure. You've granted me trust where I had not yet earned it, you've raised my station higher than I could have hoped to rise in a lifetime, and if you want to help this young fellow change his luck, then put him on the Raptor. She is a lucky ship with a lucky captain, serving a lucky queen."

"So be it," laughed Meera. "Drado of Sabine, come here please." He was kneeling before her in a heartbeat. "Lady Oona has explained some of your situation to me. I, also, will refer to that other as the Usurper. When I speak the name Drado from now on, I'll be referring to Drado of Sabine."

"Lady Meera, how can I ever thank you for this?" His voice caught and there were tears in his eyes.

"You can be a loyal servant to Lady Oona. She chooses her people carefully Drado. You're in august company, see that you bring only honor to that company."

"I swear it, Lady, by any oath you wish, I swear it."

"Enough," smiled Oona. "Drado, Captain Tallon has a berth for you aboard the Raptor this coming spring, if you wish it."

"My lord, would you truly take me aboard your ship?"

"Lady Oona's placed great trust in you, Drado," smiled Tallon, putting a friendly hand on the young man's shoulder. "Prove worthy of that trust and you'll sail on the Raptor when next she puts to sea. Now, go about your business and keep your ears open. Runners hear more than they should, and we would know what you hear."

"Aye, Captain." The boy grinned as he leaped to his feet, saluted the queens, and then vanished from the room.

"Well, I guess that's that," sighed Kellan. "All we can do now is wait."

WHILE THEY WAITED FOR news of the plot, another plot was hatching. Born plodded over the snows, traveling from hut to hall, from crib to castle, slowly but surely building up support for his war.

The lies he told were terrible indeed, but they were effective. Every place he visited, every time he spun his tale, all men agreed. They had to put a stop to Red Meera.

It was all bad enough she'd raided them for years, stealing food and supplies, but now she'd seized the great wheel. They'd all be taken slave just as had the companion of this brave man. There were promises of food and supplies, as well as fighters, as soon as the planting was finished. Born would have his army.

Far away, Kreeg continued to drill his people and to strengthen his defenses.

First

After many days of waiting, they learned the extent of the treachery that was afoot. Everyone's nerves were on edge, and it was getting harder and harder to keep up the pretense that nothing was wrong. Nearly a half moon cycle had passed before Dor made contact, for they had not seen or heard from him in that long.

Tallon was walking along the docks when he saw Dor in the distance. He was talking to a group of men, but Tallon caught the look in his eye. "Dor!" roared Tallon, causing all Dor's friends to flinch. "Dor, blast your eyes, you're two days overdue for your turn at ship's watch. Haul your lazy carcass onto the Raptor right now before I have you keel-hauled."

"Aye, Captain. Sorry, Captain," exclaimed Dor as he trotted away from the group. "I lost track of the days, being in port and all." He ran to the Raptor and leaped aboard while Tallon continued his stroll. It was over an hour later when Tallon returned to the ship where Dor was busy rubbing grease into the oar locks.

"News, Dor?"

"Aye, Captain." Dor spoke in a voice so soft, even Tallon had trouble hearing it. "They'll attack tonight. They plan to kill the Ladies Meera and Oona, then escape aboard the Jira. She's a small ship, and she's tied nearest the open water. There are at least twenty of them or more. Ten will attack the great hall, the rest will take the Jira and prepare for flight."

"How do they plan to get into the great hall?"

"Cordun of Linor will let them in. He's captain of the guard tonight. I'm to be one of the attack party."

"Very good, Dor. I'll get the word to Lady Oona right now. We have little enough time to prepare."

As Tallon left the ship, Dor called out to him. "Captain Tallon, surely there's no need to report my absence to Lady Oona."

"Sorry, Dor," Tallon called over his shoulder, "but you know what she's like. You'll be lucky if you don't spend three years guarding the walls of Castle Oona for this one."

"Awe, Captain..."

No more was said, but Tallon saw the group of men out of the corner of his eye. They had believed the ruse. Tallon was only halfway to the great hall when he spotted Drado trotting by. Obviously the boy had been watching for him. "You there, Runner, come here."

Drado ran to him with a look of anticipation. "They'll attack tonight. I've more information still, but that is enough to start with. Ten will come in the night. Dor will be one of them. He's managed to warn me in time. Go now." The boy sped away towards the great hall.

Tallon was escorted into the private chamber as soon as he arrived. The ladies were there, as were Tella and Kellan. The twins were there as well, standing guard at the door, for they were rarely more than an arm's length from Oona these days. As soon as Tallon entered the chamber, Drado took up his listening post. No unwelcome ears would come close unnoticed.

"Tonight, Tallon?" asked Meera. "Who and when? How will they enter?"

Tallon sighed as he sank to the floor with the rest of them. "Cordun of the House of Linor will grant them entry, Lady Meera. Ten in all will come. Dor will be among them, so we have nine assassins and one ally in the group. They plan to kill you both, and then escape aboard the Jira. She's tied closest to open water, and can easily be sailed by twenty men."

Meera had a wolfish grin on her face. "Take your crew and thwart the men at the Jira, Tallon. Go under cover of darkness, don't alarm the assassins. I want them here."

"Aye, Lady, it shall be as you require." He rose easily and vanished from the room.

Meera continued to lay her plans. "We'll pretend to be asleep, but Kellan and the twins will be hiding in the shadows. Young Drado, come here." He was there in an instant. "Kellan tells me you're quite proficient with weapons. Your task tonight will be to protect Lady Oona. If any get past Tella, you must finish them before they can harm Lady Oona, understood?"

"Understood, Lady Meera. I'll guard the Lady Oona with my life."

"Then go arm yourself, but let none see you do it. Return as quickly as you can."

"Should we bring in more men, Lady?" asked Kellan after a few moments silence.

"Nay, Kellan, for we don't want to sound the alarm."

A few moments later Drado returned. "Lady Oona, there's a man here asking for you to heal an old wound. His name is Eggar."

Oona's face brightened with a smile at that. "Bright him in, Drado."

Eggar entered and saluted Oona and Meera, then shook off his cloak. He was armed to the teeth under that cloak. "The captain said you might like some company this night, Lady Oona."

"Did he tell you why, Eggar?" It was Meera who had spoken.

"He did, Lady."

Meera nodded her approval. "He's right, Eggar. We would enjoy your company this evening. Let's all prepare now. This is what we'll do..."

OONA WAS A NERVOUS wreck as she cuddled into Meera's arms. It seemed like forever, but eventually she heard Drado's soft hiss of warning. A moment later shadows crept into the room. Just as they entered, Oona rolled away from Meera who sprang to her feet. As Meera leaped up the twins jerked away a curtain, allowing torchlight to flood the chamber.

The first man into the room died on Dor's blade, the second on Meera's. The battle was swift and savage, but in less time than it would take to tell it, the would-be assassins lay dead at Meera's feet. She had killed four herself, and her companions had made short work of the rest.

"Bring Cordun of Linor to me," commanded Meera, and the twins set out to find him. It took them until after daylight, but find him they did. As Meera turned to see if Oona was unharmed, she was suddenly hit with a wave of excruciating pain that sent her to the floor. Oona was instantly there, cradling Meera's head in her lap, and crooning softly.

"That won't help her now," coughed one of the dying assassins, "the blade was poisoned." He chuckled and coughed at the same time, blood leaking from his lips.

Oona turned to the man with a look as cold as a winter wind. "What was the poison?"

"Ask the gods," he gurgled.

Oona sighed as she laid her hand on his head. He breathed easier as a wave of healing energy swept over him. Suddenly she withdrew her hand, and his pain returned. "I'll keep you alive until you tell me what I want to know; and you will tell me." Oona's voice was so cold and deadly that even Tella shivered. "The only question is, how much pain you will endure before you talk. Tell me now, what was the poison?"

"The venom of the white-finned fish," he gasped. "Few have survived it, and none with a whole mind."

He tried to laugh again, but instead he coughed out his last breath as a blade entered his heart. With tears in his eyes, Kellan withdrew his sword from the assassin's chest. "So this is what she saw," he sighed.

Oona was still cradling Meera's head and crooning. She looked up at this for a moment. "What do you mean, Kellan?"

"When first we found you, Lady Oona, Lady Meera had a vision. That's why she brought you to us at great risk to herself. She knew she would die, and she needed to provide us with a new queen who would keep the people alive and safe."

"Meera's not dead yet, Kellan," admonished Oona, "nor will she be any time soon. Drado, fetch me Nora and quickly. Tell her to bring every dried blossom of the red meera she can find. When you have her, fetch Cora as well. Quickly now." The boy was gone like a shot.

Oona was working steadily on Meera's wounds while Meera herself writhed in pain. Oona sighed deeply as she finished bandaging the last of the cuts on Meera's chest. "Dor, do you know why they did this?"

"Aye, Lady Oona. The man you first saw, that one there of the poisoned blade, was once captain of the ship Tallon now commands. Many of his followers were former captains as well. They were unhappy with their change of fortunes."

"I knew damned well we should have marooned the lot of them," muttered Kellan.

"Yes, Kellan, and I should have listened to you." Meera gasped through the waves of pain that swept through her. She was growing weaker by the moment.

"As should I," agreed Oona. "Ah well, live and learn. No more mercy for the enemy, not from me. So they were afraid to return to the Usurper in defeat were they, but with a success... Where in blazes is that boy with...?"

At that moment Drado entered with Nora and Cora close behind. "Cora, take four blossoms of the meera to a jar of water. Make a warm tea and bring it to me. Make as much as you can, for the longer it steeps the stronger it will be."

"Aye, Lady," replied the cook as she took the herbs from Nora, and slipped out of the room.

"Nora, the venom of the white-finned fish, tell me all you know of it."

"Little is known, Lady, as the fish lives in warmer waters. Few have seen it, except those who fight the half men. They say that the broad-leafed oka plant can ease the pain, but little else."

"Bring me as much as you can, quickly now." Nora hurried away as Oona returned to her crooning.

"Dor, get some men in here and clean up this mess," growled Kellan as he took charge. "Hang the bodies from posts by the hall gates." A grim faced Dor hurried out of the room, but soon returned with several of the royal guards. They instantly set to work as they saw the fury in Kellan's eyes.

A few hours later Meera was resting easier. Oona's healing touch, along with the oka plant leaves, had relieved some of her pain. Cora appeared with the tea of red meera, and Oona kept giving her sips of it. When the sun arose Meera was still alive, but she had slipped into a fitful sleep.

"Lady Oona, you must come now," said Kellan gently as he entered the now clean chamber. "The chieftains are assembled in the hall."

"I don't understand, Kellan. I must remain here to tend Meera."

"Forgive me, Lady Oona. My heart is heavy with the pain of this, but it must be done. Lady, you are now the First. As such you must be acknowledged by the council of chieftains."

"I'm the Second, Kellan. Meera yet lives. I'm the Second."

"Lady, you are now the First. It is unlikely that Lady Meera can recover her strength. Even if she does, she will not awaken as Lady Meera. She will awaken as a madwoman. The people need their queen, and you are that queen now, Lady Oona. Lady Meera foresaw this, that's why she brought you to us. Come, Nora can tend her while she sleeps."

Reluctantly, Oona allowed herself to be led to the great hall where she took her high seat. She started for her normal throne, but Tella steered her to Meera's, the highest seat of all. As soon as she was settled, everyone rose from one knee to their feet. "All hail Lady Oona," they shouted in unison, "all hail the queen, First among us." Oona rose to her feet as well, tears staining her cheeks.

"Lady Oona stands before you as the First among us," declared Kellan. "The house of Kellar swears loyalty to Lady Oona." Each chieftain in turn pledged his loyalty and that of his house. In less than half a year, the condemned slave had risen to queen of the most powerful fighting force in the known world, and she had only one thought; to find a cure for Meera.

"Lady Oona, the people have pledged loyalty." Kellan turned and knelt to Oona. "Will you accept us?"

"Since I was found and set free by the folk of these houses, I have loved you one and all. If this is your desire, then I accept my role here. I pledge to do all in my power to protect the people of Lady Meera's empire."

"We are yours to command, Lady Oona. We thank you for accepting us, and we embrace your protection. What are your desires?"

"I will return to Meera now," replied Oona. "Seek out Tallon and learn of his success or failure. Bring to me any of the rebels who have survived. Bring as well every man who served with Borad. I've had enough of this nest of vipers in our midst.

"Drado!" she called, and he instantly appeared before her. "Hear me good people. From this moment forward, this land we have claimed for our own shall be called Meerasland." There was a round of approval from the gathered chieftains. "This young man is Drado of the House of Sabine. From this moment forward, when the name Drado is spoken, it shall be in reference to Drado of Sabine. He's done us great service this night, and has proved himself loyal and true. That evil man who sits on a stolen throne to the west of here, shall be known as the Usurper, and by that name alone." With that she turned on her heel and hurried back to Meera. She sank to the floor beside her and began her healing song anew.

It was only moments when Tallon appeared in the chamber doorway. Dropping to one knee he too pledged his loyalty to the new First Queen. "What news, Tallon?"

"Twelve men in all came for the Jira, Lady Oona. Eight were killed and are hanging on her yardarm as we speak."

"And what of those who lived?"

"In the great hall, Lady, awaiting your justice."

"Nora, please tend her carefully," sighed Oona, as she reluctantly released Meera and rose to her feet. "Lead on, Tallon, dear friend."

As Oona returned to the hall she saw four men in chains. At her approach they were forced to kneel before her. Oona stepped up to the first one and gazed into his eyes. "Why? Why did you do this?"

"Because you and Meera have killed all our families."

Kellan struck him a mighty blow, knocking him over backwards. "Put some respect in your voice when you address Lady Oona." He snarled as he jerked the man to his feet. "And that is Lady Meera to you. Now, answer Lady Oona respectfully, or die, in pain." He thrust the man back onto his knees before Oona.

Oona fixed her cold gaze upon him. "Explain what you mean that we have killed all your families."

"They are defenseless, Lady," spoke up one of the other men. "Borad brought the last of the great fleet here. There are no ships left to protect the isles from the half men. They will come with the warm winds of summer, and all will die."

"So you sought revenge against us, rather than the fool who sent you?"

"Nay, Lady. Arkon sought to kill Lady Meera to curry favor with King Drado. The rest of us just wanted to make the fleet return home in time to save the people."

"So, you believed that with both Meera and myself dead, the fleet would have no choice but to return to the Usurper?"

"That was the reasoning, Lady."

"Speak to me of the venom used against Lady Meera. Where did he get it? What is the antidote?"

"Arkon took the venom from one of the halfman ships. Borad claimed a great victory against them, but that was a lie. We barely escaped them with our lives, but we did manage to hold them off until the winds turned against them. Their ships rely more on sail and are not so good with oars. They cannot attack when the winds flow against them."

"A fine lesson, but speak of the poison."

"Yes, Lady. We captured one of their ships, and took a few of the half men captive. Arkon tortured them to death, but he managed to learn of the poison before the last one died."

"What is the antidote?"

"I know not, Lady, for if there is one, Arkon took that secret to the next land with him."

"Which ship was his?"

"The one you now call the Raptor, Lady."

"Tallon, go back to the ship and bring to me anything unusual you may find."

"Lady, we cleansed that ship over twice to make her ready as your flag ship. There is little hope, but I will try." With that he was gone.

Oona turned to the others then. "Tella, find the body of this Arkon. Bring to me everything in his possession. Kellan, I appoint you my chief of justice. Deal with these men as you see fit." With that she marched away to return to Meera.

Battle Plans

Oona fell asleep with Meera cradled in her arms. She awakened from time to time, and when she did, she resumed her healing song. The day was nearly gone when Kellan approached her again. "They are here, Lady Oona."

"Who is here, Kellan?"

"The men you requested, Lady. All the men who served with Borad."

"I see," she sighed, as she gently disentangled herself from Meera's arms. Meera moaned softly in her sleep, but did not awaken. "Pain brings bad dreams to her, Kellan. Where are these men?"

"Outside the hall, Lady."

Oona rose as Nora took her place beside Meera. "Lead on, my friend."

Oona's face was grim as she approached the men. The line was long indeed, and although they were not in chains, there were many armed men watching them carefully. She stepped up to the first and asked about the poison but he knew nothing. Oona looked him over then sent him on his way. She stepped to the next.

Oona was three parts of the way through the line of men when she got lucky. She had let most of them go, but had thrown six of them into chains. She was using her special sight to full advantage now, and all of the men trembled in fear under the gaze of the new witch queen.

As she approached one smaller man, he seemed almost eager to speak. He was all too easy for Oona to read. "What do you wish to tell me?" The hard look in her eye said he'd better have something important to say.

"Lady, Arkon was a user of a certain intoxicant," he began slowly.

"So, what do I care of that?"

"Lady, he got it from the half men. They use it to ward off the effects of the white finned fish, which they like to eat. It returns the mind to the body after the poison has run its course."

"Where is that intoxicant?"

"Lady, Arkon has already used most of what he had."

"Most?"

"Earlier this night past he came to me, and asked me to hold the rest for him. I was to meet him at the Jira."

"Where is it? Give it to me now."

"Lady, there is only this small bit left," stammered the man as he held out the small leather bag. At first glance it seemed to be empty, but upon closer inspection Oona could see a small bit of powder in it.

"Is this all there is?"

"Yes, Lady, that is all of it."

"How is it used?"

"He places it under his tongue, Lady."

"You knew what he planned to do, but did nothing to stop it. You also guessed he would fail, and so you held this back, as a means to bargain for your life. Throw him in chains."

Oona stepped to the next man. Three more wound up in chains before she finished with them all. She turned back toward the hall then, and noticed for the first time, the bodies hanging near the huge doors. One was a man she recognized as one of the guards from the great hall. Oona nodded her approval, then returned to Meera. She was settling down beside Meera when Kellan arrived.

"Lady, what do you wish me to do with those men you put in chains?"

"Kellan, dear friend, they mean me great harm. I can see it clearly."

"Sadly, they have committed no crime, Lady."

"The short one who saved that bag to bargain with, knew of their plan. He did nothing to stop it. You are my chief of justice now, Kellan. Do with them as you will, but keep them well away from me. They mean to do me harm if they can."

"Aye, Lady, I will do what I can." With that he rose and left her to her healing song for Meera.

WHILE OONA SANG SONGS of healing and strength, Kellan sat in judgment over those men in chains. Kellan was a fair man, but loyal to the queen, and he knew his duty. The man who had held back information was hanged with the conspirators at the gate. The rest were made to watch.

"Now then," said Kellan, as the hanging man finished twitching, "what shall I do with the lot of you?"

"Hang them as well," suggested Dor. "Let's clean out this nest of traitors while we can."

One man spoke up defiantly. "What have I done? What was my crime?"

"Lady Oona can see into the heart of a man, even as Lady Meera could sing up the mists," growled Kellan as he went nose to nose with the man. "She has seen that you wish harm to her, and she's left it to me to choose your fate. Still, as you say you have committed no crime, at least not yet."

"Kellan," sighed the man who'd spoken, as he allowed his shoulders to sag, "I have a companion and five children back on Ilsa. Do what you will with me, but for the love of the gods, man, convince her to take the fleet home to protect the Isles. You're the chieftain of my house, Kellan. You owe it to me to try." The other men in chains muttered their agreement.

It was at that moment that Kieran spoke up. "Give them to me, brother."

"Why do you want them, Kieran?"

"They've committed no crime, but still they must be watched. I'll take them aboard the Raven, and put them to the oars. If they prove true, perhaps Lady Oona might relent one day. Right now she's in no mood to be merciful."

"Aye, that's the truth of it. If any of these men had known of the attack, she'd have seen it and hanged them herself. All right, you're all sentenced to the oars of Kieran's ship. You'll remain on that ship until the snows fly again next year. If you can pass the Lady Oona test by then, you may well be set free."

"Thank you, Kellan, we will prove true."

"Don't thank me yet, she might just hang me along with you for being so easy on you. Go ahead, Kieran. Take them away."

"You all owe me your worthless lives," growled Kieran. "Don't make me sorry for what I've done."

As Kieran led his charges away, Kellan returned to Oona to report. She nodded her approval, but did not pause in her healing song. Meera was now resting more peacefully.

Many days passed, and Meera grew weaker as the air grew warmer. Oona spoon fed her the special herb broths that Cora made for her, but still she weakened, and she did not awaken. One day, a troubled Kellan approached her again. He requested that she come to the great hall to meet with the chieftains.

"I am busy here, Kellan, as you can see."

"Lady Oona, please, you must speak to the people. They need to know what your plans are for them. They wish to speak to you of a very important matter. They..."

"Alright, mother hen, I'll come. Nora, tend her carefully please." Nora nodded and slipped into Oona's place beside Meera. Since the night of the attack, Nora had not been far from Meera's side unless

Oona was there. Even little Bekka would come with her mother to sit with them, Bekka holding Meera's hand the whole time.

"Alright now, what's so very important?" demanded Oona as she took her high seat.

"Lady," began one of the chieftains slowly, "we wish to petition you about the Old Isles. As you know, we all have family there, and..."

"Hold, I thought those loyal to Meera were all here. Is that not so?"

"Those who could come are here, Lady. Many are still in the Isles, and are now defenseless. Lady, can we not help them?"

"Good people, we have enemies of our own here. I know my former captor well. Even as we speak, Born will be plodding through the length and breadth of this land, spreading his lies, making great promises. He'll raise an army against us. Mark my words. He'll cause this whole land to rise up against us. Meera wouldn't believe this when I told her, but it's true.

"When the snows leave the hills, and the crops are planted, he'll march on the castle at the great wheel, for that's where he believes me to be. We have a garrison of our own people there. Are we to abandon them to their fate? We also have allies at the place where Meera found me, the Trogs? What of them? Do we abandon them as well?"

"Lady Oona, of course we must not abandon our people here..."

"Lady Meera wanted this land as a home for those who were loyal to her," Oona went on relentlessly. "Are we to abandon her dream as well? Now that you believe she will die, are her dreams so easily cast aside? Will you now return to the Usurper to kneel at his feet and beg forgiveness? Where are the great courage and loyalty I first saw in Meera's people? Where is..." Oona stopped speaking and burst into tears. Gods, how she needed Meera now, but Meera could no longer help her.

"Lady Oona," Tella said gently, as she lightly put her arm around her friend's shoulders. "Lady, we are yours to command. It is for you to choose which battles shall be fought. Do not doubt our loyalty to you, or to Lady Meera's dreams."

"Forgive me, Tella, all of you," sniffed Oona. "Please forgive me, I'm tired and overwrought. Alright, I need more information. I'll gather to me those whose advice I trust most. We'll see if we can find a way to deal with this. If there is any way possible we can help those folk still in the Isles, then we shall. But we must first protect our people here. Is this acceptable to you?"

"Lady, it is all we ask, for we know you will hold true to your word," said the first chieftain to have spoken. "If there is a way, you are sure to find it."

"Then I will now be about the task. Drado!" He appeared almost instantly. "Fetch me Tallon, Dor, the twins, and Kieran. Kellan, Tella, come with me." She left the great hall and returned to her chamber where Nora was trying to feed Meera. "Here Nora, let me do that," she said gently, as she slipped into her position beside Meera and cradled the woman gently in her arms.

The advisers were soon in the room with her. "People, I know well the enemy I face here in Meerasland. I know little enough of the half men. What can you tell me?"

"Lady," sighed Kieran, "we here have fought them most of our lives. What would you know of them?"

"Do they always come with the first warm winds?"

"Aye, that they do, and it will soon be time."

"What do you mean, Kieran?"

"Lady, the winds will change there in about one moon cycle."

"So soon?"

"Aye Lady, the world is warmer there."

"The snows will not fully leave the lands for two more cycles here," she mused. "It will take another half cycle for the lands to dry enough for the planting. Another half cycle for the planting to be completed. Born will not be able to march against us until that time.

"Lady?"

"The men we face here are farmers and fishermen. They won't leave their homes until after the planting. Our folk are safe for about three cycles of the moon. Do you think we can get to the Isles, drive off the half men, depose the Usurper, and return in time to face Born and his army?"

"It is possible, Lady Oona," grinned Kellan. "The winds will be in our favor if we leave now so we could reach the Isles within a cycle. That's plenty of time to head off the half men. By then the winds will have changed, and they will favor us on the return trip as well. It'll be close, but I do believe we could make it. There is only one problem."

"What is that, Kellan?"

"Lady, if we go a-warring all season, who will gather provisions for next winter?"

Oona sighed as she lightly stroked the sleeping Meera's brow. "I see."

Oona was lost in her own thoughts for a while, and no one tried to disturb her. Finally she raised her head, her eyes as hard as flint. "Kieran, prepare Meera's fleet. We sail west. I will sail on the Raven."

Oona saw Tallon's face fall and she melted. "Tallon, dear friend, this is not a doubt of your worth, or your skill as fleet commander. No, I fear I have a much more difficult task for you, and you're the one I trust most to do it. You're going to break the back of Born's army for me. I'll take Meera's fleet to the Isles.

"Hear me well, my friends, this is my plan. Tallon will remain here as my representative while we are in the west. Tallon will wait until the snows have gone and the crops are well planted. As soon as the men begin to march away to join Born's army you will strike, Tallon.

"Hit every town and village on the coast. Don't venture far from your ships, but hit them hard. Burn their homes, tear down their walls, rip out their crops, and make sure they understand. Meerasland is ours. Any man who leaves his home to fight against us will be killed, his home destroyed, his family driven off. Those who return home will remain unharmed. Tell them this. Take whatever provisions you can find to restock our larders for the next winter. Be brutal, Tallon, show no mercy to any. Their fear must be stronger than Born's lies.

"If you find men at home who would not join his war against us, treat them well. Inform them of our cheaper rates for the grinding of grain. Tell them that we'll bring them the new laws in another year. This is the more dangerous mission, Tallon. I trust you to represent me well."

"Lady, I will do all in my power, but are you certain of this?"

"I am, Tallon. These men are farmers and fishermen, not warriors. The women will rush to the army to find their men. The men will abandon Born to return to, rebuild, and protect their homes. If we time this right, Born will be left standing alone before the gates of Castle Oona, just as we return from the west. That's when we grab him and stop him for good."

"Lady, we should sail immediately," said Kellan softly. "Even if we get there in time, it could take a cycle to find the enemy fleet."

"Tella, tell Kellan what you would do if you realized that your mortal enemy had lost his weapons and defenses," smiled Oona.

"I'd strike at his heart."

"So you think the half men will attack at Gapo. That would be a stroke of luck, and I think you might be right about that. It's sure worth a try."

"Nora, pack swiftly now, I'll need you to help me care for Meera on the voyage."

"Lady, is that wise?" asked Kellan softly. "Perhaps Lady Meera would be more comfortable here, where..."

"Meera comes with me," declared Oona flatly. "We need both of the elder races to make the luck work. Besides, the thing I need most lies to the west. Lady Meera stays with me. Kieran, prepare the cabin aboard the Raven for her. Make ready, we sail on the morrow. Drado, call the chieftains together for me now."

Everyone set to work swiftly, as Toole took over at Meera's side. Oona marched to the great hall and took her high seat, Tallon standing close by her side. As soon as the chieftains were assembled she told them of her plan. "Tallon is my voice and my hand here until I return. I ask that you give him the same respect and loyalty as you would me."

"It shall be as you require, Lady Oona," smiled one of the chieftains. "Many of us will sail with you, but, here in Meerasland, Tallon's word shall be as your own. Lady, we thank you for this effort to save our folk back in the Isles."

"It's my hope to reunite the empire. I wish to blend Meerasland into the empire of isles, so we will no longer have to fear attack from behind. I'd prefer to live in peace, trading back and forth with our brethren in the west."

"Lady, to do that you would have to depose..."

"Exactly so. He who has visited so much grief upon us, will meet his fate before I return to Meerasland." The steely glint of her eyes sent shivers through the assembled chieftains. They realized too late that they had pledged themselves to a madwoman. Ah well, perhaps the gods would sort it all out. Life had certainly improved since Meera had found her. They decided to trust in the luck of the new Chieftain of the House of Lothar.

THE TIDE ROSE WITH the sun, and the bulk of the fleet set sail. The Raven led them from the harbor with Meera sleeping fitfully in the cabin, her head pillowed in Oona's arms. "It won't be too long now, my love," whispered Oona as she cuddled Meera closer. "That man said the half men use the intoxicant to return the mind from the fish's poison. We'll soon have more of this intoxicant, have no fear. I'll bring you back to me, Meera, my beloved. I will bring you back. I promise."

As Oona crooned softly to Meera, the wind caught the sails and the men put their backs to the oars. The fleet meant to arrive at the Isles in record time.

The Isles

They had been at sea nearly half a moon cycle, and Meera lay still as death. Her body wasted from lack of food, and the effects of the poison. As usual, Oona was crooning her healing song, to the slow beat of the great oars. She was nearly asleep herself when she heard a soft voice. "Mamma?" Meera had opened her eyes.

Oona hugged Meera closer. "Meera! Oh, thanks be to all the gods. Meera, you have returned to me."

"You're not Mamma," declared a small frightened voice as, weakly, Meera tried to squirm out of Oona's grasp. Terrified, Meera started to scream. Nora and Kellan came hurrying into the cabin to see what was going on, but Meera only became more frightened, and screamed louder. She struggled harder but to no avail. Oona held her gently, but firmly, softly crooning her healing song. Exhausted, Meera slipped back into sleep once again.

As soon as Meera was sleeping soundly, Nora took over, and Oona went out on deck. She stood leaning over the rail, her eyes as hard as flint, and her jaw set tight. "Lady, I'm so very sorry," sighed Kellan as both he and Kieran approached her, "but Lady Meera cannot return to us. Even if her body survives, she will not return."

"Can't this damned ship go any faster, Kieran?"

"Lady, the men are near death already. We have pushed too hard. If we keep this up, we will be too weak to fight once we sight the enemy."

Suddenly Oona burst into tears and buried her head against Kellan's shoulder. Great racking sobs shook her thin body. Truly, she had eaten little more than Meera since they had left port. Kellan held her gently, crooning soothing sounds as she wept. Once her emotion was spent she composed herself and stepped back, shaking her new short blonde curls.

"Forgive me, Kellan. Once again you have brought me comfort in my darkest hour."

"Lady..."

"Kieran, rest them. We can rely on sails for a day or two until the crew is rested."

"Aye, Lady, and thank you." Kieran turned and gave the order for the fleet to ship oars, and gratefully they did so.

The fleet continued on under sail, barely slowing at all. The crews had been so exhausted that the rowers had not been much help anyway. Oona sighed and signaled Kieran to approach her. "Lady, how can I serve?"

"Kieran, be at ease, I don't bite. You must be more forthright with me. I'm no sailor, and I've no wish to kill my people with my mad desire for haste. I'll leave the sailing up to you from now on. If you feel there is need, please feel free to speak to me. I can easily see that these men have been pushed too hard."

"Lady, thank you."

"May I ask why those men are in chains?" Oona actually noticed the group of men for the first time.

"Lady, these are the men you chose from all those who sailed with Borad. Since they had committed no crime, we couldn't decide what to do with them. Kieran brought them onto the Raven. We had to put them in chains when you decided to come on board. Truly, we expected you'd take the Raptor."

"I am so sorry to cause you such trouble." Suddenly, she laughed. It was a beautiful sound and every man on board smiled to hear it. "Let me have a word with them."

Oona made her way down to the rowing benches, and along the rows of oarsmen. She made eye contact with each man and smiled at him, touching a few on the shoulder as she passed. Tella was right at her side. Finally she reached Dor and the twins who sat among the chained men. She smiled at the twins and made a few swift hand gestures. They burst out laughing and returned her signal.

"You've been practicing again, Lady Oona."

"Yes I have. Dor, I see that your seat mate is in chains."

"Aye, Lady, he works so hard, and is so strong, I had to do something to slow him down before he killed me with overwork."

"You are a most resourceful man, Dor. I've always liked that about you. You there, what is your name and house?"

"Lady, I am Lanon of the House of Kellar," replied the man chained beside Dor.

"I can see that you have had an attitude change. Am I going to have any more trouble out of you?"

"None, Lady. I swear it."

"If you lie, you die," snarled Tella, as she fingered the dagger in her belt. "That goes for the rest of you."

"Kieran," called Oona. She turned to see him right behind her. "What do you think? They aren't much use in chains. Shall we set them loose?"

"Aye, Lady." Kieran grinned as he tossed a huge key to Dor who began unlocking the chains that held the men prisoner.

"Lanon, come with me," commanded Oona, as she turned back and returned to the upper deck. She turned as she reached the rail to find him a respectful distance behind her. "Speak truly now, what'll we find as we reach the Isles?"

"Lady, there's no fleet left to defend the Isles. The southern Isles will be empty now except for the animals left behind. Everyone will have left on small fishing boats."

"Why?"

"The half men will come from the south, Lady. Those islands will be completely defenseless. The people will move to the inner islands near the capitol. There they'll prepare to defend themselves, as best they can, on land."

"I see. What are their chances?"

"The westerfolk are fierce fighters, Lady Oona, but without ships, they will soon starve. The half men need only wait until hunger and disease destroy their enemies."

"I see. Thank you, Lanon. You may return to your oar now." Oona spent much of the rest of the day at the rail, her mind racing over and over what she must do, and what she needed to have happen. Somehow she had to reunite the empire, add Meerasland to it, defeat the half men, and return Meera to herself. She had only one moon cycle to get it done.

Tella had remained silently at Oona's side throughout the day, until Oona sought her bed with the sleeping Meera. Only then did Tella leave to seek her own bed with Kellan. The twins of terror settled down beside the cabin door to sleep. None would dare disturb Oona's slumber.

Once again Oona awakened to the soft sound of Meera's voice, but this time it was different. "Oona, please hear me, my Oona," breathed the soft voice.

"Meera? Oh dear gods, Meera, do you know me?"

"Of course I know you, silly Oona. Please, Oona, you must let me die. Already I feel my mind slipping away again, and I am so very weak. You must..."

"Hush now, my Meera." Oona spoke gently as she took out the small pinch of the precious powder. "Put this under your tongue, and hold it there."

"Oona..."

"Under the tongue, that's it now. Keep it there. That's it, my love."

Oona continued to croon to Meera until suddenly Meera began to laugh and sing a bawdy song. Oona shouted for Nora to bring food and she was soon there. The now intoxicated Meera ate some, sang some more, ate another bite, and then fell asleep again.

Nora sat with the sleeping Meera while Oona went up on deck. "Kellan, this will be a lucky day," she smiled as Kellan and Tella approached her.

"Lady?"

"She awakened again, Tella. This time she knew me. It was only for a moment, but she knew me. I was able to get some food into her. She'll recover, I tell you. Meera will return to us."

"Lady Oona," Kellan sighed sadly, with a fatherly tone.

"Fine," laughed Oona, as she patted his shoulder, "believe what you will, Kellan."

She had no more chance to speak, as the call came from high in the rigging. "Land! Land ahead!"

"Where?" bellowed Kieran, as he raced from the lower deck to the rail beside Oona.

"There lies Kron Isle," replied the man in the rigging, as he pointed out what the others could not yet see. A few moments later they all saw it, the tall mountain rising out of the sea. Several small fishing boats were suddenly rowing towards the fleet.

"Speak to me, Tella."

"We have arrived, Lady Oona. Kron Isle is the first we see. There will be others as the day wears on, and the day after tomorrow we will reach Gapo Isle. There the Usurper sits on a troubled throne, high within the walls of Castle Lothar."

"Then our destiny will soon be upon us," sighed Oona. "I hope I have not misplaced my trust."

"Lady?"

"Tella, I know what has to happen next, and I fear in my heart that it will not."

"Why, Lady?"

"I'm not truly of the westerfolk. I wonder, will the men and women of this fleet truly go to war against their own kinsmen, at my command?"

"If they don't, I'll keel haul the lot of them," growled Kieran, as he approached. "Fear not, Lady Oona, we're your people. I've trusted in Lady Meera since she first took the throne. I trust that she passed that throne to you for a good reason. Fear not, your fleet will be true."

"If things happen the way I want them to, Kieran, it may not be necessary to fight our own, but I must have your complete trust."

"You have it, Lady."

"Then I'm at peace. Kieran, why are those boats approaching us? What do they want?"

"To welcome us, Lady Oona. They want to see who we are. They don't recognize the red meera, but they do recognize the style of ship. They're curious."

"As am I. Bring some of those folk to me. They may have information I can use."

"Aye, Lady," grinned Kieran, as he leaned over the rail and cupped his hands around his mouth. The first of the small boats was getting close enough to hear him. "Hallo, the boats. Name yourself and your house."

"Hallo, yourself," came the reply. "I'm Tarn of Innshe from the Isle of Kron. Name yourself, your ship, your house, and your monarch."

"Snotty little bugger," muttered Kieran, which caused Oona to giggle, "just who the blazes does he think he is? And what in the nine hells does he think he is sailing?"

"Now, Kieran, be polite," giggled Oona.

"Aye, Lady," grinned Kieran, "if I must." He put his hands to his mouth and replied to the man's hail. "I am Kieran of the House of Kellar. This ship is the Raven, and I serve Lady Oona, Healer Queen of the Golden Hair, Chieftain of the House of Lothar, as does every ship, man, and woman in this fleet. Bring your boat alongside the Raven and you will not be sunk." Oona was still laughing as the men from the boat clambered aboard the Raven and dropped to one knee before her.

"Forgive me, Lady," said the first man, a tall fellow with gray hair. "I didn't recognize your standard. I'm Tarn, chieftain of the House of Innshe."

"Whom do you serve, Tarn of Innshe?"

"Drado is King in the Isles, Lady."

"Wrong answer," growled Tella, her daggers leaping to her hands.

Oona put her hand gently on Tella's arm. "Easy, Tella, dear friend. You are not speaking the truth, sir. So I will ask again."

"Lady?"

"Lady Oona sees into the heart of a man, even as Lady Meera could sing up a fair breeze. She knows when you're lying and she knows if you wish her harm. One twitch from her hand and I'll hang you from the yardarm," growled Kieran. "Speak the truth and do it now."

The man sighed deeply then raised his eyes to Oona. "Lady, most of our young folk took the last of our ships to follow Lady Meera into the east. I stayed behind to do what I could for the elderly and the very young. Since that time we have had no contact with Gapo, except for the tax collectors. Even they didn't come this year. In full truth, I'll serve any monarch who can protect the last of my people from the half men."

"Much better," smiled Oona. "Please rise, Tarn of Innshe, you are welcome aboard the Raven."

He grunted as he climbed back to his feet. "Thank you, Lady. May I ask what's happened to Lady Meera?"

"She was cut with a poisoned blade. Lady Meera lies very ill, but she will recover. I'm Oona, Lady Meera's companion and her Second."

"Lady Meera was cut with the venom of the white-finned fish. Lady Oona has been proclaimed First, even though Lady Meera still clings to life."

"It was rightly done," agreed Tarn. "None survive that venom. Lady, may I ask why you have returned to the Isles? Have you come to stop the half men?"

Oona's eyes went hard. "We have, that and more. Before the next cycle is finished I mean to end the half man threat once and for all. I also intend to reclaim that throne that is rightfully mine as the Chieftain of the House of Lothar."

"Lady, for what it is worth, I pledge myself, and my house, to your cause. Innshe is yours."

"Did you not make the same pledge to the Usurper?"

"I did not, Lady. For it was beneath his notice to come to Kron. Since all my ships were in the royal fleet, or gone east, I could not go to him. Lady Meera was the last Monarch I swore loyalty to."

"Then I accept you, Tarn of Innshe. Kieran, give Tarn what news you can of the past years. I must check on Lady Meera."

Oona left them there and returned to the cabin. She found Kellan cradling Meera's sleeping form in his arms. Tears stained his cheeks as they ran freely from his eyes. "She's like my own child," he whispered softly as he lightly kissed Meera's hair. "She was very young when she came to the throne. Her father chose me as her champion, and I've been at her side ever since."

"She will recover, Kellan."

"Lady, no one has ever..."

"The half men do it all the time. They have the antidote."

"Lady Oona, can this be true?"

"One of the traitors told me of it. He had a tiny pouch of it with him, but I need more."

"So that's why you brought her with you."

"Yes, Kellan. The half men have the means to restore Meera to me. And by all the gods, I'll have it from them, one way or another. Kellan, the things I'm about to do may not make a lot of sense at first, but I beg you to trust me in this. We don't have a lot of time if we're to return to Meerasland before the war begins there."

"Lady Oona, I'm your man. I'll trust, and I'll do all in my power to see that everyone else does as well."

It was at this point Meera moaned and began to stir. Kellan went to find Nora and some food for Meera while Oona held her gently. "Oona?" breathed Meera.

"I am here beloved."

"I can't hold my mind in place, Oona. I'm so very weak. Even now I feel my thoughts slipping away."

"I know love, I know. Bear with me but a little longer and I will restore you, I promise."

"Mamma?" came a small frightened voice. Meera began to struggle, but Oona sang a healing song, and Meera quietened in her arms.

Even that small pinch of the antidote had helped, but it was not enough. Nora soon appeared with herbed food for Meera. Somehow Oona managed to get her to eat it. Once Meera had eaten, Oona sang her back to sleep. Oona left Meera in Nora's care and returned to the deck where the men were still gathered.

"Tarn, I have a task for you, if you're willing," she smiled.

"You have only to ask, Lady Oona."

"The chieftain on the next Isle is known to you?"

"He is, Lady, we are old friends."

"Will he listen to your council?"

"I believe he will, Lady."

"Lady Oona, what are you up to?" asked Kellan.

"I want my standard flying on as many isles as possible as quickly as possible, Kellan. Kieran, send Tarn with a ship to every island between here and Gapo. Will you do this for me, Tarn?"

"With pure delight, Lady."

"Then I name you my ambassador in the western isles. Your task is to spread the word that the true monarch has arrived, and will soon claim her throne. Give him a fast ship, Kieran, there is little enough time, and we must hurry."

"Aye, Lady, it shall be as you require."

Tarn was soon aboard the Sprite, one of the faster ships in the fleet. His small boat returned to Kron, with a new red meera to fly from the castle walls. Tarn had several more with him for his mission.

Another Fleet

As the day passed, and then the next, they sighted more and more islands. Many times small boats tried to approach them, but Kieran warned them off, saying only that Lady Oona of Meerasland had come to defend her people, and that an ambassador would soon arrive to speak with them. Eventually they dropped anchor, well out of sight of Gapo. Oona wanted to wait until daylight returned before showing herself to the Usurper.

WHILE OONA CRADLED Meera in her arms and sang healing songs, a haggard man sat on his troubled throne, brooding. Most of the people from the southern islands had managed to get to Gapo, and the three big islands close by, but he knew it would do no good.

His fleet was gone now, only three ships left, and few enough seasoned warriors to man them. He had sent two of them out to spy out the half men, hoping to at least have a bit of warning before the savages arrived to sack his empire. The third was secretly being provisioned for his escape.

Shaking his head, he wondered how it had gone so very wrong. By rights that witch should have been bound to bear his children. Instead, she had defied him and fled with the best of the royal fleet. In the ensuing years, half of what was left had followed her to the east. The half men had destroyed two thirds of the remainder.

In his desperation, he'd sent the last of the great fleet with Borad to bring her, and the rest of the fleet, back with him. Borad wasn't much of a warrior, but he was cunning and treacherous, the best he'd had.

Only one ship managed to return from that expedition. The news had not been good. Borad was dead, and that witch Meera had found a golden-haired healer woman somewhere. She'd taken her as a Second. The fleet would not return, and the half men would come with the summer winds. That time had now arrived.

His spy ships had returned with news of a great fleet of half man ships, well in excess of a hundred and fifty, but the news had come too late. Before he could get to his ship, the half men had arrived. Their numbers choked off the harbor. He could not escape. They would surely attack with the dawn.

"Sire, Sire, I have news," gasped a runner, as he dropped to one knee before the king.

"Now what?"

"Another fleet has arrived, Sire."

"Another fleet? Whose? Have the westermen returned at last to defend the empire?"

"It was a small boat that spotted them, Sire. They outnumber the half men. They look like ours, but he didn't recognize their standard."

"How did it look?" demanded the king as he leaned forward toward the young man, seizing him tightly by the shoulder.

"It is a red flower on a green field, Sire."

"A flower? Hmmm, an herb I'll wager," he muttered as he released the boy and relaxed back into his high seat. "That must be the golden-haired healer. So the golden-haired warriors come to the isles once again as in ages past. What can this mean, I wonder? Hmm, perhaps there is an opportunity here. When will this fleet arrive? Will it arrive in time?"

"Yes, my lord Drado, it will arrive at dawn, or sooner."

"Excellent, bring to me the mightiest crier. Quickly now, or I'll have your head."

The young man sped away while the mad king made plans. Something had obviously happened to Meera, and the great fleet had pledged themselves to the healer. Good, he could play a bit of history to his advantage. He would offer the golden hair a throne in the isles. She could help him restore the old bloodline. He chuckled to himself at the thought of it. The half men destroyed, and a golden-haired healer to bear his children. He was still cackling with glee as the crier arrived.

OONA'S SLUMBER WAS disturbed by Nora, gently shaking her shoulder. "Lady Oona, Lady Oona, you must awaken."

"Hush Nora, you'll waken Meera."

"Lady, you are needed on deck."

With a deep sigh, Oona disentangled herself from Meera's arms. Meera whimpered in protest, but settled down again as Nora cradled her gently. Oona went on deck to find it still dark, and the sky full of stars. "What is it Kieran?" she asked as she approached the brothers and Tella.

"Lady, the harbor at Gapo is already full of half men ships," replied Kieran.

"How do you know this?"

"I sent the Jira ahead, under cover of darkness, Lady. They say the harbor is full of half-man ships, but they have not landed as yet. They will probably attack at dawn."

"Alright then, here we go. Let's show ourselves to the enemy so they know we have them trapped, but don't attack until I give the command."

"Aye, Lady, it shall be as you require."

Kieran hopped to the lower deck, and soon the oars were in the water again. Orders were given, signal lanterns waved and acknowledged, and the great fleet got under way with hardly a sound. When the sky began to lighten there was a sudden alarm shouted among the half-man ships. Oona's fleet had been seen.

The sun was beginning to break over the horizon as the Raven led the fleet into the mouth of the great harbor. As they passed the headland, a voice rang out from the rocks. A crier stood there, with his hands cupped around his mouth.

"Hear me great golden-haired warriors, I speak the words of King Drado the Mighty, ruler of all the isles. Our gracious king greets you, and thanks you, for destroying his enemies. Our great king welcomes the golden-haired healer queen, and offers her a throne in the Isles. Together they will restore the ancient bloodline, and rule the empire as in the days of yore. What greeting shall I take to the mighty Drado?"

Kieran already had his hands to his mouth, and a remark on his lips, when Oona's hand caught his arm and stopped him. "Ignore that, Kieran."

"Aye, Lady, if I must."

"Kieran, I have to be serious now. You're not allowed to make me laugh just yet."

"Forgive me, Lady. Whatever was I thinking? What is our course now, Lady Oona?"

"The half-men, can they see our whole fleet?"

"Aye, I believe they can."

"Good, stop the fleet."

"Lady Oona?"

"Stop the fleet, please."

"Aye Lady, it shall be as you require." Kieran began bawling orders and the entire fleet backed oars, coming to a swift halt. "Now what?"

"Give them a few moments to look us over. Tell me Kieran, can we defeat them?"

"Aye, Lady, that we can. In truth, they look a bit ragged. Wouldn't you say, Kellan?"

"I agree, Kieran. I expected to find a bigger fleet, with a lot more fighters than I see here."

"Agreed. They can have no more than a hundred eighty ships to our two hundred." Kieran began bawling orders again and three ships turned about to face outwards. If the half-men had more ships on the way he didn't want to be caught between them.

"Alright, they've had enough time to think things over," said Oona. "Kieran, move the Raven forward slowly. Just the Raven, if you please, and slowly. Head for whatever looks like their flagship."

Kieran gave her a strange look, but he complied. A moment later the Raven moved slowly, regally forward then stopped two ship's lengths from the largest of the half-man ships.

"Call out to them, Kieran."

"Aye, Lady. Hallo, the ship. Can you speak our language?"

"Talk some," came a harsh reply. "What want?"

"A man of few words," grinned Oona, "I like that. Invite him aboard to confer."

Kieran nodded and cupped his hands about his mouth again. "Come aboard. Talk. No harm will come to you."

"You lie."

"Fool, if harm we meant, you would be dead now. Come aboard, talk, no harm."

"Kieran, you're a natural diplomat."

"It's a gift," grunted Kieran as Oona broke out in nervous giggles. "Well, bless me for a sea dragon. Here he comes."

A small boat was lowered from the large ship, and the three occupants rowed over to the Raven. Oona was still giggling as they clambered over the side. They were indeed a savage looking lot. Very short dark hair covered much of their visible skin, and their snouts were a bit longer than a man's. They were dressed in well-crafted skins mostly, but they were heavily muscled, and they looked to be quite familiar with the weapons they wore, even though they were much shorter than most men. Oona could see that they had the knowledge of metal working as well as shipbuilding. There was intelligence in those dark eyes, and she was secretly praying her guess was right.

As Oona stepped toward the newcomers, all her people dropped to one knee. Kieran waved at the half-men, and gestured that they do the same. The larger male grunted in derision, but the female, and younger male complied. As Tella's daggers leaped to her hands the female struck the male with the back of her hand. She growled something. Grudgingly, he dropped to one knee before Oona.

Tella replaced her daggers and stepped forward. "Tella," she said as she patted her chest. "Kieran," she said as she touched his shoulder, "Kellan, Lady Oona." As Tella introduced Oona, she dropped to one knee beside her. They nodded that they understood. "Who you?"

The large male as he slapped his chest. "Hekkat." He turned and placed his hand affectionately on the female's shoulder. "Peta. Orga."

Oona smiled as the introductions were concluded. "Rise please."

"What want?" grunted Hekkat, as he regained his feet.

Oona held her hand out to Kellan. "Kellan, your dagger, and your arm please." As she took the dagger, Oona made a cut along Kellan's arm. There were gasps from both the half-men, and her own sailors. Smiling sweetly, Oona placed her hand over the wound. She sang a high sweet note that hung on the air like a child's laughter. When she finished, she removed her hand, and showed the arm to her guests. The wound was sealed. There was a round of approving sounds from the sailors, and a nod of grudging admiration from Hekkat and company.

"What want?" he demanded again.

"Your healer."

"What *healer* mean?" he asked but, Peta suddenly began to jabber at him. She turned to Oona and pointed her finger. "Healer, you?"

"Me, healer." Oona smiled, then she pointed to Hekkat's ship. "Healer there?"

Peta said something to Hekkat again, and he nodded. He turned to Orga and barked a command. The youngster was over the side in a heartbeat, and rowing toward the ship, calling out as he went. Once he reached the ship, another person was lowered carefully down to the small boat. He then rowed back to the Raven.

As the boat came alongside, an old female was seen in the stern. "Help her up lads," commanded Kellan. The old one tried to slap away the hands, but in the end, she was forced to accept the help. She could not climb aboard herself.

Peta helped her over the rail, jabbering at her the whole time. She led the elder to Oona, where she introduced her as Keete. Keete grudgingly tried to kneel, but Oona caught her arm and helped her to stand again. "Healer?" she asked. "Keete healer?"

"Keete healer," replied Peta. "What need?"

Oona spoke softly as she took the old one by the arm. Keete made a frightened sound and tried to pull away from Oona. "Come. No harm Keete. Peta come too. Come."

Reluctantly, they followed her into the cabin. Meera was just waking. Frightened by the newcomers, Meera started to scream and struggle. Oona restrained her gently, and sang a soothing song. As Meera began to quieten down, Oona held her gently. "This is Peta, and this is Keete," said Oona softly. "This is Nora, and this is Meera."

The two females gasped and shrank away from her. Meera! Obviously they knew that name. "Meera Bloody Hand." Peta made a sign in the air before her.

"Meera not harm," soothed Oona. "Keete fix Meera."

"No!" spat Keete and Peta in unison.

"Why? Meera sick, need help. Keete fix."

"Meera Bloody Hand kill all people, long time."

Oona shook her golden curls and sighed. "Fix Meera," she said softly. "Fix Meera. Meera not kill people again. Oona not allow. Keete fix Meera."

"No!" The response was emphatic.

Oona sighed deeply then leaned toward Peta, her eyes hard as stone. "Hear Oona. Hear Oona and fear. Fix Meera, no harm to people. No fix Meera, all people die. All ships burn. None left alive. All die. Fix Meera, Oona help people, feed people, be good to people. No harm."

The two females looked at each other for a long moment. The idea of healing their worst nightmare terrified them, but the look in Oona's eye said she was telling the truth. Their fleet was trapped in the harbor. They couldn't fight the bigger ships in such tight quarters. They needed open water to fight an enemy like this. Reluctantly they agreed to help Meera.

"What wrong Meera?"

"Fish with white fin," said Oona carefully. "Need white powder."

She showed them the empty pouch, with a few precious grains still stuck to it. Old Keete sniffed at it then grinned broadly, nodding her head. She rummaged in her pouches for a long moment. Finally she surfaced again with a bag of the precious powder. Passing it to Oona she made gestures to indicate that Meera should take a huge pinch under her tongue.

Peta translated as Keete gave Oona instructions. "She take, she wild, foolish. All day foolish. Sleep long, next day good. You see. Next day all good. Oona promise, Meera Bloody Hand not kill people no more."

"Oona promise." Oona reassured them, the relief clear in her voice.

Oona took a large pinch of the powder, and convinced Meera to take it under her tongue. It was a struggle, and Oona almost had to force her, but they got it done. It wasn't long before Meera relaxed completely in Oona's arms. Soon she began to laugh. It was a full rich laugh that Oona hadn't heard for so very long. It brought tears of joy to her eyes to hear it. Meera began to sing a bawdy song and tried to rise, but she was too weak and unbalanced.

Old Keete cackled at that and reached out to help Meera to stand. Oona looked worried, but Keete said something and Peta translated. "Sooner stand, sooner sleep, sooner sleep, sooner fix." Oona got the idea. The sooner Meera exhausted herself, the sooner she would sleep, then awaken renewed.

"Nora, fetch Kellan." Oona helped Keete get Meera on her feet. Nora scurried away then swiftly returned with Kellan in tow. "Kellan," laughed Oona, "Meera wants to dance with you." She released Meera, who was still singing as she fell into Kellan's arms. "I'll bet you taught her that song, Kellan."

"I did no such thing, Lady." He laughed as he gently hugged the singing Meera. "It was Kieran."

Meera danced Kellan about the cabin for a while, then began a new song. Laughing, Oona retrieved Meera from Kellan. "Kellan, take our guests out to the deck and feed them until they beg for mercy. Learn what you can of their situation. I'll be out as soon as she falls asleep. If I understand things correctly, we will have our old Meera back on the morrow."

Kellan indicated to the two females that they should follow him. He took them back to their kinsman, then sent for food and plenty of it. He saw them jabbering among themselves, and saw the look of rage and terror that crossed Hekkat's face as they spoke. He recognized Meera's name. Obviously they knew who they had healed.

Taking a large bowl of food from a sailor, Kellan sat facing Hekkat and offered the food. Hekkat eyed it suspiciously until Kellan took a bite himself, then Hekkat dug in with a will. "These people must be near starvation."

"Food good," declared Hekkat as he and his companions finished the bowl. "More?"

Kellan nodded and more food appeared. "Your ship, what name?" asked Kieran.

"Koddok," replied Hekkat, the pride clear in his voice. "This one?" he asked as he patted the deck beneath him.

"Raven, know you that word?"

"Hekkat know, is good name, good ship. Why Kieran not attack?"

"Lady Oona say no," replied Kellan, as he passed more food to Keete who seemed to be a bottomless pit.

"Fix Meera first, kill Dorand next?"

Kellan was surprised at the calm with which the man had asked the question. Clearly these people believed they were going to die, and soon. "Fix Meera, all good, Lady Oona say so. Meera good, no kill."

"Meera no fix?"

"All die." Hekkat just nodded his head.

"All Dorand die anyway," sighed Hekkat, as he took another bite of food.

"Why all die, Hekkat?"

"Starve."

"Why?"

"Scaled men come from hot lands. Take food, hunt us, kill us, all Dorand flee. Long time scaled men come. Long arms, big claws, big heads, long teeth, hunt Dorand. Cold come, scaled men go away. Warm air come back, scaled men come back. Always more scaled men; less and less Dorand. Once Dorand many, like fish in sea, but scaled men kill. Dorand try to flee, find new place, tall men in ships kill. All time more scaled men, more tall men, more Dorand die.

"One time close, but, Bloody Hand Meera come with tall men. Fierce warrior, Meera. Kill many Dorand. Dorand go back, scaled men come again. One time no Meera, Dorand come closer, see many islands. Be safe there, but tall men fight. No Meera, tall men not fight so good, Dorand have chance. Dorand send one ship, see no tall man ships. All Dorand get on ships, come here."

"Most isles are empty now, why come here?"

"Tall men weak, drive away. Leave alone, tall man grow strong, kill Dorand. Dorand live, need islands."

"Why?"

"Scaled men no thumbs," grinned Hekkat, as he wiggled his thumb in the air. "No build ship. Safe on island."

"It all makes sense to me," sighed Kellan.

"And to me," agreed Oona, who had come up behind them. "No no, sit, sit." She sank down beside them. "Hekkat, more Dorand back there?" She waved her arm to the southward.

"All still alive, here." He waved his arm at his fleet.

"Hekkat chieftain of Dorand?" Oona smiled at his puzzled look. "Oona speak, all folk do. Hekkat speak, all Dorand do?"

"Hekkat speak, all Dorand do," he replied, nodding his head. "Why ask?"

Oona looked deeply into his eyes. She sensed no true malice from this man. He was just a man trying to save his people, in the only way he knew how. "Hear Oona now, Hekkat. Meera good, all good. Meera good, Hekkat do Oona speak, Oona protect Dorand."

It took a moment for it all to sink in, but it did. Oona saw the defiance and resentment on his face, but she saw something else as well. Before anything else could be said, the Jira moved swiftly toward the Raven. As she did the entire Dorand fleet turned to fight.

"Get that bloody ship back," bellowed Kieran.

The reply floated across the water. "Kieran, there is great need."

"Send a small boat."

"No time, Kieran, no time." The Jira came on as did the Dorand fleet.

"Hekkat, come Oona," she said as she grabbed his hand and leaped to her feet. He jerked away and whipped out his short sword. Tella was on him in a heartbeat, but Oona managed to get between them.

"Stop, stop. Hekkat, no harm. Tella, easy, easy. Hekkat, no harm. Show Dorand fleet, Hekkat no harm." Understanding reached his eyes. He turned from Oona and leapt to the high rail, waving his arm and bellowing at his ships. It took a bit of time, but he got them stopped.

As Hekkat was trying to control his fleet, Oona rounded on the Captain of the Jira, who was now on the deck of the Raven. "What is it that makes you defy my orders and put us all at risk?"

"Lady, I'm Ogor of Tongot. Lady, a messenger came to us from a small boat on the headland. They've built great catapults on the shore, and are about to send fireballs into the half-man fleet. They want us to attack them from behind. I thought you needed to know."

Oona nodded her head as she absorbed this new information. "You acted rightly Ogor. I do thank you for it." She patted the man's shoulder then turned her gaze back to toward shore.

"What he say?" asked Hekkat as he reappeared beside Oona.

Oona swiftly explained to Hekkat what was going on. "Oona obey land king? Kill Dorand? Meera no fix yet, what Oona do?"

"Oona protect Dorand. Hekkat return to Dorand ship. Move all Dorand ships beside Oona ships."

Hekkat hesitated for a moment then decided to trust Oona. If she lied he would be in a better position to fight than he was right now. He nodded and leaped over the side to his own small boat, leaving Peta and Keete with Oona as a show of trust. There was something going on in his brain, and Oona could not figure it out.

Hekkat reached his ship and began jabbering at the crew. There was a lot of wild fussing, but he soon brought them under control. As his ship began to move slowly toward Oona's fleet he was busy bellowing orders to the rest of the ships. There was a lot of hooting and jabbering to be heard, but the whistle of a fireball from the shore caught their attention. The fireball struck the water right in the middle of the Dorand fleet. They got the idea and began to move out.

While Hekkat was getting control of his people, Kieran had sent the signals to his own ships. They began to spread out to make room for the Dorand. "Kieran, take the Raven close to shore. I want to speak to the people gathered there," Oona growled through clenched teeth.

"Aye, Lady Oona." Kieran grinned as he gave the orders. As the Raven moved closer to the great docks, her men-at-arms were ready. Signal flags were flown and the rest of the fleet prepared for battle. All they needed was Oona's command. "We are close enough now, Lady Oona." Kieran gave the signal to back oars.

"Be my crier, Kieran?"

"A pleasure, Lady Oona." Cupping his hands about his mouth, Kieran called out to the shore. "I am Kieran of Kellar. This ship is the Raven. This is the Lady Oona's flagship. Hear me well. I speak the words of Lady Oona."

"What do you want?" asked a voice from shore.

"The head of the man who ordered that fireball to begin with," bellowed Kieran.

"That was ordered by King Drado himself. Why did you not attack the half-men?"

"We do not attack our allies," roared Kieran. He gave them a moment to absorb that information while Oona spoke softly to him. "With pleasure, Lady Oona."

"Hear me people of the isles, I speak the words of Lady Oona, Chieftain of the House of Lothar. Lady Oona has come to bring peace to the empire, and to reclaim the throne that was stolen. Lady Oona is queen of all the isles, and you must recognize her as First. Bring the Usurper, and his allies, to this dock in chains. Do this and all will be well. Lady Oona will bring peace to the isles. You will be able to return to your homes without fear. Fail in this, and she will set the half-men, as well as her own fleet, against you. None will survive. You have until dawn on the morrow to decide."

There were shouts and threats, as well as pleas from the land, but the Raven backed oars and left the harbor. "Well, that's that," sighed Oona, as the Raven cleared the range of the catapults. Not one shot had been sent their way. "All we can do now is let them make up their own minds. Let's go back out and see what I can do about bringing Hekkat into the fold."

Oona didn't have to worry, Hekkat was waiting for her. As soon as the Raven came alongside the Koddok, he leaped aboard the Raven and dropped to one knee before Oona. "Ladyee Oona is one foretold. Ladyee Oona talk true, protect Dorand. Ladyee Oona speak, Hekkat, all Dorand do."

Hekkat had just pledged loyalty to Oona. He was sincere and she knew it. "Rise Hekkat. Tell me, what Hekkat mean, Oona is one foretold."

"Old story," he replied as he regained his feet. "Very old story. Long time gone is foretold. One will come, child of Dorand. Kill many Dorand. Another will come, child of sun. Child of sun tame child of Dorand, protect Dorand, take to new home. Dorand be safe in new home, grow strong again. Ladyee Oona is sun child foretold."

"So, Meera is child of Dorand?"

"Is so. Long time gone sun people take some Dorand away. Long time after tall men appear, part sun people, part Dorand. One day tall woman come. Kill many Dorand. Was Meera Bloody Hand. Now Ladyee Oona, sun child, come save Dorand."

"Hekkat, did you leave any people on the other islands?"

He looked a bit puzzled for a moment then replied. "No, Ladyee Oona. All Dorand still alive, here."

Oona was impressed with the speed he seemed to be grasping the language. "Why not take empty islands?"

"No trees. Need trees to hunt food, build ships to catch fish."

"Hekkat, I can take all Dorand to a land far away. Many trees, much game, but cold winters. Sometimes bad men come, take slaves, but only come with one or two ships at a time. Other men live there, but they do as Oona say, or they die. This be a good place for Dorand? Dorand could defend this place?" He nodded so she kept going. "Oona's people help Dorand. Dorand help Oona's people against enemies?"

"Agreed," he said nodding his head. "Meera Bloody Hand?"

"Meera good, all good. Meera not good, Oona not angry with Dorand. All good with us, Hekkat."

"Meera all good," he grinned, as he turned to the rail, "you see. Daylight come, Meera all good." With that he leaped back to his own ship, and Oona returned to the cabin where Meera was still sleeping soundly in Keete's arms.

A New Day Dawns

The usurper king was beside himself with impotent rage. Not only had the fleet ignored his crier, but even after he had engaged the enemy, that golden-haired baggage had protected them. She demanded he be put in chains? He? Drado the Mighty in chains, before a ... The rage took complete control, and his thoughts scattered. He raved and ranted until exhaustion brought him to a stumbling halt.

"A single fireball," he muttered at last. "They launched only a single fireball. I gave orders for a hail of..." he trailed off as a messenger raced into the throne room and skidded to a halt before him. "What?"

"You must flee, Sire."

"Speak clearly, boy. What do you mean I must flee? Where the nine hells do you suggest I flee to? That damned witch has every ship in the known world under her control. I..."

"Sire, you must go quickly, they are coming..."

"You dare to interrupt me... What do you mean they are coming? Who is coming?"

"We are," replied a tall, gray-haired man, as he strode swiftly into the throne room with a score or more of armed men behind him.

"Just who are you, and how dare you enter this room uninvited? Name yourself and your house. Guards! Guards!"

"Your guards will not answer, for they've abandoned their post. I'm Tarn of Innshe, Chieftain of the Innshe and lord of Kron. A place you did not think worthy of your presence. I'm also ambassador for Lady Oona, Queen of Meerasland and all the Isles. You're under arrest for murder and treason. Seize him!"

The Usurper was unceremoniously hauled from his throne, and dragged off to the dungeon, where he was clapped in chains. He was thrown into a cell with several other men and women. They were all his advisers and favorites at court. There they languished, until the soldiers came for them at dawn.

IT WAS NOT YET DAWN when Meera awakened Oona. "Oona, my Oona."

"Meera, you're awake," breathed Oona, as she cuddled Meera closer. "Oh my love, how are you feeling?"

"I feel awful. I feel like crap on a boot, but my mind is restored. My body is so very weak, but my thoughts are clear at last. How have you managed this miracle, my Lady Healer?"

Oona then began to cry great sobs of relief. Meera held her gently until the storm of emotion passed. "It wasn't me, Meera, not really."

"It seems that you have much to tell me, my Oona. How long have I been in the lands beyond?"

"A moon cycle and more, Lady. Everyone thought you dead, but I wouldn't give up. I had to bring you back to me."

"Why, Oona, you were completely safe. Why work so hard to bring me back?"

"I like you, Meera. I want to keep you," smiled Oona.

"Good," chuckled Meera, "because I do want to be kept. Tell me, did they make you the First?"

"Yes, but that is your place now. I'm delighted to be your Second once again."

"Alas, that cannot be, my Oona. If all the people have pledged loyalty to you, then you're the First, and I'm just Meera now."

"Meera, stop this foolishness. You promised to keep me near you always, and I insist you keep that promise."

"But..."

"Do you not want me close...?"

"Of course I want you close. I like you, Oona."

"Then you must keep me, Meera."

"Truly I would like nothing more, my Oona. However, now that you are the First, you will have to declare me, and make me your Second."

"I'll do that at the rising of the sun, my beloved Meera," sighed Oona, as she cuddled Meera closer.

"Oona, what has happened in my time of delirium? Who healed me if you did not?"

"I could only keep you alive, my Meera. It was Keete who healed you."

"I remember a half-man female. Was that Keete?"

"Yes, those you call half-men are truly the elder race from which you sprang, my beloved. Listen now, and I will tell you everything..."

Oona spoke softly to the weakened Meera, until she had full knowledge of all that had happened since she was poisoned. "So I was right all along," sighed Meera as Oona finished speaking.

"What do you mean, Meera?"

"When first I saw you, my Oona, I knew you were the one to save the people, and return peace to the empire. I knew I wasn't to be the one, and then I saw you, and knew it was you. I saw you as First, with a mighty fleet behind you, and the whole world kneeling at your feet."

"Is that why you took such a chance to save me, and again in battle against the assassins?"

"It was. I knew you'd never take command if I was alive."

"Is that also why you would never...?"

"I didn't want the parting to be any harder than necessary for you, my Oona."

"There will be no partings, Meera, promise me. You swore to keep me safe, and I want you to keep that promise until old age takes me from you."

"It shall be as you require, my Lady Oona." Meera suddenly got a wicked little smile on her face. "Oona..."

"Meera, not now for pity's sake, you're too weak, and..."

"Oona," purred Meera, "I'm hungry."

Oona laughed with delight as she released her hold on Meera. "Yes, my Meera. Come, let's find some food, and get you into the fresh air once again." She helped Meera to stand, then steadied her as she led her from the cabin. The twins leaped to their feet, grinning, as Oona helped Meera out through the small door.

"Kellan, Kellan," shouted Oona. He was there in a heartbeat, Tella at his side. "Kellan, somebody wants to see you."

Tears flowed freely down the old warrior's cheeks as Meera fell into his arms, laughing. "So, you thought you were free of me, did you? Well, you're not so lucky after all."

"Lady Meera, my luck holds no bounds," breathed Kellan, as he hugged her fiercely. Tella was pulled into the hug as well, and a smiling Oona called for food for the starving sailor queen. Food swiftly appeared, and the dawn arrived as Meera's ravenous appetite departed.

Once Meera had eaten her fill, Oona stood and helped Meera to her feet. "Hear me, good people, this woman is Meera, my chosen companion, and my Second. I ask that you show her the same respect, and loyalty, as you show to me." There was a resounding cheer aboard the Raven, which caught the attention of the rest of the fleet. Messengers were soon dispatched, and the entire fleet informed of Meera's return, and new status.

The Koddok came close to the Raven, and, with a leap that Oona would have thought impossible, Hekkat left the rail of his own ship to land on the deck of the Raven. He half snarled, half chuckled as he saw Meera. "Meera Bloody Hand all good, Ladyee Oona?"

"Meera all good, Hekkat," Oona laughingly replied.

"Told you so. All good now?"

"Hekkat, Oona say, all do. Meera say, all do. Oona, Meera, all same. Hekkat agree?"

"Meera no kill Dorand no more?"

"Meera no kill Dorand no more," replied Meera. "Meera wish she had talked to Dorand long ago."

"Hekkat too," he grinned, "fewer scars." He lowered himself to one knee before Meera. "Ladyee Meera say, Dorand do. All same Ladyee Oona."

Meera tried to help him to his feet, but Oona had to steady her as well. "Meera Bloody Hand not so scary now," chuckled Hekkat.

Meera laughed heartily with him. "Hekkat tell Keete, Meera all good. Keete good healer. Meera say thank you to Keete. You tell Keete."

"Will tell," he replied as he hopped to the rail and made the leap back to his own ship. Soon there were messengers moving throughout the Dorand fleet with the news as well.

A few moments later there was a call from the rigging. "Sail ho!"

"Where away?" bawled Kieran. "What colors?"

"It's the Sprite. She flies the red meera."

The Sprite made straight for the Raven and came along side. Her captain leaped aboard, and gave Oona her special salute. "Ambassador Tarn sends his greetings, Lady Oona. Every island from here to the east carries the red meera on her poles. This includes Gapo Isle, Lady. We came to Gapo from a back harbor, and found a ship leaving. We took her into custody and learned of all that had happened, and of what you desired, from the folk of Gapo Isle. The folk were willing and gave Ambassador Tarn command.

"The ambassador awaits you on the docks, Lady. He also says to inform you that the Usurper is in chains, as requested, and so are his minions. They await your pleasure at the castle."

"Well, there you have it." Oona sighed as she allowed her relief to show. "We've averted the threat from the Dorand, and we have the throne of the Isles back where it belongs. Best of all, we didn't have to wage war against our own folk."

"The luck holds true, Lady Oona." Kellan was smiling broadly. "Bringing Lady Meera was indeed the right choice."

"Take us ashore, Kieran," smiled Oona. "I want to see Meera on her proper throne."

"Aye, aye, Lady Oona." Kieran turned and began issuing orders. Slowly, regally, the Raven, followed by the entire combined fleet, moved through the harbor to the docks where Tarn was waiting. So were everyone else who could cram into the area. The docks and the road to the castle were blocked with people.

As Oona stepped ashore, everyone dropped to one knee. The pledge of loyalty was nearly deafening. She stepped up to Tarn, supporting Meera by the arm as she did so. "Rise, Tarn, my good ambassador. You seem to have everything well in hand."

Tarn rose to his feet with a grin of delight. "I do try to please, my Lady. Lady Meera, it is good to see you whole and sound once again. I was told you were poisoned by the venom of the white-finned fish."

"I was, Tarn old friend. My Lady Healer is a most resourceful woman, and she refused to let me go to the summer land. Oona tells me you have a gift for me, Tarn. Is this true?"

"It is true, Lady Meera. Your throne awaits in Castle Lothar. The Usurper and his cohorts are guests of the lower levels. They also await your pleasure."

Meera sighed and leaned more heavily on Oona's arm. "This is all quite wonderful, Tarn, but it is Oona's throne now."

"Stop this silliness, Meera," Oona chided gently. "You're still too weak for all this. Can someone find a cart for her to ride in?" A cart was soon produced, and Oona sat beside Meera, supporting her, as they were carried to the Castle that had once been Meera's home. Tella, Kellan, and the crew of the Raven marched along beside, keeping the teeming crowds back from the two queens.

Oona was like a child in wonderland as they entered the castle gates. Before this moment, she hadn't dreamed that such splendor could exit. Meera smiled delightedly at her the whole time, as she pointed out things of interest. Finally they reached the towering doors of the great hall. Two uniformed guards opened the doors and held them for the queens and their entourage.

The gigantic room was three times the size of the great hall in Meerasland, and ever so much grander. The path to the thrones was lined with people. They all dropped to one knee as the two queens entered. Oona gently supported Meera's arm as they made their way slowly to the twin thrones. As they reached the raised dais, Oona tried to put Meera on the throne of the First, but she would not. "Oona is First. I am her Second." She accepted Kellan's help to reach the throne of the Second, then gratefully sat down. Reluctantly Oona took the high seat herself, Tella close at her side.

As Oona seated herself, everyone rose to their feet. Tarn approached and gave Oona her special salute. That brought a big smile of delight to her face. "The crew of the Sprite taught me," he grinned. "Lady Oona, there is a matter of business that must be attended to."

"And that is?"

"The chieftains wish to pledge loyalty to you, Lady Oona."

"Tell them to step forward." He signaled and nearly fifty people stepped forward. "Kellan of Kellar is my chief of justice. There are many house chieftains in Meerasland whose people are still here in the Isles. Those folk in Meerasland shall have preferred claim to the title of House Chieftain. Kellan, look them over and weed out the unworthy."

"That has already been done, Lady Oona," said Tarn. "I took the liberty myself last night. The unworthy are in chains with the Usurper."

"I see. You're one efficient fellow, Tarn my friend. I think I like you, and if you're willing, I have a great task for you."

"Your wish is my command, Lady Oona."

"Kellan, inform these good people of my special talent."

"Aye, Lady." Kellan stepped out from behind Meera's throne. "Lady Oona has the ability to see through a man's heart. She knows when you're lying, and when you're true. She will now hear the pledge of loyalty from you all. Any who are insincere will be tossed in chains with their former master." Three men bolted for the door, but they didn't make it. The crew of the Raven had them in a heartbeat.

Oona came down off her throne and walked among the rest, Tella right at her side. She pointed out seven more who were seized and clapped in chains, then she returned to the high seat. "I will hear you now." Of the men who were left, each in turn stepped forward and pledged loyalty to Oona and Meera. When all had spoken Oona rose to her feet.

"Lady Meera and I accept you and thank you. We inform you now that it is safe to return to your homes. The Dorand fleet will be leaving for the east with us very soon. No one is to harm a Dorand in any way for any reason, and no Dorand will harm you ever again. The threat of the half-men is no more."

There was a rousing cheer at that. Oona let it go on for a moment then held up her hand, a bright smile on her face. "We have urgent business in the east, but we hope to return for a proper visit before the summer is completely gone. It will be late but we'll come if at all possible, if not, expect us to spend next year with you here in the isles.

"The land to the east is called Meerasland, and it's now a part of the Empire of the Isles. Trade will soon be established between Meerasland and these western isles. There is much more to tell you, but I'll leave that to others for now. Suffice it to know that the folk who went east prosper there." She smiled again then resumed her seat.

"Now then, Tarn, bring forth the accused."

"Aye, Lady, we have had them brought from the dungeons already." He signaled again, and several men and women, bound in chains, were herded into the room where they were forced to kneel before Oona and Meera.

"How dare you," snarled one man as he tried to get to his feet. A guardsman struck the back of his knees with the butt of a spear, and the man was instantly on his knees again. The guardsman then smacked him up side the head with the back of his hand to keep him silent.

"Who is this man, and what is his crime? Who accuses him?"

"He is Drado the Usurper," purred Meera as she rose to her feet and approached the man in chains. "His crimes are murder most foul, and high treason. I have witnessed these actions myself. It is I who accuse him."

The man gasped as he saw Meera. "It cannot be. You're dead."

"I was dead, uncle, but my Lady Oona, who was my companion and my Second, is a healer of great and terrible power. Once she was declared First she grew lonely, and so she recalled me from the land of the dead." There was a gasp heard throughout the hall at that. "I am now Lady Meera, companion to Lady Oona, and her Second. Lady Oona, I accuse this man, and ask that he face justice for his crimes."

"Kellan is my chief of justice. What say you, Kellan?"

A hard eyed Kellan stepped down to face his old enemy. "Hang the lot of them, Lady Oona. They're all traitors. You can't trust any of them."

"You've heard the sentence of the chief of justice," declared Oona. "So be it. Take them out and hang them from the walls for all to see. All except that one." Oona was pointing to a richly dressed woman who was chained to the Usurper.

"Lady?"

Oona stepped down from her throne again, and approached the women in chains. She reached out her hand and raised the woman to her feet. "Who are you?"

The poor woman was trembling in fear, tears running freely down her face. "I am Freela, Lady."

"Why are you here with these people?"

"I was his companion, Lady," was the terrified reply as Freela pointed to Drado.

"By choice or by force?"

"By force, Lady, but how could you know?"

"It takes one to know one," Oona smiled gently. "Tell me, Freela, did you bear him any children? Carefully now, I will know if you lie."

"I did not, Lady. There are certain herbs that will prevent the birth of a child."

"I know them well. She speaks truth, Kellan," said Oona as she turned away from the woman. "As you well know I, too, was once companion to a man, but only by force. A slave by any other name is still a slave. High Chief Justice, your word in this matter is law, but I plead for mercy in her case. Still, it is up to you to decide."

Oona resumed her seat while Kellan mulled over this new development. Suddenly Meera rose to her feet with a smile of delight. "Chief of Justice, I too beg mercy for this woman." She had seen the snarl of hatred that Drado had sent the woman's way. Meera knew that it would hurt him more to know she would go free.

Kellan caught the glint in her eye and nodded his head. "What should I do with her, Lady?"

"You're Chief of Justice, Kellan dear friend. Do with her as you will."

With a deep sigh Kellan turned to the woman in chains. "You're of my own House, are you not?"

"Yes, my lord," she replied with downcast eyes.

"Look at me, woman. My name is Kellan, nothing more. I'm chieftain of your house, and as such, I am bound to help you if I can. Both the Ladies Oona and Meera have begged mercy for you. You'll have it. You shall tell me what I should do with you."

"Me, my lo..., I mean, Kellan?"

"You Freela, as in the old days and the old ways. Tell me what you were before this traitor's eye fell upon you."

"I was a healing woman on the Isle of Toron."

"Were you happy with that lot in life?"

"I was. That man," here she pointed an accusing finger at the Usurper, "had my companion slain so he would be free to take me himself."

"He'll hang this day for his crimes. Very well, Freela of Kellar, you may return to Toron, or not, as you wish. You are a slave no longer. Remove her chains, hang the rest."

There was a great scuffle while the struggling prisoners were dragged out to the walls and executed. Freela stood rubbing her wrists, hardly daring to believe she was finally free of her servitude. Oona came down and put her arm about the woman's shoulders. "He held you prisoner for a long time, didn't he?"

"Four years, Lady."

"You know, it occurs to me, Kellan, that Freela might be of more use to us as an adviser here."

"Advisor here? Lady Oona, what are you up to?"

"I must return to Meerasland as quickly as possible, and well you know it. I also need someone here to represent me, and to get things running smoothly again. I can think of no better man for the task than you, Kellan. Freela has been held here for years, she will know who you can and who you cannot trust."

"Me? Lady Oona, you can't leave me here," Kellan's face was a wide eyed look of protest.

"Why not?"

"You'll be taking Lady Meera back with you. I'm Lady Meera's champion, and as such I must go with her. Besides, you'll be taking your own champion with you, and I can't bear to be parted from her for that long." He was grinning broadly now.

"He's got you there, my Lady Healer."

"Alright my trusty advisers," laughed Oona, as she placed her hands on her hips, "what do you suggest I do?"

"You could give Tarn the job," replied Meera. "He was once chief steward to my father."

"You remember that, Lady Meera?"

"I well remember the young man who slipped sweet treats to me, even though I wasn't supposed to have them."

"Well you certainly seem able to get things done in a hurry, Tarn," smiled Oona. "What do you say? Will you be my regent here in the western isles?"

"I'd be honored, Lady Oona."

"Tell me what you'll need, Tarn."

"A few ships would be a great help, Lady. If you could spare five or six well manned..."

"Kellan, give him forty ships, well armed, and well manned. Tarn, each half moon cycle send a ship to me with all the news. I'll send one to you as well, so your fleet won't be depleted."

"You are most generous, Lady. Can you spare so many?"

"I've just added nearly two hundred Dorand ships to my fleet, Tarn. I have still another fleet awaiting us in Meerasland. We'll be just fine. Kellan, we'll spend the next two days here so Meera can rest, and recover some of her strength. Let as many men ashore as you see fit, refit and re-provision our fleet, feed the Dorand until they split, and make sure their ships are well provisioned. Assign Tarn's ships to him and get us ready to go. We leave for Meerasland in three days time."

"It shall be as you require, Lady Oona."

"Tarn, what say you? Will you keep Freela as adviser?"

"Freela is a free woman of the isles, Lady. She will come or go as she desires. Freela, I see by the returning of the guards that you are fully at liberty once again. You may now go about your business as you choose. My companion passed of the fever two winters past, and I have sorely missed her company. She too was a healer and a gentle soul. I do need you to advise me. Will you stay?"

Freela sighed deeply. Her one true desire was to get as far from this accursed castle as she could. "Ah well, why not? At least I won't have to pretend to be a queen when I'm not. Perhaps I'll learn to enjoy this place in your company, good sir. I'll stay."

"Enough of this," laughed Oona. "My poor Meera is starving right before our eyes. Bring us food before we all perish." There was a sudden rush of activity in the great hall.

The rest of the day was filled with the business of greetings, and letting the people of Gapo get a look at the golden-haired healer queen. They marveled at she who had recalled Meera from the land of the dead, and then removed the half-man threat forever. Later that night, as they retired to the sleeping room, Oona snuggled into Meera's side and started to weep.

"Hush now, my Oona," soothed Meera, as she cuddled Oona closer.

"Oh Lady, I was so afraid this day would not ever return for me."

"Lady?"

"Stop it, Meera. We can play whatever game you like for the people, but you're the First. I'm the Second, you're my rescuer and my protector. I like it that way. I want it back like it was."

"Oh, my Oona." Meera lightly kissed Oona's hair. "I am so sorry, my love, but it cannot ever be that again."

"Please, Meera, even if it is just at night when we sleep. Please let it be as it was again."

"Tell me what you need, my Oona. I shall make it happen for you if I can."

"Meera, you were so strong and confident then. You made me feel safe and you protected me. I want that back again, please?"

"Yes, my Lady Healer," sighed Meera, as she gave Oona a gentle squeeze, "it shall be as you require, but first I must regain my strength. Once I'm strong again, I'll be your protector as before."

"You promise?" asked a soft, sleepy, voice from near Meera's breasts.

"I swear it, my Oona."

"Then I am content."

"Are you sure you're content? I could..."

Oona's laughter was rich and genuine. "Lady Meera, behave yourself."

"Yes, my Oona."

"Save some of that for when you regain your strength." This time it was Meera's laughter that rang out sweetly.

A Troubled Land

For two days Meera rested and grew stronger. Oona had brought peace to the Isles and now she could relax for a time. Meera acted as tour guide for Oona, showing her all the places in the castle, and surrounding lands, that had been special to a young growing princess. In one certain nook of the castle, Meera had a small shrine erected to the brother she had lost so long ago, and finally avenged. She also visited the tombs of her parents, and silently told them of her adventures, and of Oona's success. She knew her mother would approve.

While Meera rested, many of the sailors spent as much time as they could with family they had not seen for a long time. The few who had no family to visit on Gapo, voluntarily took on the task of provisioning the ships.

The Usurper had amassed a vast supply of provisions and wealth within the castle. Oona directed Tarn to take the excess and provision the Dorand ships with it, then distribute the rest as was needed. Hekkat was now fully Oona's man. She had prevented a battle, protected them, promised a new safe homeland, and now was providing more food than the Dorand had seen in years.

The news spread throughout all the Isles very quickly, and by the second day there was a massive celebration going on, with the red meera flying everywhere. However, while there was celebration and rejoicing in the western isles, trouble was brewing and threatening to boil over back in Meerasland.

WHILE THE PEOPLE OF the Isles rejoiced at the demise of the harsh king, and the return of their beloved Meera with her golden-haired companion, Born was also rejoicing. He had spent the entire winter trudging the length and breadth of the land, spreading the word, and raising the promise of an army. He had even managed to get a boat and reach a few of the outer islands.

Born had been lucky there as well, for he'd encountered a large band of golden-haired warriors, led by an old woman. She was as fierce as any he had met, and when he told her of Red Meera's intention to enslave every man, woman, and child, the woman went into a fine rage.

Born had managed to strike a raw nerve with these people, as they had all lost many of their own folk to the slavers of the south. He carefully didn't mention that he had kept a golden-haired slave himself for a number of years, or that she was now with Red Meera. He left that place with a promise of a full hundred warriors, as soon as the planting was finished.

Born sat nodding by the fire, his belly full of food and his mind full of thoughts. Thoughts of revenge against Red Meera and Porga, that miserable slut. Outside the farmhouse where he had been a guest for the last of the winter, the snows were already gone. The weather was warm this year, and the planting was already beginning. Born was well pleased.

"What about home?" Broc sat beside the fire as well, for he had accompanied his brother through the winter.

"Home?"

"Born, you know that damned animal is still in our home. What are you going to do about that?"

"Nothing, why should I?"

"It's our home, dammit."

"We'll take the castle at the great wheel, Broc. That'll make us a fine home. Who cares about that other one?"

"I do. It's my home, and I want it back."

"Alright then, here's what we'll do. Once the army forms up, I'll give you a hundred men, and you can go take it back. Skin that damned animal alive and bring me the hide for a blanket. We'll chain the rest of them to the wheel with those accursed pirates."

Just as Broc chuckled at this, the farmer who was their host, returned from the barns. "All is well, the fields are ready, and we'll begin the planting on the morrow. It looks like fair weather, and now is as good a time as any. The sooner we plant, the sooner we can take back the wheel. Remember, you promised me a cheaper rate."

"That we did," grinned Born, "and that we'll do. Better yet, we'll help you with the planting. Many hands make light work."

EVEN AS BROC SAT PLANNING his demise, Kreeg sat listening to a man Born had sent to him. Born had sent as many men as would go, to all the towns and villages they could find, spreading the word of the great army going to war against Red Meera. One of those men had found his way to Kreeg's castle.

Kreeg sat and listened for as long as the man talked, then he looked to his advisers. "What think you?"

"Bad idea," replied one of the Trogs. "Meera has too many ships, too many men. Better stay here."

"No, we can't remain neutral," spoke up another. "Remember the bargain. We get the castle. Meera goes to war, we go to war. We were lucky last time when we fought beside the Dorand. She could have drowned us all, but didn't. We'd be foolish to challenge her again."

"It's a bad idea. I remember Born all too well, Kreeg. He's a boastful fool. Meera will slaughter him and his army. It would be suicide to oppose her."

"Bad idea," said another Trog. "This is a good home. I say we stay here, defend our new home."

"Agreed," chimed in the other two men in the room, as did the rest of the nine Trogs.

"It's a trick to get us to come out in the open," grunted one of the men. Several of the men who had stayed in the town, had fully embraced the Trog's defensive tactics. They fished under watch guard, they hunted as though they, too, might be prey, and their homes were snug and safe, their families well fed and warm.

Kreeg rose to his full height, flexing his gigantic shoulders. "Agreed. Go back to that fat fool. Tell him we will remain here and defend our home."

"What will we do if Meera calls us to go?" asked one of the Trogs.

"We will decide that when the time comes. Throw this one out into the storm. You go back to that fool, boy. Tell him we will never let him get his hands on this castle again. Go." The emissary was unceremoniously thrown out the gates into the darkness of the spring rainstorm.

THE PREPARATIONS FOR war were not exclusively Born's domain, for he was expected. Gerrit had been busy all winter, beefing up the castle's defenses. He didn't know for sure that the castle would be attacked, but he wanted to be ready if it was. After all, what was the point of a garrison if it was completely unprepared to defend its walls?

The winter had been long and cold, by the standards of the westerfolk, but the former slaves assured them that it was actually a fairly good winter. They also said it was a short one. Under normal circumstances, this would mean an early return to the labor of planting and then to the wheel. This time it was different. There would be many men to help with the planting, and, by the queen's order, the wheel would be turned by beasts, not slaves.

Through the winter, Konnor had worked tirelessly with the former slaves. He was not only able to convince them of their freedom, but managed to instill a determination to keep it. As the months wore on they learned, to one degree or another, the language of the western isles, and the use of weapons. By the time the snows were gone, some had even managed to convince a few of the garrison to speak to their chieftains on their behalf. Life was good.

The former slaves had all chosen names for themselves by the time the Night of Candles arrived. It was a new ceremony to celebrate an old familiar time of year, and they all embraced it. As the winter grew old, and signs of spring were in the air, Morel was great with child. One night, as Konnor returned from his shift on guard duty, he found her weeping.

"Morel, my beloved, what has disturbed you so?" he inquired softly, as he took her in his arms.

"Oh Konnor, I'm so afraid."

"Of what, my love? What brings this unnatural fear to you?"

"I'm with child, Konnor. Swear to me you will never hurt our child."

"I swear it, by any oath you require, Morel. What makes you afraid I might hurt our child?"

"It may not be your child, Konnor," she sobbed. "The guards took me many times as you well know. It could be one of theirs."

"My sweet Morel, any child that issues from your body will be my child. There's an old saying among our people. Let me raise your child for six years, and she will be mine forever. Any child of yours will be my child, Morel."

"You won't kill it if it isn't yours?"

"By all the gods, Morel, I swear I'll not harm a child of yours, not ever. Why would you think such a thing?"

"My father killed one with black hair. He claimed it wasn't his, and he sent my mother to the wheel. I didn't see her again. Many of the people say that Born killed Por.., I mean Lady Oona, killed her children because he thought they might not be his."

"By all the gods, Morel," sighed Konnor, "I don't understand why your people fear my own and call us cruel. No westerman in his right mind would ever think of such a thing. My love, you must put all this from your mind. Besides, the child you carry is my own, as you will see as soon as she comes out to talk with us."

"Oh you think so do you?" giggled Morel, some of her natural good cheer rising to the fore. "What makes you so certain of that?"

"Morel, before our people came and set us free, we were nearly starved to death. Do you not remember? It was only after you were freed, and regained some of your strength, that you began to bleed again, as a woman bleeds with the moon. It happened only once, and then stopped as you began to grow with the child within. The child is mine, Morel. You know that's true."

"You're right, Konnor. I'd forgotten that. Is it really true that a westerman would not harm a child, even if it wasn't his own?"

"A complete waste of a good warrior," chuckled Konnor. "A westerman would cherish the child and make it his own, thereby increasing the strength of his own clan."

"I am very happy to have fallen in with such a civilized folk. Konnor, forgive me for my fears and doubts. I know in my heart that you wouldn't harm a child."

"Your fears are born of the folk you grew up with, Morel, nothing more. These folk have harsh ways, but they can't harm you anymore. You're safe with us, and with me, as will be all our children. They'll be born to the House of Lothar, and will have the full might of the empire to protect them. Sleep now, my lady love, you're tired and need to rest. Sleep now. Tomorrow will be an exciting day, for the Lucky Lady is expected to return with all the winter news from the great hall."

The Lucky Lady did indeed return the next day with news, most of it bad. Lady Meera had been felled by a poisoned blade. Lady Oona was First queen now. She'd taken half the fleet and returned to the isles. Tallon had retained the rest of the fleet. Tallon had waited until the snows were gone, then he took his fleet and went a-raiding. Worse yet, an army was forming, and it planned to attack Castle Oona. War was coming, and Gerrit was woefully undermanned for a prolonged battle.

Preparing as best he could, Gerrit called for every scrap of edible food, and anything that could be used as a weapon, to be brought into the castle. He also sent men, with many beasts, to dismantle the wheel and bring the great stones into the castle as well. Guards were posted, the Lucky Lady was sent to find Tallon, and the garrison settled down to wait.

WHILE THE GARRISON waited, Born fumed. It was taking a lot longer for the army to arrive than he had hoped. They were coming in by twos and threes, but there were barely six hundred men so far. Just as he was about to sink into a deep pit of despair, a watchman called out. The golden-haired warriors had arrived; over two hundred of them.

"Gurda, it is good to see you. Welcome," called Born, as he rose from his seat at the fire. "You've brought many warriors with you, I see."

"I promised to help you rid this land of the slavers, and I mean to do just that," replied the gray-haired woman with the deep scar across her forehead.

"Choose any camp you like." Born waved his arm expansively at the small valley he had chosen as a marshaling ground.

The blonde warriors moved off to a vantage point, and began to set up their camp. "What are you going to do about them?" asked Broc. "As soon as they realize that you're planning to use slaves to work the wheel, they'll turn on you."

"We won't wait that long, brother. We'll let them take the brunt of the clash when we engage the savages. Once the pirates are defeated, we turn on them and clap the last of them in chains with the savages. They're strong and can push the wheel as well as any. We'll have enough slaves to last us for years."

"I DON'T TRUST THAT fellow, Gurda," muttered a tall golden-haired warrior, as he sat beside her while she was gazing into the fire.

"I know, Lonn, I know." She didn't take her gaze from the dancing flames. "He's too easy with his words. He probably wants us to be in the vanguard, so he can spare as many of his own people as possible. Who knows, he may even turn against us in the end."

"Then why are we here?"

"We're here to kill as many slavers as we can. We're here to make it known to all slavers; the yellow-haired folk are too dangerous to raid for slaves. That is why we are here."

"And while we're here, our homes and families are vulnerable to attack," he muttered softly.

"I know, Lonn, I know. We won't stay long. We won't partake in any siege, and if this army of his doesn't march within two days, we'll go home anyway." Satisfied, he left her to her own thoughts and sought out his sleeping place under a tree.

Luck was again with Born. The next day brought him another three hundred men. With the new arrivals, he declared that they'd march on the next dawn. "Ten days or less should bring us to our enemy's stronghold. Two days after that it'll be ours."

Another fifty or so men straggled in over the next few hours, and no one at all missed the tall, lanky, runner who slipped away in the dead of night. Gerrit would know of their coming. Hopefully the Lucky Lady would find Tallon in time.

Homeward Bound

"I almost hate to leave again," sighed Meera, as she gazed out from the window of their sleeping chamber. It had once been her mother's and father's, before the Usurper had used it for his own. It had taken very little time to restore it for Meera and Oona, who now stood beside her. "I know we must hurry, love, but I'll miss this place."

"Lady Meera, if all goes well we should have little or nothing to do next summer. I'd like to return here, and visit every single one of these isles with you."

"I'd love to show them all to you, my Oona. Alas, we have much to do back in Meerasland. If I understand your plan fully, we'd better get ourselves to Castle Oona as fast as we can."

"I hope the Dorand fleet can keep up with us. They need the wind for their sails while we can use the oars in slack weather."

"There will be wind, my love," laughed Meera. "Enough of this moaning, I can see that the fleet's ready. Let's get going before we lose the tide."

They left the chamber, and the castle gates, marching swiftly down the hill to the docks where the Raven was waiting for them. Tarn walked with them, and a throng of well wishers lined their path. "Remember, Tarn, send me a ship every half moon cycle and I will send one to you."

"I understand, Lady Oona. It shall be as you require."

"Keep my high seat warm, Tarn, we'll return next summer to stay for a while. Lady Meera has promised to show me each and every island in the Empire." Smiling, Oona turned and followed Meera onto the deck of the Raven. "I do so want to see them. Kieran, put up the sea dragon. I want everyone to know that Lady Meera is back."

By the time the Raven reached the rest of the fleet, it was flying the sea dragon just below the red meera. The Dorand fleet now had the red meera on their masts as well, and insisted on keeping it there. Together, they set out for Meerasland.

Once the fleet was well away from the harbor, Meera strode to the bow of the Raven. Raising her hands to the sky she began to chant. Oona approached from behind and put her hands on Meera's shoulders. Meera's voice grew stronger and a stiff breeze sprang up, then grew into a strong wind carrying them due east.

Meera wanted to pull an oar with the crew, but Oona talked her out of it, insisting she needed to fully regain her strength for the coming battles. Reluctantly, Meera saw the wisdom of this argument, and complied. She spent her time resting and singing up the winds. After a few days of rest, she began to practice all her warrior skills with Kellan and Tella.

Half a moon cycle and more passed, and the crews of the fleet had barely put an oar in the water. Meera had the advantage of the natural winds at this time of year. All she had to do was enhance them a bit. With her help, the winds were strong all the way back to Meerasland.

"Land ahead!" The call came near midday, and Oona raced to the deck right behind Meera. Meera was fully recovered now, and her natural take charge nature had reasserted itself. "Where?" she shouted to the rigging as she reached the deck.

"There, Lady, ahead to the starboard."

"If Tella is any sailor," grinned Kieran, as he joined them, "that should be the headland where the river spills out into the sea."

A few moments later they could see that he was right. As soon as the fleet was sighted a small boat set out from shore. It rowed swiftly toward them. In short order the boat was alongside, and a man swarmed over the rail to drop to one knee before Meera.

"Lady Meera, we heard that you had been killed. I'm well pleased to see that the news was incorrect."

"Rise, Konnor, my kinsman." Meera smiled as she helped him to his feet. "I did indeed walk the edge of the great abyss for many days, but my Lady Oona is a powerful healer, and she called me back to her side. Oona is First among us now, Konnor, and she is Chieftain of the House of Lothar."

"Lady Oona, it is good to see you well," he smiled, as he turned to Oona and gave her the special salute.

"You seemed to be in a hurry, Konnor. Have you news for us?"

"A great army marches on Castle Oona, Lady. They'll arrive in two days or less. We believe there are well over a thousand warriors coming."

"What news of Tallon?"

"They say he went raiding a cycle ago, Lady. None have heard from him since, but there are rumors. Many of them are quite unpleasant. Gerrit sent the Lucky Lady to find him, but they haven't returned."

"Tallon has done what I asked of him, Konnor. Don't fault him for obeying me. He may yet prove to have been the dagger that strikes through the heart of the enemy."

"Lady?"

"I'll explain later. Lady Meera, you must take over now."

"Forgive me, Lady Oona," grinned Meera, "but you're First among us now. It's you who must take command."

Everyone snickered as Oona stuck her tongue out at Meera then burst out laughing. "Very well then, as First Queen of the Empire of the Isles and Meerasland, I, Oona, do hereby command you, Lady Meera, to take control of all my fighting forces, and to defeat my enemies."

"It shall be as you require, my Lady Healer," laughed Meera. "Kieran, Kellan, Tella, advise me now. Someone bring me Hekkat."

Oona noticed the bemused look on Konnor's face, and she smiled. "What is it Konnor?"

"Forgive me, Lady Oona, but is that not a fleet of the half-men flying your standard?"

"It is."

"I'm not even going to ask how you managed that." He grinned as he shook his head in amazement.

"Our new chieftain is quite resourceful, don't you think, kinsman?" Meera asked as signals were sent and the Koddok moved up beside the Raven.

"I would say I'm a very lucky man to have been adopted into a house whose chieftain can tame the half-men and raise the dead."

Both Meera and Oona were laughing as Hekkat made the leap from one ship to another. Konnor flinched, but Oona caught his arm. "They're allies, Konnor," she said softly.

"Bring me charcoal," commanded Meera, and a piece appeared as if by magic. "Hekkat, Dorand fight good on land do they?"

"On land is best, Laydee Meera. Ladyee Meera Bloody Hand come ashore, Hekkat thump good." Everybody had a good laugh at that.

"Alright, point taken." Meera was laughing with them. She gave Hekkat a friendly thump on the shoulder. "People, here is what we face. Castle Oona is on a hill overlooking a broad valley, here." As she spoke, Meera drew a map on the deck with her piece of charcoal. "The enemy is coming by land, so they will most likely arrive from this direction. There is forest here, and here. Konnor says they're nearly upon us, so we must ferry as many fighters up river as possible in a very short time. I want to put more fighters in the castle, many fighters in the forest, here and over here. This way we'll have them surrounded. Any questions?"

"What means ferry?" asked Hekkat.

"Most ships too big for river, scrape bottom. Smaller ships take fighters up river then return for more."

Hekkat thought for a moment before he spoke again. When he did it surprised them all. "Dorand take all fighters up river. Put old, young, sick, on Oona ships. Take all Oona fighters up river on Dorand ships."

"Are you saying your ships can all go up that river?"

"All Dorand ships go where smallest Oona ship go. Not need so much water as bigger ships with long oars."

"Well I'll be a sea dragon. What do you think, Kellan, Tella?"

"It sounds good to me, Lady Meera," smiled Kellan. "I've come to trust Hekkat."

"All right, Hekkat, we'll do it. When we get there, Dorand go here, Oona fighters go there and there. Let's get busy people. I want to be in that castle before dark." There was a sudden rush of activity as the ships were readied and crews moved about. The day was growing late as Oona and Meera stepped aboard the Koddok. Peta beamed widely as she greeted them, welcoming them to her own ship.

"Tell me, Peta, what does Koddok mean?"

"Koddok is white-finned fish, Laydee Oona. Very fast, very deadly to enemies."

"Then I'm happy that we are now friends."

"Ladyee Meera Bloody Hand, come," called Hekkat, as he stood in the bow of the ship.

Meera approached him slowly. "Hekkat?"

"Sing up good wind, Ladyee Meera? Ship go faster with good wind." He was grinning and so was she. Somehow, she too, had come to trust this wild man from the far western jungles. Meera raised her arms and began to chant. She was a bit startled to hear him join in the chant. A stiff breeze sprang up and filled the sails. The Dorand fleet, loaded to the gunwales with fighters, moved into the mouth of the wide river.

"Hekkat know wind song too?"

"Is old song of our people, daughter of Dorand," he replied gently. "Is good no enemy no more. Better friends."

"Aye, Hekkat," smiled Meera, as she slapped his shoulder in a friendly gesture. "Much better friends."

The Dorand fleet moved upriver until it became too difficult to use the sails. The sails were brought down and long poles appeared. There was a great fuss until the westermen understood that they had to get back from the rails. Once the rails were cleared one Dorand tucked his pole into his shoulder, jabbed the other end into the river bottom, and began to push with all his might. There was another man on the other side of the ship and every ship had men with poles. As soon as the ship began to move there was room for another man to use his pole. As more and more men got their poles into the water, the faster the ships moved. As a man reached the stern of the ship he removed his pole from the water and ran back to the bow to start again.

As soon as the amazed westermen got the idea, they too began to take turns with the poles. As a Dorand got tired, a westerman would take his pole and join in. In this manner, the ships moved upstream against the current with more speed that Meera could have imagined. The day was just growing dark as they reached the landing place. There was no sign of an invader. They had arrived in time.

As the Koddok bumped gently on the riverbank, Konnor leaped ashore and sped away to the castle. By the time the ships were all tied up, and their crews ashore, Gerrit had arrived to greet the queens.

"Lady Meera, Konnor said you were here, but I dared not hope."

"The rumors of my death are somewhat premature, Gerrit," grinned Meera.

"And I'm delighted to hear that. Ladies, you're a most welcome sight indeed, for I have word that nearly two thousand fighters are marching against us. They'll be here on the morrow, the next day at the latest. My spy's told me that they have a band of golden-haired warriors with them, led by an old woman with a long jagged scar on her forehead. I think he said her name was Gurda Bloodaxe. He says they're the fiercest looking of them all."

"Did you say a woman named Gurda? With a long jagged scar on her forehead?" inquired Oona softly.

"Yes Lady, that is what the man said."

"What is it, Oona?" asked Meera.

"That was my mother's name, Lady Meera. I saw the slaver strike her with a sword. It cut her forehead and there was a lot of blood as she fell. I thought her dead, but I wonder..."

"Well, we should soon find out. Gerrit, take Lady Oona into the castle where she'll be safe. Hekkat, take the Dorand that way." He nodded and, with his people, disappeared into the gathering gloom. "Kellan, let's go while we can."

"Lady Meera," called Oona. "Be patient and give Tallon's efforts a chance to take hold. Keep yourself safe."

"I will, my Oona." Meera came back and hugged Oona gently. "I will keep myself safe, I swear it." She turned and led her fighters into the forest. Oona was left standing with Tella at her side. Dor and the twins were there as well. Somehow they had all appointed themselves as her personal guard, and Oona liked it that way.

"All right, Gerrit, take me home and lock me inside." He saluted then turned and led the way back to the castle.

"So, Gerrit, where did you get a spy that Born wouldn't suspect?" asked Oona, as she marched alongside him on the way to the castle.

"One of the former slaves, Lady Oona. Jonn's his name, and he was quite willing to spy on his former masters. He said he walked right past Born, and the fool didn't recognize him. He did tell me that another man led a strong force away to reclaim their first home."

"That would be Broc," snarled Oona. "He's on my list of men I want to see dead. Oh well, at least I'll know where to find him. He'll hole up in there like a frightened rabbit."

"Forgive me, Lady," laughed Gerrit, "but that place is held by the Trogs."

"What exactly are Trogs, and what does it mean that they have that place?"

"Trogs aren't human, Lady, yet they're close. We first encountered them a few generations ago in a land far to the southwest. Trogs are poor farmers, and worse fishermen. They prefer to hunt and gather their food. They aren't so great at open warfare, but give them a place to hole up, and the demons themselves won't dig them out. There's fifty Trogs there. So, unless he has several hundred men, I doubt your man Broc will succeed. Kreeg will probably bring you his head, and demand a high price for it."

"If he does, I'll gladly pay the price he asks. Well, here we are behind closed doors once again. I guess there is nothing to do now but wait."

"I'll escort you to the most comfortable quarters we have, Lady Oona. You might as well rest until they get here."

"Actually, I would like to see Morel, if I may. Konnor, where have you hidden Morel?"

"Forgive me, Lady Oona. I'm sure Morel would like nothing better than to see you again, but she is somewhat busy giving birth right now. It is a bit early and the healer is concerned. Lady, could you...?"

"Show me where, Konnor. Quickly now." With Tella right on her heels, she followed Konnor to a small hut near the castle wall.

There was a woman standing guard. She put her hand on Konnor's chest to stop him. "You may go no farther." Just then there was a moan of pain from within the hut. Oona moved toward the door and the woman stepped aside, giving Oona the special salute. "You are most welcome, Lady," she said as Oona passed through the door.

Oona found Morel squatting beside a small fire. She was sweating profusely, and weak from exhaustion. "Lie back here, Morel." Oona crooned soothing sounds as she helped Morel to lie back. "Let me see what is going on here."

"Por... I mean, Lady Oona, how did you get here?"

"I came on a ship actually," giggled Oona. "Lie still now, Morel." Morel tried, but another contraction racked her body, causing her to writhe in pain. "Easy now my darling, Morel." Oona sang a healing song and Morel melted into her arms.

Oona felt all along Morel's belly, singing to her the whole time. She gently poked and prodded as she sang, and the baby kicked and squirmed inside. All at once the women in the hut saw Morel's abdomen move and twist, then a great contraction hit her, and the baby started to come. Still singing her healing song, Oona helped Morel back to her squatting position and the baby came with the next contraction.

Konnor was pacing back and forth outside, muttering the whole time. Suddenly there was a primal scream from Morel, and then a scream of protest from very small lungs. Oona was cradling Morel and the baby, as the other healing woman went to inform Konnor that he was a father, and that his companion and daughter would soon be ready to return to their quarters.

EVEN AS OONA HELPED Morel to bring a new life into the world, Broc reached his old home with full intent of ending a great many lives there. Kreeg was called to the wall as Broc and his small army arrived at the gates. "Open up, I say," bellowed Broc.

"No!"

"Then we'll break it down." Several men began to hack at the wall when suddenly there was a rain of boiling fish oil and burning embers falling on them. With screams of pain, rage, and terror, the men fled the gates. A hail of heavy stones followed their retreat.

"Stones only," admonished Kreeg, as he directed the defenses. "Stones only, save your spears." A few moments later there was not an attacker to be seen.

"What will happen now?" asked one of the men who had manned the wall.

Kreeg grunted with what passed for a laugh. "They're in the forest now. They'll cut trees to make a ram and shields. When dawn comes, they'll attack again. Some men will hold shields over the heads of the men who wield the ram."

"What can we do then?" The fear was to beginning to show in the man's voice. There had been a lot of men at the gates.

"We will open the door and let them in." Well pleased with himself, Kreeg marched away to his home for a meal and a night's rest. Tomorrow would be a long day.

Reunion

Ella pushed herself hard. She'd left the children with her mother, hiding in the barns, while she tried to catch up to Bronn. She had to catch him and bring him back before the wild men returned. Ella had met several other women, each as desperate as herself to find their men, but she'd managed to leave them behind. Ella had ever been a hard worker, and her great stamina would bear her in good stead now. If she could bring Bronn home, they still had time to replant the fields, but there was a need for hurry if there was to be a crop for the winter.

As she ran on, Ella once again played the words of the marauder through her mind. "This land is now called Meerasland, and it belongs to Lady Oona of the House of Lothar. Your men have gone to make war against Lady Oona. For this reason your whole family is being punished. It grieves me to do this, but I must." That was when he had given the order to burn her home.

Ella had begged him not to do it, but he said that it was the fault of her men. Lady Oona wouldn't tolerate rebellion or resistance. Those willing to embrace Lady Oona, and her ways, would prosper greatly, and have her protection. Those unwilling had only one season to abandon the lands, or be killed. If Ella could get Bronn to see reason and return, they could rebuild.

She had wept bitterly as the marauder's men chased her own livestock through the newly sown fields, destroying the planting. Ella had been surprised to see real compassion in the man's eyes as she wept. "I'll leave you the barns," he had said softly, "even though she'd skin me alive if she knew. Find your man, girl. Bring him to his senses. Lady Oona will charge less for the grinding of the grain, and our ships will patrol the waters to keep away slavers. Find him and bring him home."

At that he had turned to the young man at his side. "Drado, call them back to the ships." The boy had sped away at alarming speed. They had already destroyed the rest of the village, and, according to some of the other women she had met, they had destroyed every town and hut they could find. This Lady Oona would not go easy on the men who marched against her.

"The bloody fools," thought Ella as she ran on, slowly gaining on another group of women in the distance, "how can you march across land against a people who strike from the sea?"

Darkness had fallen, and Ella was near exhaustion when she caught up to still more women. They agreed to rest for the night and stay together for protection. They had little food with them, but they shared what they had. As they settled in for the night, they exchanged stories. Ella wasn't the only one who'd seen the regret in the wild man's eyes. Some fully believed that he hadn't wanted to do the things that he had done.

One woman spoke of her sister's house and her men folk. Her sister's companion had kept his folk back from the war, and had stayed home to tend his fields. The ships of the wild men had yielded up better tools for working poor soil, and the ship's crews had actually helped with the planting. It had all been done in a day.

Tallon the Terrible was the name she had called the wild man. Yes, that had been his name, Tallon. His ship was the Raptor, a fitting name and ship for so harsh a man. Ah well, the ground spoke of many feet passing a short time ago. They'd catch the army on the morrow. They must, for they were nearly to the great wheel, and there they would find their men.

AS THE WOMEN RESTED in the forest, their men were resting on the banks of the great river. They would reach the castle of the wheel before the end of the next day. As they marched, their numbers had grown to nearly two thousand men. In a land so sparsely populated, it seemed impossible that so many could actually be found, but here they were. Born was well pleased with himself. He was about to become a king. He smiled broadly at the thought, and wondered how Broc was making out.

THE GOLDEN-HAIRED WARRIORS had kept to themselves, and marched in the vanguard of the army. Gurda's plan was to march out onto the field of battle, then turn to the right, taking up the flank and still be able to keep an eye on Born. She didn't trust him, and something else was beginning to bother her.

"What troubles you, Gurda?" asked one of the men who shared her fire.

"I'm not certain, Lonn, but I swear I can feel eyes watching from the forest, counting my every breath, as though counting out the last breaths I'll ever take."

"I know, I feel it too. It's as if there was an army of unseen eyes out there. Ah well, probably just the nerves before a battle. I always get them."

"As do I," muttered Gurda as she settled down to sleep, "but this is different."

As Gurda's people settled down for the night, young Orga crept silently into their camp. He cut the string of an amulet from the sleeping Gurda's neck. Grinning his delight at the prize, he melted back into the forest and returned to report to Hekkat. As soon as he'd made his report, Ogra went with Hekkat to find Meera. Hekkat translated Orga's findings to Meera, then Orga showed her the amulet as proof of his deed. She smiled brightly and praised his stealth and courage.

"He took this from the leader of the golden-hairs?"

"Yes, Ladyee Meera."

"That was well done indeed, Orga, you do your people proud. Kellan, hold our folk here. I'll go with Hekkat and his fighters, as they're closer. I want a word with the leader of the golden-haired warriors. Hekkat, ask Orga to take me to this woman." Hekkat spoke to the young man for a moment, then, beaming with pride, Orga led the way. As they passed through the Dorand campsite, all the Dorand fighters rose and followed them.

Gurda was awakened from her slumber by a feeling of being watched. She opened her eyes to see a figure crouched beside her fire, slowly poking life back into it. Before she could move, the figure spoke softly so only she could hear. "Move slowly and make no alarm. Look all about you; my fighters are all through your camp. One sound of alarm and all will die in their blankets. Do you understand?"

"I understand," replied Gurda, but two of the men nearby awakened anyway. There were daggers instantly at their throats.

"Make no sound, all good," whispered Hekkat, as he held a knife to one of the men. "Make sound, die quick." Lonn didn't understand the words, but he got the idea.

As Gurda and her men gazed all around their camp, they could make out the figures of the Dorand fighters in the pale moonlight. Gurda had chosen a campsite a bit away from the rest of the army. She was now regretting that decision. "Who are you, and what do you want?"

"I'm Meera, of the House of Lothar, Second Queen of all the Empire of the Isles. I want to ask you some questions. Answer truthfully and you will not be harmed this night."

"Ask then."

"Are you Gurda, companion of Handor the Fairhair, mother of Oona the Healer?"

"I am that woman. Although, Handor is long dead, and my poor Oona was taken slave many years ago. I pray that she died swiftly, for slavery is no life worth living."

"On that we agree."

"Oh really?"

"The things you have been told about us are all lies, Gurda. Why have you come here to this place, armed for war?"

"We have come to kill as many slavers as we can. We believe you and your people intend to enslave us all, and put us to the wheel."

"Our first queen has decreed that the wheel shall be turned by beasts. The westerfolk do not keep slaves. Gurda, I do believe you are the woman I seek. Would you know your daughter's fate?"

"Oona? You know of my Oona?" exclaimed the woman, as she rose up on one knee to look Meera in the eye. From this close Meera could easily see the resemblance to Oona.

Meera nodded her head slowly. "Your daughter was taken, and sold to a man who named her Porga. It is a foul name for anyone, for it is a beast's name. She was held by this man for many years, and bore him three children. On the day I first saw her, he had slain her children, and staked her out across a cask for the use of all men. Her head had been shaved, and she had been beaten nearly unto death. As the tide rose high he threw her into the sea, bound hand and foot."

"Name this man, and he will die on my blade before the moon comes full again," hissed Gurda, the rage clear in her eyes now.

"The man's name is Born the Strong."

"That's a lie. You're just trying to create dissension between us."

"Why would I bother, Gurda?" Meera continued to stir the embers of the fire. "Look around your camp. If it was trouble I wanted to cause his army, I'd just have killed you all in your sleep."

"She's right, Gurda," sighed Lonn, as he relaxed back on the ground. "They could have easily killed us all and let Born find us in the morning. You know we can't trust him, but for some reason, I believe this woman."

"I can prove to you that what I say is true, Gurda."

"How can you do that?"

"I dove into the sea that day, and took Oona from the waters myself, killing several of Born's men as I did so. Oona and I have been constant companions ever since that time. In a nearby place, there is a small songbird who would like to sing for you, Gurda."

Gurda burst into tears and sank back onto the ground. "Handor used to say that whenever Oona wanted to show me a new song she had made up. I believe you, Meera."

"Forgive me, Gurda, but you must call me Lady Meera, or one of my folk might kill you for disrespect before I could stop them. You must also call Oona, Lady Oona, for it is she who is First Queen of the Isles."

"What???"

"When I took Oona from the sea, I made her my Second and life companion. Earlier this year we were attacked by assassins, and I was cut by a poisoned blade. Since no one had ever survived that form of poison before, everyone thought me dead. As I weakened, they proclaimed Oona as First, but Oona wouldn't let me die. She brought me back to life and made me her Second and life companion."

"I don't believe a word you say, woman."

"It is truly a strange tale, I know. Come with me to the castle. You can see for yourself. I swear to you that you won't come to any harm."

"I believe her, Gurda," sighed the big fellow, as she sat pondering what to do. "Go with her and learn the truth of this thing, before we let some lying fool get us all killed."

"Alright, Lonn, I'll go. Lead on, Lady Meera. If you truly have my Oona safe and sound, I'll worship you for the rest of my days."

"It's always good to have your companion's mother in your camp," chuckled Meera. "Lonn, when the march on the castle begins, keep your folk in the fore. March right up to the gate. Gurda will meet you there, and the gates will be opened to you so Born can't strike at you from behind. If you don't see Gurda at the gate, you'll still have time to turn aside without harm."

"Thank you, Lady Meera. Call off this savage with a dagger at my throat, and I'll be happy to follow your instructions." Hekkat saw Meera's signal, grinned, and danced away.

Hekkat made a soft bird call, and, with a sound like a sighing wind, the Dorand withdrew back into the forest and vanished. Meera took Gurda's hand and led her through the darkness beneath the trees. "We can see in the dark quite well." She grinned as Gurda stumbled again. "It can be most helpful when sneaking into an enemy camp."

"I can easily believe that," grunted Gurda, as she struggled to keep up.

The night was half gone when Gurda realized that she and Meera were alone, and had been for some time. She could guess where the rest of Meera's fighters were. She shivered, hoping Lonn would do as he'd said he would. Suddenly they were out of the forest and into a broad valley. Gurda could see a bit better now, and the going was easier.

As they neared the castle, Meera called out and the gates were slowly opened, just enough for them to squeeze through. "Lady Meera, what's happened?" asked Gerrit, as he came pounding up to them just inside the gate.

"All is well, old friend. I'm sorry to disturb your slumber, but I've brought a gift for my Lady Oona. Could you ask someone to..." she got no further as Oona shouted her name and ran into her arms.

"Oh Meera, I am so glad you're safe. When the guardsman came to say you were here I thought you..."

Oona stopped speaking as she noticed the woman standing nearby. She disentangled herself from Meera's arms, and stepped over to the woman who was smiling at her with tears flowing down her cheeks. As Oona came closer, Gurda reached out to run her fingers through that full head of golden curls. "I was told that a small songbird wished to sing for me."

"Mamma," cried Oona, as she seized the woman in a bear hug. "Oh my oath, it truly is you. I saw you fall when the slaver struck you. I thought you dead."

"So did they all, Oona my child," whispered Gurda, "but I remained alive to avenge the theft of my daughter, and the death of my companion. I gave up the ways of a healer, and took the path of the warrior."

"That time is now past, Mamma. You must return to the ways of a healer, for the folk need good healers. We already have plenty of fighters. Meera..."

She turned to Meera, but Meera wasn't there. "Where is Lady Meera?"

"Returned to the forest, Lady Oona. She said she's brought you one gift this night. She will soon bring you another." He smiled and spoke to Gurda. "Forgive me, I am Gerrit. By the grace of Lady Oona, I am commander of this garrison. Lady Meera said to keep you close to the gates when the army arrives."

"I'm Gurda. Yes, she said if I wanted I could lead my folk inside to safety or turn them aside from the fighting."

"Indeed, which would you prefer?"

"That all depends." Gurda's voice took on a hard edge. "Oona, may I ask the name of the man who held you slave, if indeed that was your fate?"

"The slavers sold me to a local chieftain for half a shipload of grain," Oona replied harshly. "He claimed that I was his companion, but a slave by any other name is still a slave. On the day Lady Meera found me, he slew my children, beat, and shamed me, then threw me into the sea. His name is Born the Strong."

"Then Meera spoke truly. Gerrit, I want to bring my fighters into the castle to help you defend it."

"You will be most welcome, Gurda. However, I must caution you to speak of, and to address, this woman as Lady Oona, and to speak of her companion as Lady Meera. To do elsewise will surely shorten your days considerably. It is considered most disrespectful, and an act of treason."

"M...Lady Meera did mention that. I'll do my best to remember. Please forgive me, Lady Oona. Truly, I meant no disrespect."

"Stop now, Mother, it's just the way of the people. I, too, had a hard time adjusting at first, but you get used to it. Come, we can spend the few hours before dawn catching up. You can tell me all about what's happened since I last saw you. How is our home these days?"

"It no longer exists, Lady Oona," sighed Gurda, as she allowed herself to sink to the ground beside the gate. Oona sat beside her to hear the rest of her tale. "After I recovered, I had to beg a place at another man's table for the winter. He was a good man and taught me the use of weapons. The next year the slavers came to us there, but we fought back and a few of us escaped them. The next year we fought and killed many.

"Over the years we've been pushed back into the cold islands to the north and east of this land. It seems that golden-haired slaves bring a high price in the southern lands, and they come with more ships each year. We now try to grow crops in barren places, hidden from sight, and in lands where no one would suspect a people could live. There are over two hundred fighters here with me, but they're all we have. Most of the women and the children are hidden on a barren island awaiting our return."

"Far to the west of here is a chain of islands that are a large part of our empire. The world is warmer there, and since so many of our folk have come to Meerasland, several of the islands are nearly empty. If you wish it, I'll send messages to my commander there, and ask him to find space for your people.

"Believe me, Mamma, the sight of so many golden-haired folk would bring great joy to the islanders. There would be no enemies there to fight, as the only fleet in those waters is mine. If you wish it so, I'll send you all there on my ships."

"Oona, I mean, Lady Oona, my own beautiful daughter. Are you truly queen of the entire world?"

"Well, a big piece of it, that's certain, Mamma."

"We have so longed for a place of peace," sighed Gurda, "but we've lost hope."

"Then we will bring that hope back to you, Mamma. I promise. As soon as Lady Meera deals with this army, we will see about getting your folk a new home."

A Day of Reckoning

As the dawn broke in a cloudy sky, Kreeg was already on the battlements. "Make ready, here they come," he bawled with a sense of satisfaction. Now he would show that loud-mouthed human what defending a castle was all about. Below him, near the wall, there were nearly twenty Trogs gripping a thick rope. The gates were well manned, and a gauntlet of fighters stretched along the path from the gates on the inside. They were ready.

"Hold. Let the ram pass the moat first. Hold! Hold! Pull! Pull!" As the huge Trogs heaved on the rope there was a sudden grinding sound outside, and a large ravine appeared where solid ground had once been only a moment before. "Open! Open! Shut it! Shut it!"

As the light grew strong enough, Broc and his men attacked. Twenty men or more carried a huge log for a battering ram. They were planning to break down the gates. Several more men ran alongside, holding shields over the heads of the men carrying the ram. There would be no defeat from above this day.

As they neared the gate, they were at a full run. Suddenly there was a rumbling sound and the land beneath their feet started to give way. The hindmost men almost didn't make it past the landslide, as a large portion of the roadway slid off toward the beach below, carrying several men away with it, and leaving a deep ravine behind. The warriors following the ram were cut off, and could not aid the rest of their fellows.

Carried on by their momentum, the men with the ram reached the gates at a dead run. Instead of the expected shock of the ram meeting the timber of the gates, the gates swung open and they charged right on through.

As the gates opened the Trogs dropped their rope and swept up their weapons. The men carrying the ram were suddenly inside the gates, confronted on one side by armed men and armed Trogs on the other. The gates swung closed behind them as they dropped their tree and reached for their weapons, but it was too late.

The carnage was brutal and swift. No invader within the gates survived. The few warriors trapped outside, between the now closed gate and the new ravine, were pelted with rocks, oil, embers, and a rain of their dead fellows. The last of the bodies was dropped over the wall just as the men outside scrambled through the loose rock of the ravine to safety.

"How many?" demanded Kreeg.

"Two humans dead, six wounded, five will recover."

"Ours?"

"One dead, eight wounds, none serious."

"Life is good. Throw the rest of the enemy bodies over the wall, so these fools will know what they're dealing with."

A turn of the glass later there was a shout from the roadside. "Hallo, the walls."

"What do you want?" bellowed Kreeg. Unseen by the men on the road, he was waving his arm wildly at his men who were swiftly disappearing into a tunnel.

"We're leaving," shouted the man in the road. "Here's the fool who wanted to attack you. We thought you might have a use for him, as we do not."

With that he and his fellows dumped Broc, bound hand and foot, into the ravine. They turned to leave and met a wall of fighters pointing spears, blocking their escape. They were now trapped between the ravine and the castle's defenders. "Drop all weapons," commanded a large Trog. They did so, even though they still greatly outnumbered the Trogs. These men were farmers and fishermen, not hardened warriors.

"Go now, do not return," snarled the Trog, and the now unarmed men fled back toward the forest. They didn't stop until they reached their burned out homes far away.

With effort, they finally managed to drag Broc inside the gates. "What shall we do with him?"

Kreeg grunted and waved his arm. "Kill it. Stick its head on a pole at the gates for all to see." Broc's scream of terror was cut short as a man with a long sword separated his head from his shoulders. Within moments his head adorned the gates he could not force open. The fate he had planned for Kreeg was now his own.

BORN COULD NOT KNOW of his brother's fate, but he had an uneasy feeling as the sun rose over the hillside. Ah well, this was the day, time to get a move on. He began rousing his troops and headed for the camp of the golden-haired warriors. Even as he reached them, a half starved Ella arrived at the back of the mass of men. Even as Born sought for Gurda, Ella sought desperately for Bronn.

"Where is Gurda?" demanded Born, as he gave up searching for her himself.

"She went into the forest. She said something about hearing a songbird."

"What???"

"I don't think she was feeling all that well." Lonn shouldered his pack and his weapons. "Let's go, men." The golden-haired warriors set out along the trail. Grumbling to himself, Born slowly dropped back to the rest of his army. He was completely unaware as several more women arrived at the back of the marching horde.

As the army began to pour out of the forest and onto the wide valley floor, Ella found Bronn. Clinging to his arm, and babbling almost incoherently, she tried to drag him out of the marching column.

"Ella, Ella, calm down for pity's sake," exclaimed Bronn as he tried to shake her off his arm. "What are you doing here, girl? You should be at home with the children."

"That's what I'm trying to tell you, Bronn. There is no home. None of you have a home anymore. While you were all running about the countryside playing at war, the raiders came. They burned all our homes and tore up all our crops."

"What???" Ella had the attention of a good number of men now.

Ella gasped as she caught her breath. "His name was Tallon the Terrible. They destroyed the home and fields of every man here. He said if you go home and rebuild, no harm will come to you or your family, but if you make war against his queen he'll return and kill everybody he can find. They'll take our lands and kill us all, Bronn. You have to come back with me now. Don't let them see you here."

"You lie woman," snarled one of the men nearby.

Bronn rounded on the man instantly. "Ella never tells lies. Say that again and I'll rip out you foolish tongue."

"It's not a lie," shouted Ella. "Look there. There come the other women to bring the same news to their men. The road through the forest is full of women as desperate as I am. They've come to find their men and take them home before they can get us all killed. Bronn, you must come now."

"If we leave, Ella, they will make us all slaves."

"No, Bronn, no. He swore to me that they don't keep slaves. It's against their queen's law. They freed our two slaves and let them leave."

"They didn't keep them?"

"No, they set them free."

"How are we supposed to get the crops replanted without the slaves?"

"Tallon said his men would help. I believe him Bronn, for they did help those who didn't march away. Please, you must come home with me now."

By this time several more women had arrived, and two other men could be seen leaving. Bronn slowly nodded his head and complied. He'd always prospered by her council before; he would trust her instincts now. Bronn shouldered his pack, and, putting his arm around her shoulders, left the field with Ella. It would be a long walk home, best to get started. As they walked, they passed many more women hurrying toward the valley of the wheel.

Born was blissfully unaware of the commotion at the back of his army. He had his eyes fixed on the castle atop the hill. They'd reach it in less than a turn of the glass. He smiled as he watched Lonn lead the golden-haired warriors in the vanguard. The fool was playing right into his hands. Born held his own troops back slightly, giving the men in the castle time to come out and attack Lonn's men.

Born planned to let them fight it out themselves. The golden-haired warriors would certainly lose. There were too few of them to bring a victory, but they were fierce fighters, and would surely weaken the castle forces considerably. Everything was going according to plan; and then it all went to hell. Born's jaw dropped as he watched the castle gates open and Gurda emerge. She stood aside and Lonn marched his fighters inside then the gates closed once more.

Seeing the castle swallow up the golden-haired warriors caused confusion among the remaining men. They began to mill about, and slowly the great army came to a halt just out of bow range of the castle. They were still somewhat unsure of what to do next when a voice rang out from the castle.

"Hear me, people in the valley." The army fell silent to hear what the voice had to say. A man stood atop the wall, his hands cupped about his mouth. "Hear me! I am Gerrit, of the House of Lothar.

By the grace of Lady Oona, I am commander of this castle garrison. Hear me and fear, for I speak the words of Lady Oona. Leave this place now and return to your homes. Do this and no harm will come to you. If you stay, you will all be slain."

There were many shouts of defiance, and the army began to surge forward. They got right up to the gate before the voice called out again. "Look behind you, people. Your women have come to take you home. Do you want them to be killed as well?"

This caused a great uproar among the army as the truth of that statement became clear. Born was nearly incoherent with rage. He could feel his dreams slipping away. "Get those bloody women out of here. What the blazes is wrong with those foolish women? Get them out of here."

"Hear the words of Lady Oona," called the voice from atop the walls. "Leave with your women now. We will give you time to sort yourselves out, but you must leave. You must also bring Born the Strong to the gate, bound hand and foot, and stripped naked. Do this and you may leave unharmed. Refuse and we will attack you."

With a bellow of rage Born attacked the gate with his axe. Suddenly he yelped and leaped back as a huge stone falling from above nearly brained him. He looked up to see a head of golden curls and a bright smile looking back at him. "Porga, you miserable useless slut, I'll skin you alive for that." She only laughed at him and climbed up onto the wall in plain sight.

"Hear me, people. I am Lady Oona, first queen of the Empire of the Isles. This land is now called Meerasland. It is mine. Bring me Born, bound and naked, and I'll let you live. Refuse me, and you will not see another sunrise." With that she hopped back to the safety of the walkway.

With a look of deep compassion on her face, Gurda took Oona in her arms. "Porga, is that what he named you?"

"Two of us bore that name," snarled Oona. "Me and his favorite breed sow. I swear I'll see him dead for the killing of my children, if for no other reason."

"How long will you wait before you attack?"

"If they haven't delivered Born and left the field before nightfall, Meera will attack in the darkness."

"Ah yes, these folk can see in the dark." Gurda turned her attention to the men on the field below. There were a number of women among them now, haranguing them to leave the field. Many more women could be seen arriving.

Born wasn't about to see things fall apart so easily. "Don't be foolish," he bellowed, as he struggled to regain control of his men. "We can defeat them, and then it won't matter. Are you men, or are you a bunch of frightened women. Come on, get those rams up here. Let's get that gate down. We'll show them whose land this is. Come on, where's your spines?" It was beginning to work, as men shooed the women to the side and gathered up their weapons, preparing to attack.

"Well, that's cracked it." Gerrit hopped down to the walkway from his perch on the top of the wall. "Here they come! Brace the gates! Man the walls!"

Two dozen men, carrying a freshly fallen tree, charged forward, others running alongside to hold shields over their heads. With a resounding crack the ram struck the gates then bounced off. "Again!" They backed off then struck again with the same results.

Suddenly the terrified screams of the women drowned out Born's voice. He turned to see what was going on. He blanched as he saw a wall of fierce looking creatures, pouring out of the forest. They were heavily armed, and moved with a precision and speed that spoke of years of training. A shout drew his attention to another direction where he saw a second horde of warriors streaming out of the trees towards him. They were led by Red Meera herself.

The entire army was thrown into a near panic. Born struggled to get some form of order back, but he failed. A great many men dropped their weapons and fled the field with their women. They were terrified, but the onrushing wall of small savage warriors ignored them completely and passed them by. Any unarmed man leaving the field was ignored.

Hekkat and his fighters reached the army first and drove so deeply into the main body that they effectively cut it in half. The Dorand swung around on themselves encircling one half of the army while Meera and her warriors struck the remaining half. Meera charged straight at Born, with her men right behind her. They hit Born's men as sledge would strike a post, driving them back against the wall of the castle. At that point the gates opened and a combined force of westermen and golden-haired warriors poured forth.

Meera cut her way through the men before her as a farmer scythes grain. She didn't even seem to see the men in front of her, as her eyes were fixed on Born. He was in the middle of the fray when, suddenly, the westermen swept everyone away from him. He stood alone, facing Meera.

He lunged at her with a spear but she dodged it easily, then came at him with her two short swords weaving a curtain of steel before her. He dropped the spear and tried to parry with a sword of his own, but he was outclassed and he knew it. With a scream of pure hate he charged at her, swinging wildly with his weapon.

He came to a stop, realizing Meera was no longer in front of him, and there was a great pain in his leg. He turned to see her grinning at him, her long canine teeth gleaming in the sun.

"You won't escape me this time," she snarled, as he tried to charge at her again. Born swung his sword with all his might as he came at her. That blow should have cut her in half, but it struck only air. Meera was on the ground with her legs tangling up his own, and he toppled forward.

As Born hit the ground face first, Meera was on him, cutting his tunic and twisting it around his arms. Her mighty legs squeezed the air from his lungs and slowly he went limp. A moment later he was naked and bound with the remnants of his own clothing. He regained his senses to see the last of his army drop their weapons and surrender. Meera was standing over him smiling toward the castle.

"I warned you, Born. I told you that before I was finished with you, you would kneel to Oona and face her justice. That day has now arrived."

Born tried to regain his feet but he failed. Meera had tied his legs together as well. He cast his gaze in the direction she was looking, and he saw a golden-haired woman stride from the castle. She was flanked by a tall, fierce-looking, warrior on each side, another close behind, and a female warrior leading the way. As the woman reached the field of battle, everyone except Meera dropped to one knee, including the prisoners. She smiled and strode right up to Meera.

"Are you harmed, Lady Meera?" she asked in a clear, sweet voice, using the language of Meerasland.

"I remain unharmed as you can see, my Lady Healer."

Oona grinned and signaled everyone to rise. "Kellan, are you here? Are you unharmed?"

"I am here, Lady Oona." Kellan stepped up to her, giving her the special salute. "I'm unharmed as well. The blood you see is that of my enemies only."

"I'm well pleased to hear that, dear friend. Lady Meera, what have you here?"

"Another gift, as I promised, my Lady Oona. Before you kneels the man who slew your children then threw you into the sea. What do you want to do with him?"

Born tried to protest, but a westerman jammed a gag into his mouth and yanked it tight, causing him to fall silent. "Speak only when Lady Oona commands it," snarled a voice in his ear. All the prisoners were listening carefully now, wondering what would happen to Born.

Oona continued to use the language of Meerasland. "My Lady Meera, I can't imagine enough punishments, or sufficient torture, to repay this man for his crimes against me. Hear me, people. Since my own hatred for this man is so great, he will not face my judgment. Instead, he'll stand before the chief of justice for all of the isles. Kellan."

"Get him up," barked Kellan, and several hands jerked Born to his feet. "Who accuses this man?"

"I do," declared Oona. "This man held me slave for many years. He beat and tortured me. He killed my children. He tied me across a cask so all men could use me. He had me bound hand and foot, then thrown into the sea."

"Can anyone verify these accusations?"

"I can and do," replied Meera.

"As can I. Lady Oona is right. There are not enough tortures to fully repay this man for his crimes. It's enough to be rid of him forever. Hang him from the castle wall." Born tried to protest and to struggle, but it did him no good at all. A rope was placed around his neck and tossed to a man high atop the battlements. Kicking and begging, Born was hauled halfway up the wall. He was left there many days before Gerrit ordered him cut down.

"Is there other business here?" asked Oona in a loud voice.

"There is the matter of the prisoners, Lady." In truth there were few enough of them. Of the mighty horde that marched into the broad valley that morning, there were not more than eighty prisoners. Half the force had fled with their women while most of the remainder had fallen in the battle.

"So I see. Hear me well, men of Meerasland. Do you now see the folly of the path you chose?" There was not a sound so, smiling, she continued. "I told you what would happen, did I not?" Still no sound.

"Very well," she smiled as she switched into the language of the westermen, "Hekkat, what shall I do with your prisoners?"

"Ladyee Oona very generous," grinned Kekkat. He turned to his prisoners. "Ladyee Oona say, Hekkat, all Dorand do. Ladyee Oona say, all you do?"

"What's he saying?" one man asked another softly.

Kellan stepped closer and spoke to the men. "He's asking you if you will swear loyalty to Lady Oona, and obey her laws. He's offering you a chance. I'd take it if I were you. He'll kill the lot of you and eat your children if you don't."

There was a round of protests from the prisoners. "What will happen if we do?" asked one of the men.

"I have no idea," chuckled Kellan, "but you'd better decide. He's getting impatient."

"All right, I'll do it. Just don't let him harm our children." There was a round of agreement at that.

"If I were you, I'd make that pledge of loyalty to Lady Oona a bit more convincing."

"Lady Oona, I swear to be loyal to you and to always obey your laws," said one man as he knelt facing Oona. In a moment all Hekkat's prisoners had pledged to Oona.

"Well, they've done it, Hekkat. Now what do you want to do with them?"

"Kellan tell go home, behave." Grinning, Kellan relayed the message. To their great amazement the men were released and set free. "Go," commanded Hekkat as he pointed toward the forest, and the road away from the castle. They did not understand the command, but they got the idea. They left on the run.

"And now, Lady Meera," smiled Oona, shifting back to the language of Meerasland again. "What do you wish to do with your prisoners?"

"Hang the lot of them," growled one of the westermen.

"It's good that they can't understand what you said," laughed Meera. "Alright, men." She turned and faced the prisoners that her men had taken. "I'll offer you the same chance Hekkat gave to his prisoners. Swear loyalty to Lady Oona and you are free to go, but I warn you. You'll never receive this mercy again. Should you prove false in future, you'll meet the same fate as Born did this day.

"What if we don't want to...?" The question was cut short by a blow to the side of the head from a fellow prisoner. "Lady, we accept your terms, and if this one proves unworthy, I'll hang him myself." There was a rumbling of agreement from the rest. They were feeling shamed. They had not meant to show any mercy to these people had they been the victors. Had they been victorious, all would have been enslaved and put to the wheel. This luck just might not come again. To a man they swiftly swore the oath of loyalty to Oona and were set free. They fled back along the path taken by the others.

"Well, my Lady Healer, are you pleased?" asked Meera, as she took Oona's arm and led her back inside the castle.

"Truly, I had hoped to escape any bloodshed. Ah well, it was much better than it could have been. At last I'm free of Born, and that's a relief."

"Even with the whole empire to protect you, you still feared him, my Oona?"

"Lady Meera, that man was the biggest fool I have ever known. He didn't know when to stop. He was like a bull when he got an idea in his thick head. I knew that as long as he lived, he'd be trying to find a way to kill us. Thank you for finally putting a stop to him, and for keeping me safe from him."

"It was my extreme pleasure, my Oona. Well, that's two of the three on your list. I'm afraid that one has escaped us. Broc left the army several days ago taking a small force to reclaim that town that was once his home."

"Then we know where to find him," said Oona in a cold, determined voice.

"I've already sent a ship my Oona. They'll bring him to us, do not fear."

"Then I'm well pleased and content. Shall we retire to our rest?"

"Are you sure you want to rest? I could..."

"Meera," hissed Oona, as she slapped playfully at Meera's arm. "My mother is here, for pity's sake." Meera's laughter was full and rich, bringing a bright smile to Oona's face. Life was good.

Still another Threat

The sun had barely risen the next day when there was a great commotion at the castle gates. Yawning, Oona rose to see what was going on. She arrived to find Meera already there, and a man gasping for breath, Tallon grinning at him as he did. "Tallon!" Oona flew into his arms and gave him a bear hug.

"Lady Oona, it is good to see you well." He smiled as he gently returned her embrace then released her. "Today is truly the luckiest day of my life so far."

"What is that supposed to mean?" she demanded, her hands on her hips and a stern look on her face. The stern look faltered as she broke into a bright smile. Oona had truly missed Tallon's brash playfulness.

"The sun is barely risen, and already I've been embraced by the two most beautiful women in the empire."

"Oh really?"

"Absolutely. Lady Oona, however did you manage to bring Lady Meera back to us?"

"Ah, ah, ah, healer's secrets, Tallon." She smiled as she gripped his shoulder affectionately. "Tallon, dear friend, your mission was a great success. I know that it was a hard thing for you to do, but it had the desired effect. Hundreds of lives were saved as a result. Tell me how I can reward such a service, for I can see in your eyes what the cost has been to you."

"I have already been amply rewarded, Lady Oona," he grinned. "However, I fear I bring another matter for your attention."

"Tallon, I swear..." Oona shook her finger at him, which brought a smile to every face there. "Oh alright, what is it?"

"I believe my companion here has regained his breath now, Lady. I'll allow him to tell his tale."

The man was already bent over, his hands on his knees, as he drew in great lungfuls of air. He didn't understand their words, but at Tallon's pat on his shoulder he dropped to one knee as Tallon had coached him. "Lady Oona, I have dread news."

"Who are you and what news do you bring?" Oona's good cheer vanished instantly to be replaced with a feeling of fear as she switched to his language.

"My name is Hant, Lady, and I was born to these lands. Lady, I was taken slave many long years ago by the men of the southlands. They took me to their homeland and there I was sold to a man of status among them. I served him for many years."

"Rise up, Hant, and finish your tale," sighed Oona, resignation replacing her fear.

He thanked her as he regained his feet. "Lady, I loathe everything about those people, yet I do fear them. I managed to gain my master's trust, and for years I proved worthy of that trust. Last full of the moon I was serving drinks as they laid their plans, and it sickened me. I had to warn the people here of the danger."

"Hant, you're as hard as Tallon to get a straight answer from," sighed Meera. "Get to the point."

"Yes, Lady," the fear clear in his voice as he replied to Meera's demand. Hant was well accustomed to responding to a voice of command.

"Hant, what is the danger you speak of?" Oona asked softly as she took pity on him. She too, had responded fearfully to an impatient voice when she was a slave, and she still did.

"Lady, they are coming."

"Who, Hant, who is coming?" Meera was even more impatient now.

"The slavers, Lady. They've heard of a great war in this place, and so my master has called together all the ships of the land. They're coming to enslave everyone who manages to survive the war. I heard them planning to wait until the battles are over. That's when they will attack and capture everybody. They will sail to every town and village, taking all away to be sold at the great market."

"How many ships, Hant?" asked Meera. "Think clearly now, this is the most important part. How many ships are coming?"

"The night I stole a boat and rowed out of the great harbor, it was full of ships, and more were coming. I rowed toward the lone star as long as I could, but I was lost and near death when Master Tallon found me."

"That's just Tallon, Hant. Tell them about the ships now."

"Lady, I have seen all the ships in Tallon's fleet, and those who await you at the river mouth, as well as all on the river. Lady Oona, there are many more coming, at least two to every one you have."

Oona had blanched white at this, but Meera had a cold smile playing at the corners of her mouth. "When will they arrive, Hant? Do you know when they will sail north?"

"Lady, I was on the water for nearly a cycle of the moon. They planned to wait two moon cycles before sailing. They want the battles to be over and the people to be back at their homes. I believe they will wait another cycle before sailing."

"Tallon, your best guess?"

"Lady Meera, I believe we can get there before they sail, if the winds favor us, but we must be swift."

"Tallon, what are you saying?" gasped Oona. "Meera, they have so many ships, you're not thinking about..."

"Oona, my Oona," soothed Meera as she took Oona in her arms. "Think like a queen, my Lady Healer. This is your land now, and these are all your people. We have settled here, taken these lands for our own, and we have even brought the Dorand here to live. Can you abandon these folk to their fate?"

"No, I can't. Forgive me people, it is a slave's fear I feel still. Lady Meera, what must we do?"

"That is for you to decide, my Oona."

"Then I have decided that it is your responsibility to deal with this situation for me. You may now begin." Meera's full rich laughter was infectious and soon everyone joined in, including Oona. "Stop this foolishness, Meera. This is not a time for teasing. It is a time for action."

"Yes Lady Oona, and it's action you shall have. Tallon, get back and ready your fleet. Tell Kieran to make ready as well."

"He prepares even as we speak, Lady Meera. My fleet is all ready to sail. We shall await your arrival." With that he vanished back through the gates, leaving a nervous Hant still standing by the queens.

"Kellan, take the tale to Hekkat and ask him to join us would you? Tell him he can leave his elders, children, and a small force to protect them, here in the castle. We need him in the fleet."

"Aye, Lady," Kellan replied over his shoulder as he disappeared through the gates.

"Gerrit, keep as many of your garrison as you need, but give us every fighter you can spare."

"Lady, they are already packing."

"Good, now somebody find Konnor for me."

"Lady, I am right here." Konnor skidded to a halt and dropped to one knee. He was dressed for travel and bristling with weapons.

"Going somewhere, Konnor?"

"Lady Meera, please, I was held slave for two years, unable to defend myself or to help my kin. Morel has given me a child. I will not let that fate befall my family again. I beg you, allow me to defend my house and family."

"Konnor of Lothar, we'll be delighted to have you accompany us on our journey. Alright people, there's no time to lose. Let's get packing."

In the end, it took three days to get the entire fleet provisioned and ready to sail. Oona stood at the rail of the Raptor, gazing back at the mouth of the river. "I had truly hoped that this would be finished right here," she sighed.

"Lady, you know full well we dare not wait until they come to us." Tella was right beside her, as always. Tella had remained tight to Oona's side since Hant's arrival. Dor and the twins were never far away either. Meera was busy making battle plans and organizing the fleet, and Oona was content to let her. If they were to survive at all and protect the people they were sworn to protect, then Meera had to lead this expedition. Oona well remembered Tella's words, "All too often it has been swift obedience to Lady Meera's commands that has kept us alive on the high seas."

"Tella, tell me the truth. What are our chances?"

"Better than average, Lady Oona." Tella grinned wolfishly. "Especially if we can catch them bottled up in some harbor. We're a sea-faring folk, Lady Oona, and we don't depend on slaves to do everything for us. Slaves make you weak. Slaves make you dependent. They rob you of courage and strength. Hant has told us that it's slaves who pull the oars to drive their ships. Our ships are manned by free men and thus are much faster. We will defeat them, Lady Oona, do not fear."

"You're right, Tella," declared Oona, as she straightened up from the rail and turned away from the land. "It's time for me to stop acting like a slave, and to act like the First. Take me to Lady Meera."

"As you desire, Lady Oona, so shall it be. Come, they're on the Koddok."

As Oona stepped onto the deck of the Koddok everyone there, including Meera, rose to their feet and gave her the Oona salute.

She laughed with pure delight and returned it as she approached the council of war. "Greetings, good people, may I join you?"

"My Lady Healer, you are always welcome in this company," replied Meera as she gave Oona a gentle hug then released her. "I do believe we're ready to sail."

"Wonderful, what is the plan?"

"With luck, Lady, we can catch them still in their harbor. If we can keep them bottled up, we can defeat a thousand ships. We plan to sink every damned one of them, then go home to the great hall where Cora can feed us until we split."

"Tell me all of it, Lady Meera."

"Yes, my Oona." Meera replied with a gentle smile. "If we meet them on the open waters it may well be a different story, but even there we have certain advantages."

"And those are?"

"Their ships are driven by slaves, but our are driven by warriors, so each of our ships will have two or three times the number of fighters on board."

"That is indeed a huge advantage," smiled Oona. She was beginning to feel a bit more hopeful about it all. "Do they have weather singers, Hant?"

"None Lady, the concept is unknown to them."

"Another huge advantage; people, I don't want to stop at just sinking their ships."

"I told you so, Kellan," laughed Meera as she hugged Oona again. "Did I not tell you?"

"You did indeed, Lady Meera. Lady Oona, we're also planning to sack their town. Hant has told us that the town where he was prisoner is the largest in that land. He also tells us they have no queen or king, but that every town rules itself as in Meerasland in years past."

"Good. People, I don't want this land of slavers, but neither do I want them coming north ever again."

"Agreed, my Lady Healer. We shall teach them not to seek slaves in the lands of the north."

"Wonderful. I'm well pleased. Mother, your people need not have come with us, but we're glad that you have."

"Miss a chance to hit the slavers in their own lands?" Gurda exclaimed in mock surprise. "Perish the thought. Lonn would skin me alive for even suggesting it."

"Then we're ready to sail?"

"Only one thing remains, Lady Oona."

"And that is?"

"Which ship will carry the First?" he replied with a grin. "Shall it be the Raven or the Raptor?"

"I will miss you, Kieran," smiled Oona, "but I think I should sail on the Raptor."

Meera smiled gently as she spoke. "Lady Oona, you are First now, it is I who should sail on the Raptor. You should be on the Raven."

"Forget it, Meera." Oona laughed as she realized they were teasing her. "You gave me the Raptor and I've chosen her captain."

"I'm deeply honored, Lady Oona. So much more than you know, but my uncle is a far more experienced fleet commander."

"Tallon, are you advising me to entrust the entire combined fleets to Kieran?"

"I am, Lady. Lady Oona, it's my understanding that we'll be greatly outnumbered. I'll do all in my power if you ask it of me, but I do advise you to reconsider."

"Tallon, my friend, once again you've shown why it is that I trust your advice so readily. I'll heed the advice of my fleet commander. Lady Meera, please inform Kieran that I have placed the entire fleet into his care, and that he is to look to you for direction."

"I shall inform him immediately, Lady Oona," grinned Meera, as she winked at Kieran.

"As soon as Kieran has been made aware of these developments," smiled Oona, as she leaned against Kieran's shoulder, "we can get under way." She laughed and gave Kieran's shoulder a friendly squeeze then accepted Meera's hand and stepped off the Koddok and back to the small boat.

Kieran and Kellan conferred with Tallon and Hekkat for a few moments then returned to the Raven. Tallon was already back aboard the Raptor and ready to get under way by the time Kieran's ship raised the signal flags. Meera sang up a strong breeze and the three fleets spread out, Tallon and his fleet closest to the shore, Kieran leading the way, and Hekkat the furthest out to sea.

After several days they passed Kreeg's castle, and a small boat rowed out to them. It delivered its message, then turned back to shore. The ship it had contacted sent up a signal flag. It soon conferred with the Raptor which then signaled the Raven. The two flagships moved together, then Tallon leaped nimbly from one ship to the other. He saluted Oona, then dropped a bag between them.

"Lady Oona, it is not necessary for you to look into that bag, as I have already done so."

"Tallon, please, I'm not in the mood to pry the tale from you." Oona reached for Meera's hand.

Meera smiled as she put her arm around Oona's shoulders protectively. "Start at the beginning, Tallon."

"Aye, Lady. We have a report from Kreeg, who is commanding the town where we first encountered Lady Oona. A number of days ago a small army attacked the town, but they were defeated. This bag holds the head of the man who led them."

"You've looked into the bag?"

"Yes, Lady Oona. It contains the head of the man who abused you so badly on the day we first met. As I recall his name was Broc."

"Show me," said Oona, her voice as hard as stone.

"My Oona, perhaps..."

"I want to see it for myself." Oona's eyes were hard and her voice completely devoid of emotion. Tallon nodded and dumped the head out onto the deck of the Raven. The head was badly decomposed but Oona was easily able to recognize her old enemy. "Thank you, Tallon," she said after staring at the thing for a long moment. "Throw that to the fish please, and remind me to reward this Kreeg when we pass this way next."

"Aye, Lady." Tallon scooped up the grisly trophy and hurled it over the side. He threw the bag after it, then dipped his hands into a bucket of soapy water used to scrub the decks.

"It was Broc, alright," Oona sighed, as she allowed her shoulders to slump. "I can release that part of my life now. They are both dead."

"Yes, my Lady Healer," soothed Meera as she took Oona into her arms. "Soon we'll deal those slavers a mortal blow as well. They won't dare to come north for a thousand lifetimes."

"Meera, if we're so outnumbered, can we truly prevail?"

"Oona, my delight, we have an entire fleet of the elder race with us as well as over two hundred of the golden-haired warriors. With so many folk of both elder races with us, how can we possibly fail?" Oona's and Meera's laughter floated across the waters like a song of joy. A stiff breeze responded to that song and the fleet swept southward into the night.

City of the Damned

It had been nearly a moon cycle since they sailed and everyone was getting anxious. They had expected to find land by this time. Meera was as calm as ever, and each morning she sang up a fresh breeze to speed them on their way, but even she was getting concerned. If they somehow missed their enemy in the night, Meerasland would be completely helpless.

Hant had been taken aboard the Raven, and she sent for him just as Oona emerged from the cabin. It was another sunny day with a stiff breeze favoring their sails, and Oona smiled at Meera's cheery greeting. Oona's smile faded as she saw a man bringing Hant to Meera on the fore-deck. She hurried to arrive at the same time, as did Kellan and Kieran.

"Hant, my friend," began Meera, "forgive my doubts, but I believe we should have sighted land before now. If you have lied to us to draw us away from..."

"No, Lady Meera, please believe me. I've spoken only the truth. I..." Further protestations were cut short by a call from the rigging. "Land!"

"Where?" bellowed Kieran. All eyes followed the man's pointing arm. There it was, a rocky point of land jutting out into the sea. It wasn't long until it was visible to the whole fleet.

"Alright Hant, which way now?"

"I don't know, Lady," he stammered. "I was a house slave, not chained to an oar. I have no idea at all which way to go now."

Meera fought her frustration, and didn't allow her impatience to show. "Kieran, a fast ship along the coast that way and another that.

One day only then return, I don't want any of our people getting separated from the fleet now."

"Aye, Lady." Kieran began bellowing orders. Flags were sent up, then the Lucky Lady offloaded half her crew to the Raptor and set out along the coast. Moments later the Raven was crawling with fighters and the Jira was away as well.

"Hant, describe the land around that town of yours."

"It is hilly, but has deep rich soil, Lady Meera," he replied nervously. "The coastline is gentle, and the great harbor is protected by hills. The fields are well tended and the first harvest should be happening right now."

"First harvest?"

"Yes, Lady, there are two harvests each year. There's a great festival at the time of first harvest and many ships come from afar for the celebrations. The fleet will probably not leave the great harbor before the priests of the festival have had a chance to bless its voyage."

"So you believe they will still be there?"

"I do, Lady."

"I hope for your sake that you are right," she growled, then stalked away to the bow of the ship. Oona joined her there a moment later, and slipped her small hand into Meera's. "Forgive me, my Lady Healer, but I don't like this game of blind sailor seeks harbor."

"I know, Meera, I know. I'll wait here with you until the ships return." It was a long wait.

Oona lay on the deck, cuddled in Meera's arms, sleeping fitfully, while Meera's piercing gaze continued to bore into the gathering darkness. Finally she saw that which she wanted to see, the first scout ship returning. It was the Jira. She made straight for the Raven and the waiting Meera.

Kellan and Kieran were already at the rail as the captain of the Jira clambered over the rail. He saluted them all before he spoke. "Ladies, I have seen no signs of life this day," he sighed.

"Hant has spoken of low hills and green fields being harvested."

"I saw nothing like that, Lady Meera. The lands I saw had high mountains, jagged cliffs and peaks, with some barren hills. I saw no good harbors, and no signs of life at all. It seemed to go on forever so I turned back."

"You did well. Rest your crew now. Perhaps the Lucky Lady will bring better news."

"Aye, Lady." He saluted then returned to his ship, retrieved his fighters, and moved her back into place within the fleet. The Lucky Lady returned near dawn. She had found the enemy still in their harbor.

Meera and Oona came running from the cabin where they had eventually retired for some sleep. "What news, Dalla?"

"They're still in the harbor," shouted Dalla, as she clambered over the rail of the Raven. "We sailed along the coast until we saw a small town. Dropping our sails and our banners, we kept just on the edge of their vision. None came to greet us or to warn us away, so we continued on. As the day passed we saw a few more towns, but none reacted to our presence. Just as the sun set we found a great harbor filled with ships. They're packed in so tight they can barely move. Better yet, the mouth of the harbor is narrow. We can keep them bottled up in there for years with only a handful of ships."

"Were you seen?"

"Nay, Lady. There seems to be a great celebration or something going on in the town. Lady Meera, that is one big town. It is nearly twice the size of Gapo. There were no guards posted that we could see, and we did go fairly close before we slipped away under cover of darkness. We rowed like demons to get back here by dawn."

"I told you so," came Hant's soft voice from behind them. He was startled and terrified at the speed with which Meera spun and leaped at him. He relaxed a bit as he realized she was smiling.

"Yes you did, Hant," she grinned, as she gave his shoulder a friendly squeeze. "I apologize for my doubts. Can you tell me why there are no guards posted?"

"It is the time of festival, Lady. All feuds are laid aside at this time, so there is no need to guard the harbor. There is a guard post on each of the capes that create the sheltered harbor within, and each will have a catapult, but they won't be manned at this time. At the time of festival everyone will be ashore. Only one slave master and the slaves will still be aboard the ships."

"Hant, my friend. That's the best news you've given me yet. Dalla, how soon can we arrive?"

"If we take our time, and stay out to sea a bit, we should arrive under cover of darkness."

"Then get something to eat, put fresh men to your oars, and lead the way, Captain Dalla."

"I can eat under sail, Lady Meera," laughed Dalla, as she abandoned the Raven for her own ship. She reclaimed her fighters from the Raptor and, with fresh hands to pull the oars, set out with the entire fleet following in her wake.

AFTER THREE STRAIGHT days of revelry, the host of sailors began to return to their ships. It was time to sober up and make ready. A cycle of the moon would see them in the lands of the north, filling the holds of their ships with slaves and booty. They would return by second harvest as rich men. The dawn was clear and bright, but there was a sudden feeling of foreboding spreading among them; and then the alarm horns sounded.

The first men to reach the outer ships were horrified to see a strange fleet just outside the harbor, and both catapults ablaze. That fleet hadn't been there the day before. No one could make out the banners they were flying. One was a green field with a sea monster of some sort, and the other was a green field with a red flower. They didn't look friendly. Slowly one of the strange ships moved forward, stopping just short of entering the harbor.

"Can you hear me?" bellowed Hant, as he stood beside Meera in the bow of the Raven.

"I hear you," came the reply. "Who are you and what do you want here? The festival is over. We are about to sail north. Do you wish to join our fleet?"

"Hear me well," came the voice from the strange ship, "I speak the words of Lady Meera, Queen of all the Isles and Second to Lady Oona herself. Lady Meera says to abandon your ships, and flee into the hills if you wish to live, for the wrath of the northlands is about to fall upon you." At that the ship backed oars and withdrew from the mouth of the harbor.

There was a wild series of screaming shouts from the harbor, but the Raven ignored them completely. "What are they saying, Hant?"

"It does not bear repeating, Lady Meera. They're making many boastful threats of what they will do to you, among other things."

"Threats are easy weapons to wield, but they're not very effective. We'll give them a bit of time to think it over before the fog comes."

"Fog, Lady?"

"Trust me, Hant. Mista will answer my call as readily as Sweet Wind."

"They're coming out," bellowed a voice.

"Battle stations," roared Kieran. Every fighter on the Raven knew his or her place and they took it. Oona was instantly surrounded by Tella as well as Dor and the twins.

"Dor?"

"Yes, Lady Oona?"

"Who are these men?"

"Lady, you know them as well as I."

"Not the slavers," she sighed, "I mean these two men who've become my dear friends and protectors. I know they must have names, but I've never heard them spoken."

"Come to think of it, neither have I," mused Tella.

"The man to your right with the scar under his eye is Ronan. His twin is Conan and I'm Doran. We're of the House of Kellar, Lady Oona, the sons of Turkon and Brenna. This seems a strange time for introductions, if I may be so bold as to say."

"If I'm to die this day, Dor my friend, I would like to know the names of the men who have been so kind to me." The nearest twin made several signs with his hands and Dor broke into a wide grin.

"Ronan says that if you go to the summer land this day, Lady Oona, he will have already gone ahead to clear the path for you."

Tella chuckled at that just as the first ship moved out through the mouth of the harbor. It seemed slow and clumsy compared to a western ship. It barely cleared the harbor when two of the fleet rammed it, one from each side. The westermen were over the sides and onto the enemy's deck before they could right themselves. There were many screams heard above the snarls and barking battle songs of the westermen.

It happened so fast the second ship was out of the harbor before she could stop herself. She met the same fate as the first, a quick trip to the bottom. The rest of the gigantic fleet managed to remain back in the relative safety of the harbor, or so they thought.

Suddenly there was the deep booming of the war drums to set the cadence of the oars. The Raptor sped through the narrows and cut deeply into the enemy fleet, followed closely by several of her fleet mates. They sank several and fought the rest to a standstill. Again the drums sounded, and the Raptor withdrew with her mates. As they left the harbor and moved aside, the Raven and six more drove through the narrows, slamming into the enemy fleet and forcing it closer together, further hampering its ability to defend itself, and then she too, withdrew.

Oona had watched the last from the deck of the Koddok. As the Raven withdrew, Oona was returned to her flagship. The rest of the day was a standoff. No ships attempted to leave the harbor, and none tried to enter. Only the deep booming of the northern war drums was heard; drums like the slow heartbeat of a brooding angry goddess.

The stranger's warning had sped through the fleet long before the end of the day, and under the cover of darkness, many fled the remaining ships. It was well that they did, for, deep in the night, the Hammer of the North struck with a vengeance.

As the sun sank behind the hills, and darkness fell, Meera began her chant. Darkness crawled over the harbor, and then the chill of the mist was felt. Throughout the northern fleet, fighters began to shed their clothing, keeping only a dagger in each boot as well as one between their teeth. "Where are they going?" Oona gasped as she saw Meera strip to join the other men and women.

"They're taking the fight into the harbor, Lady Oona."

"You want to go too, don't you, Tella?"

"As champion I must remain here, Lady."

"As queen, I command that you take Dor, and the boys, and go with Meera. Bring her safely back to me."

"Lady Oona, I..."

"Do it, Tella," sighed Oona, as she hugged Tella gently. "I'll remain here. None will attack me here, Kieran will see to that." With a nod Tella and the boys shed their clothes and joined Meera at the rail.

"I know, Tella. She made you do it. Are we all ready?"

Many torches signaled that all were ready. Every fighter that could be spared was ready to enter the waters. "What about the razor fish?" Oona asked softly.

"Don't worry, Lady Oona. Razor fish are drawn to blood, or to thrashing in the waters of the surface. Our folk swim silently, deep under the waters. Have no fear of the fish."

"If you say so, Kieran. I'll trust that Meera knows what she is doing."

"She does." Suddenly it seemed as though the entire fleet slipped into the water. Oona was still marveling at how the fog that shrouded the harbor didn't appear to exist outside the harbor mouth. All the fighters were gone before she fully realized it. At a signal from Kieran the drums stopped. She waited in silence with Kieran for what seemed like an eternity, and then the screaming began.

THE FOG HAD SETTLED in unnaturally, and every man on the trapped fleet felt uneasy. Scouts sent out along the land had reported that the northern fleet was as vast as their own and bristling with warriors. The two catapults had been burned to the ground. The second group of scouts had not returned, nor had the next. Two ships sunk with ease, several more right inside the safety of the harbor, and now this damned fog. Perhaps it would be wiser to heed the warning and flee into the hills. It wouldn't have been so bad if it wasn't for those damned drums that never seemed to stop; and then they stopped.

Suddenly there were screams and shouts of battle. The snarling barking battle song of the demons could be heard everywhere amid the screams of the terrified and dying. Men fought each other, as well as the enemy crawling from the waters, in their haste to escape the doomed ships. Suddenly there was fire amid the crowded ships and the panic truly set in.

As men fled the doomed harbor, the panic spread into the town. Demons had come to destroy them all. The gods were angry and had sent the demons. Flee to the hills where there was safety from the water demons. Terror spread through the town like wildfire. Hundreds of people were killed or injured trying to escape in the darkness, and then the barking song of death was heard on the land.

The sky was just starting to lighten when there was a sudden wave of fighters clambering over the sides of the ships. Meera was among the last; Tella and the boys with her. Oona threw herself into Meera's arms, tears of relief streaming down her cheeks.

"All is well, my Oona, hush now, all is well, and we are unharmed." Meera gently rocked Oona back and forth.

Meera rested her fighters through the day and the fleet sat bobbing on the waters, just out of reach of the harbor mouth. The slow beat of the drums was a constant reminder to the enemy of the presence of the northern fleet. Only one ship tried to make a run for it. It was sunk as soon as it cleared the headland. As darkness began to fall, Meera once again sang up the mist to shroud the harbor. Once again the fighters slipped over the side. The golden-haired warriors took the headlands and marched right into the town where they waited in silence.

This was a huge town, and there were still many signs of life here. Gurda gripped Lonn's arm tightly and hushed him. The battle rage was taking him over; she wouldn't be able to hold him still for long. Where the blazes were those westermen anyway? Even as she had the thought, Gurda heard the sudden cries of terror from the harbor, mixed with the battle song of the westermen. She released Lonn's arm and the golden-haired warriors exploded into the town with a burning thirst for vengeance.

Oona spent this night much like the last, as she leaned against the rail beside Kieran, listening to the sounds of battle in the harbor. She could see the fires of the burning ships and hear the cries of the terrified men. She actually smiled a little at Meera's battle tactics. Never showing the enemy their faces, but attacking from the waters in the night, was brilliant. The westermen and the Dorand could see in the darkness, and that gave them a huge advantage. Also, coming from the waters made the enemy believe they faced a supernatural foe. Absolutely brilliant.

Dawn came slowly, but it did arrive, and with it came the returning fighters. As usual Meera was among the last to return. Tella had taken a bad wound and it was the twins who bore her back to the Raven and to Oona. Oona placed her hands over the wound and sang a healing song. The bleeding stopped and Tella fell into a deep sleep.

"Take her to the cabin, gentlemen," sighed Oona as she removed her hands from Tella's chest. "Kellan, stay with her and keep her still when she awakens. Our Tella will recover, but she'll need time to rest and heal." Kellan followed the twins as they carried Tella gently into the cabin, tears of relief in his eyes.

"Meera, are you unharmed?"

"Yes, my Lady Healer." Meera took Oona into her arms and held her gently. "I'm sound and safe, Tella took the blow that was meant for me. All is well."

"Then I am content. Lady, can we truly succeed here?"

"I believe we may have already done so, my Oona." Meera sighed, as she released Oona from her arms and sank to a cross-legged sitting position on the deck. "I'm weary unto exhaustion, as are all our fighters, but I believe we have succeeded."

"You must rest now, my Meera." Oona sat behind Meera and pulled her back so she was lying down with her head pillowed in Oona's lap. "Rest now and I'll guard your sleep."

Meera was instantly asleep, and although the business of the ship went on all around her, she didn't awaken until near high sun. She awakened to find her head still pillowed in Oona's lap. "What's going on?" Meera asked as she suddenly leaped to her feet to see the abandoned and burned out ships of the enemy all around the Raven.

"They've abandoned their ships and their town, Lady Meera. They've also abandoned something else."

"What is that, Kieran?" Oona took Meera's hand and rose gracefully to her feet.

"Their slaves, Lady. Come see."

There was a ship as big as the Raven grappled to their gunwales and, with Meera to steady her, Oona stepped easily over to the other ship; it appeared to be deserted. "Kieran?"

"Down here, Lady," grinned Kieran, as he led them below decks. There sat dozens of half-starved and beaten men chained to the rows of benches.

The stench was strong, but Oona bore it as she walked along the pathway between the rows, Meera at her side and the twins right behind them. "Can any of you speak the language of the north?"

"I can," replied several voices.

"Good; now listen carefully. I'm Lady Oona, queen of the Empire of the Isles and Meerasland. This woman is Lady Meera of the House of Lothar, my companion and my Second. It is she who has defeated your former masters. Do you understand?"

"Yes, Lady."

"Very good. Now tell me what has happened here?"

"The demons you sent came in the night, Lady," said a man near her. "They killed many of the masters, then vanished into the waters where the razor fish were feasting. The rest of the masters fled to the shore, leaving us here as a sacrifice to appease the angry gods of the sea."

"Ronan, set them loose and bring them up to the sunlight. Conan, bring Hant to me. Lady Meera, please take me back into the light of day."

"With great pleasure, my Lady Healer."

By the time Oona reached the upper deck again, Conan had already returned with Hant. A few moments later the slaves stood on the deck blinking in the sunlight. "Kieran, are all the ships here abandoned like this one?" asked Oona, as she turned to her fleet commander.

"Aye, Lady Oona, every last one of them."

"Can we use them?"

"We can, Lady Oona, and we must. We lost a few of our own, and still more were left in the Isles. We can certainly use these ships."

"How many are there?"

"We sank the best part of them, but there are at least two hundred still seaworthy."

"Two hundred? Do we have enough people to man them all?"

"It'll be tight, but we'll manage."

"Perhaps we can recruit some help." They had been speaking in the language of the isles, and as she turned back to the slaves, she saw their confused stares. They hadn't understood a single word that had been said.

"All you men who were of the north, step forward." They did so. "We're returning to the north, you may come with us if you like."

"Lady? We're your slaves now, Lady. We go where you wish us to go."

"Hear me well, there are no longer any slaves in the lands of the north. That land is now called Meerasland, and it is ours. If you wish to return to your homes, and live in peace, you may do so. First you must swear loyalty to me, and to Lady Meera. If you prefer not to do that, you may go ashore here and live as you will."

"Lady, if it means I can go home and live in peace, I'll gladly swear loyalty to you and your companion," said one man as he dropped to his knees before Oona. The others followed his example.

"Then I accept you. You're my men now, and you will obey my commands. This man is Kieran. He will find work for you to do until we get you home. Now, Hant, can you speak to these other men?"

"Yes, Lady, I can make them understand me."

"Tell them to gather at the docks there. Tell them they are to be set free and will be allowed to go where they will. I want them to remain at the docks for now so our fighters don't harm them by mistake. Go to all the ships and deliver this message to all the slaves you find."

As the men set about their tasks, Meera took Oona back to the Raven where they slowly ate a small meal. Suddenly Meera spotted a huge crowd of people on the docks. "Oona, is that you mother with those people at the shore?"

"Yes, Lady. My oath, what is she doing?"

Gurda was trying to signal them to come ashore. Slowly the Raven made her way through the captured ships to the docks, where Gurda was waiting with a throng of people. "Oona, Lady Oona, Lady Meera. Look who we have here," she shouted as the Raven drew near. "We found the slave pens full to the brim."

"What?" Oona looked a bit bemused as she and Meera stepped ashore.

"Apparently they were going to have a big slave auction before they went north. They fled the town leaving all the slaves behind. We set them free, Oona, we set them free."

Gurda suddenly gulped and jumped backwards as Ronan leaped at her with a short sword drawn. He shook a warning finger at her then pointed to Oona. Gurda grinned sheepishly as she got the message. "Forgive me, Lady Oona. In all the excitement, I forgot myself."

"You are forgiven, Mother," chuckled Oona. "Ronan, stop frightening my mother." He grinned and made a hand sign to her. Oona slapped his arm and told him to behave.

Just then, Tallon and Hekkat came pushing their way through the crowd. Tallon called out to them as they came. "Lady Oona, Lady Meera. My friend Hekkat has a gift for you."

"Tell me, Hekkat," smiled Oona, as they arrived and saluted her.

"Hekkat and Dorand go this way," he replied as he waved his arm to show where he had been. "Find many big buildings, many fighters there to protect. Good fight, but many defenders. Friend Tallon come help Hekkat, all good. Defenders run away."

"What was in the buildings, Hekkat?" Meera asked, a smile playing at her lips.

"Tallon say."

"The harvest, Lady. The storehouses were full to the brim with a fresh harvest. We'll need every ship we have, and more, to carry it all back with us."

"That is a mighty gift indeed. What are your desires now, my Lady Healer?"

Oona smiled to see Kellan and Kieran arriving with Hant in tow. They saluted as they approached her. "Kellan, take what men you need and empty those storehouses into our ships. Hekkat can lead you to them. Kieran, take Tallon with you and share out the new ships between your two fleets as you both see fit. Kieran, once the ships are loaded, pillage the town for whatever else you think might be useful, then burn it to the ground. Quickly now people, I want to go home as soon as possible."

"Aye, Lady Oona." They saluted and swiftly set about their appointed tasks.

"Hant, bring me a man of this land from among the slaves."

"I have something better, Lady Oona." Hant had a snarl on his face as his gaze bore into the crowd. A man suddenly bolted from the throng and tried to flee. He did not get far as Lonn was on him in a heartbeat. Lonn dragged the hapless man before Oona and threw him to the ground at her feet.

"Hant, who is this?"

"My master's son, Lady Oona. A most cruel and vicious man is he."

"Ask him how he came to be here." Hant spoke but the man just spat at him.

"He was found unconscious, Lady," said one of Gurda's men. "We thought him just another slave."

"Good, then he is just the man I want. Put a bag over his head, he is unworthy to see my face." It was instantly done.

"My Lady Healer," said Meera softly, in the language of the Isles, "this is unworthy."

"Sometimes things must be done that are unworthy." Oona spoke gently as she gazed deeply into Meera's eyes. "Just as I have always trusted you, I beg you now, trust me. The thing I am about to do has a purpose."

"Forgive me, my Oona. I simply didn't want you to have regrets for an impulsive action. I'll trust you, as you've always trusted me."

"Thank you, my Meera." Oona turned back to the gathered crowd and switched back into the language of the north. "Strip off his clothing. Ronan, heat a blade in fire. Hant, translate my words for this man, all of them."

As the man was stripped and blindfolded, Hant translated Oona's words. A torch was lit and Ronan heated up his short sword until it glowed red then he passed it to her. Oona stepped up to the prisoner and spoke. "This is close to the first pain a young girl feels when she is taken slave," she said in a cold deadly voice. Hant translated her words and the man stiffened. He screamed in pain and terror, his body jerking horribly as she pressed the hot iron to his genitals and held it there.

"When I was taken slave by your people, I was abused by every man of the crew. That pain went on all night." Oona's voice was cold and completely without emotion. Hant continued to translate. "This is the second pain a slave feels when she is captured." Hant translated again and the man screamed once more as she put the hot iron to his chest.

Oona passed the sword back to Ronan then indicated that the man's blindfold should be removed. As his eyes showed their fear and hate for her, Oona pulled back her tunic to show the ugly brand on her breast. "I have now returned to you the pain that was given me so long ago. Be grateful the years of pain and humiliation that followed will not be your fate." Hant dutifully translated for her.

"You will now go to the hills and find your people. Take this message to them for me. Your people have taken their last slave from the north. Heed this well. Don't make me come back again, for I will not be merciful the next time. If I return, none will survive, not a man, woman, beast, nor child. All will feel the hot iron before death embraces them. Now go!" Hant translated then the man was set free, although several of the newly freed slaves struck savage blows at him as he ran past them.

As the man ran from the terrifying Oona, Meera saw the trembling in her companion's shoulders. She gently took Oona by the hand and led her back aboard the Raven, where she ensconced her in the cabin with Tella. "Stay here and rest, my Oona," she whispered softly. "I'll see to the rest of it for you."

"Please, Meera, stay with me a moment." Oona suddenly lost the battle to control her emotions and she wept. Meera held her gently until she cried herself to sleep.

Homeward Bound

It had taken two full days to load the ships and delegate new crews and captains. Over a hundred former slaves who'd been taken from the north, swore loyalty to Oona and joined the fleet. Three ships had been given to the former slaves from other lands, so they might find their way home. They left the harbor and turned south even as the great fleet turned north.

The first thing Oona had done upon boarding the Raptor was to heal young Drado's wounded shoulder. She now stood at the rail of the Raptor, watching the huge town burn behind them. There would be little enough for the former slave masters to return to.

"Share your thoughts, my Lady Healer?" asked a soft voice, as gentle arms enfolded Oona from behind.

"I was just hoping that those fires burning down, would signal the last of our wars. I grow so very weary of it all. I want to go home and help the people plant crops."

"It is far too late in the season for that now, my Oona. We can help them rebuild their homes, and harvest what crops they have managed to plant themselves. For those who have no crop to harvest, we can share what we took from the slavers. Will this do?"

"It'll do nicely, my Meera." Oona cuddled deeper into Meera's arms. "Mmm, I have always felt so safe here in your arms, Lady Meera."

"Then you must stay there, my Oona. Tell me now, what else is on your mind."

"What else?"

"Come now, my Lady Healer. I know you too well. There's something on your mind. Share with Meera now."

"If I must," giggled Oona. "I was thinking of how we can renew the royal bloodline of the isles."

"Oona?"

"You know as well as I that it must be done, Lady. It must be done to complete the sense of safety for all the people we are sworn to protect."

"Yes, my Oona, I do agree. Do you wish to choose another companion?"

Startled, Oona spun in Meera's arms and looked deeply into her eyes. She saw the hurt and resignation there, and tears sprang to her eyes. "Absolutely not, Meera. You promised to keep me near you, and that is exactly what I want. You're my chosen companion and I beg you to remain so forever."

"Then it shall be as you require, my Lady healer. Forgive me, but as I cannot give you children, I wondered if you might..." Oona placed her finger on Meera's lips to silence her.

"Stop now, my Meera. It's of your bloodline that I speak, not mine."

"What???"

"Yours is the blood royal..."

"No Lady, you are the First. It is you who must continue the bloodline."

"Actually, I have a much better idea," grinned Oona. "One that I believe will satisfy the old traditions, as well as bring new life to the line."

"Oona?"

"Listen now, my delight. Consider that we both might bear children. That would renew your line as well as add my own."

"So, you propose that a child of mine and a child of yours unite to renew the old traditions?"

"That was my thought. I won't force this upon you, my beloved. If you don't wish it, we won't."

"Is it your wish that we do?"

"Meera, it would be a great loss to the world if you don't pass along all the nobility and grace that you possess. It would be a great loss to the people, and as much as I would dislike having to share you with another for a time,..."

"There is also the other."

"The other?"

"Since the first time you fell asleep in my arms, Oona, I have desired no other to be there. I, too, would not be happy about sharing you with another but I, too, believe that you bring much to the empire. Perhaps this is the only way we can truly have a child that is part of us both."

"Then you'll consider it?"

"I see the wisdom of this, my Oona. I'll consider it. Have you chosen our paramour as yet?"

"What???"

"Have you decided who is to give us these children?"

"I was hoping you might have some thoughts on this."

"Before this moment I hadn't ever given this sort of thing a single thought. The only man I ever wanted to bring me children was murdered before my eyes many years past. Since then I've given this no thought at all. Have you given it any thought?"

"You know well my history, Lady Meera. I have never in my life given myself to a man willingly, nor have I ever wished to. If there were another way I'd be content, but I have questioned poor Tella unto madness about this, and here we are.

"Since the death of my father at the hands of the slavers, Kellan was the first man to show me gentleness and kindness. He loves you like his own too, Meera, you know this to be true. I can't name the number of times he held you and wept as the poison coursed through your body. Would Kellan be acceptable to you?"

"As chieftain of the strongest house, and since there are no living male relatives close enough, Kellan would be a good choice, but there is one problem."

"And that is?"

"Tella would skin the both of us alive just for thinking it," giggled Meera.

"Tella would skin you both for thinking what?" asked Tella's voice right behind them. Oona shrieked and Meera leaped away, blushing furiously. "Confess all to Momma Tella now, what were you two thinking?"

"Well, you see, it's like this."

"You're thinking my poor Kellan might be a good choice to extend the royal bloodline?"

"How did you know?"

"You're not as subtle as you might believe, Lady Oona, my dear friend. Your questions over the past few cycles have made it pretty clear what you might be thinking. As for me, I think it is a fine idea. Kellan is a sturdy lad. He should have enough strength left in him for the task."

"Tella? Tella, what are you saying?" asked Meera softly, as she pulled Tella into her arms. Oona, too, put her arms around Tella as tears filled Tella's eyes.

"I took a deep wound when I was quite young," she whispered softly. "There will be no children for me. Listen carefully now, it falls to the guardian to do much of the child rearing in a royal household. I would seriously like you to consider me for that task. Dor will make Lady Oona a fine champion. I..."

"It shall be as you require, Tella." whispered Meera as she hugged Tella gently.

"I agree completely. Alright, now we come to the hardest question of all."

"And that is?"

"Which of us is going to inform Kellan?" giggled Oona.

"Oh my dear, Lady Oona. That task truly must fall to the First."

"Oh really? Alright then, so be it." She raised her arm and made a sign. Ronan instantly leaped to his feet. Another signal and he fetched Tallon who was asked to bring Kellan from the Raven.

Kellan arrived to find the three women smiling at him wickedly. "Why do I feel I am about to be sacrificed?"

"Because you are," replied Oona. "Kellan, my dear friend, since the very first, you have always been at the forefront to defend me and the empire. Once again, I must call upon your loyalty and service."

"My Lady Oona, ask what you will of me. If it is within my power I shall make it happen for you."

"Oh you have the power alright; I can attest to that," grinned Tella, as she took his arm and led him toward the cabin. "Be a good lad now and listen, the Ladies Oona and Meera have a mighty task for you." She led him inside the cabin with Meera and Oona close behind.

"Ladies, are you quite certain of this?" Kellan asked as soon as Oona had finished explaining what they had in mind.

"On the day we met, Kellan, Tallon said that if I came to you with a willing heart..."

"Kellan, you are closer to me than any other man since the loss of my sweet Garnor. If you won't help me, then there will be no other, for you know well that I can't bear the touch of a man."

"I know, Lady Meera, I know."

"Since I was taken as a girl, I haven't ever known a kindness from a man until the day we met, Kellan. I need that gentle kindness for this. Please help me."

Kellan was blushing furiously as he looked to Tella who just shook her head sadly. "I can't bear your child and well you know it, Kellan my heart. These two will be far too busy ruling an empire, so the child rearing will fall mainly to me. This is my one chance to rear your children, Kellan. Come on now, you're the chieftain. Hold up the honor of your house." Meera and Oona began to giggle and Kellan blushed furiously.

"Ladies, will you not reconsider?"

"We will not," sighed Meera. "You must help us, dear friend."

"Then, as you say, I shall endeavor to uphold the honor of my house."

"Stay here with Tella now, Kellan," smiled Oona, as she stood to leave. "I'll inform Tallon that you'll remain on the Raptor to attend to Tella's needs as she recovers from her wounds." She patted his shoulder as she and Meera left him alone with Tella.

"Tella?"

She sighed as she laid her head on his shoulder. "It's the only way for me, my beloved. These are great women, and with your strength added, they'll bring new power to the bloodline. The people will be safe for another thousand generations. I love them both as sisters and you know it. All is well."

"Tella, you know that without your blessing I..."

"I know. There is no betrayal here, my Kellan. I'll lie with you all and all will be as it should be."

FOR THE REST OF THE voyage north to Meerasland, Kellan shared the cabin with the three women. A moon cycle after leaving the slavers' town in flames they sighted Meerasland again. There was a long coast with thick forests stretching out before them. As they passed by a deep harbor the Koddok approached the Raptor and Hekkat came aboard. "This good land," he said as he saluted Oona. "Many trees, no people, good hunting, many fish, good harbors. This place for Dorand?"

"Is this where you want to settle, Hekkat?"

"This good place for Dorand. Dorand ships keep slavers away. Ladyee Oona say?"

"Oona say. Send a ship north to me every moon cycle until the snows come. Ship bring news, Oona send news on ship. All good?"

"All good. Hekkat leave ships here, follow Ladyee Oona in Koddok to place where other Dorand ships were left behind. All good."

"All good, Hekkat, all good. We hope Dorand prosper here, stay friends."

"All Dorand Ladyee Oona folk now, all good all time." He turned and leaped back to his own ship. Signals were soon sent and the Dorand fleet swept into a deep harbor, leaving the Koddok to follow the Raptor north.

The fleet sailed on until they reached Oona's former home. Kreeg awakened to the sight of a fleet, larger than he had ever imagined, floating just offshore. He pulled on his best tunic and called his men. They took the largest fishing boat and rowed out to the fleet. He was swiftly directed to the Raptor.

"Lady Meera," said the huge Trog, as he reached the deck and knelt.

"This woman is Lady Oona, Kreeg. Lady Oona is First among us now. It is she that you owe your allegiance to."

"Lady Oona?"

"You are Kreeg."

"I am, Lady."

"You now command that which was my former home. Are my people well and free?"

"Ask them for yourself." He turned to the small boat and barked an order. "Come up."

Eight men, all human, swarmed over the side and onto the deck where they all dropped to one knee as Kreeg had taught them. "Lady Meera," they said in unison.

"This woman is Lady Oona. She is First among us, and as such it is to her that you owe your allegiance."

Startled they looked at the woman with the golden curls and they knew her. One man started to speak, "Por,," but Kreeg's huge paw struck him a blow that sent him flying. "Proper respect," he growled, "you know better."

"Lady Oona," they said in unison.

"I see that you remember me. If I ever hear that hateful name from your lips again there will be bodies hanging from the yardarm of this ship. Do I make myself perfectly clear?"

"Yes, Lady, very clear."

"You there, Gran, tell me the fate of the people under Kreeg's command."

"His rule is hard, Lady, but it's fair. All in all we have better lives than under Born, and we're much safer." Oona nodded her head, satisfied.

"The killing of Broc was a great favor to me, Kreeg. I am well pleased. Know you also, that his brother Born is dead as well. We hanged him from the castle walls. He will not return to this place. Commander Kreeg, what would you have of me as a reward?"

"A ship, Lady Oona."

"Why?"

"To help defend ourselves, and so we can send messages to you."

"For help if an enemy comes."

"Yes."

"Commander Kreeg, several days south of this place, you will find a new people. They're smaller, but tough and smart. Send men to them to learn how to build the ships and to help them build homes. In return they'll use their ships to patrol your coastline. This man is Hekkat. Hekkat is the chieftain of the Dorand."

Hekkat stepped up to the huge Trog and grinned. "Long time gone, your folk, my folk, friend. One time you fight beside Dorand.

You send men help Dorand build new homes, Dorand ships keep coast safe for Kreeg folk. Ladyee Oona say, Dorand do. Lady Oona say, Kreeg do."

Kreeg eyes the smaller creature for a long moment then decided to trust him. There was something almost feral about this Hekkat, and Kreeg liked that about the Dorand. "Agreed," he rumbled. "Your folk will teach us to build ships, and we will teach you how to defend your homes on land."

"That's a good offer, Hekkat," laughed Kellan. "There is none better than a Trog at defending a castle."

"Agreed." Hekkat offered his hand to the Trog, who gripped it in the warrior's grip.

"Commander Kreeg. There will be no supplies required of you this season if you help the Dorand."

"Agreed," rumbled Kreeg, "and thank you, Lady Oona." The visit was swiftly concluded and, well pleased, Kreeg returned to his castle while the fleet continued on north to the land of the great wheel.

Upon reaching the mouth of the great river, Hekkat took his leave and, with the last of his people, set out for the new lands Oona had given to him. Hekkat was well pleased with the results of this season. They had gone northwest in search of a home or to face certain death. They had indeed found a home, and Oona had left three of the supply ships with him to help his people through the coming winter. As Hekkat would say, it was all good.

By this time more than a moon cycle had passed since leaving the south, and Oona and Meera both lost all interest in a morning meal. It seemed quite unusual, but no one made mention of it. The garrison was replenished, young Konnor returned to his family, and the former slaves of the south were set ashore to go their own way.

Many days later, the massive fleet entered the harbor at the place of the ancients. Everyone came out to meet them, and Oona squealed with delight as she swept Bekka into her arms. "Lady Oona, it is so good to see you again," smiled Toole, as she managed to get through the throng.

"It is good to be home at last, Toole," Oona smiled, as she hugged her friend. "Look who I've brought with me."

"Lady Meera, it is a miracle. We dared not hope."

"I know, Toole, but all is well now, thanks to, my Lady Healer." The golden-haired folk were greeted royally as well. Lonn swore he would split if they didn't stop feeding him.

After several days of feasting, Oona called her advisers together in the great hall. "People, we must stop eating long enough to get some work done. Kieran, gather Gurda and her folk. Take them to retrieve the rest of their people, then take them all to the Isles. I'm sure Tarn can find them a safe place for them to begin anew."

"Aye, Lady, how many ships?"

"Take fifty ships and ten shiploads of supplies. Remain in the Isles and see what you can do to help Tarn there. I'm sure he can use the extra ships."

"Will you be needing the Raven, Lady?"

"She is your ship, Kieran. Take her and go. We'll come to the isles next spring. We can retrieve her then."

"Aye, Lady," replied Kieran, as he turned to go.

"Kieran," called Oona, and he turned to catch her in his arms. "Fare well my friend," she smiled, as she lightly kissed his cheek. "Be well until we meet again in the spring."

He smiled broadly as he left the hall to get on the go. Meera knew quite well Kellan and Kieran's mother was ill, and Kieran was more than happy to be banished back to the isles for the winter.

As Kieran left the hall, Oona turned to Tallon. "My dear friend, last year I laid a hard task upon you, and you didn't fail me. I now have another for you."

"Your wish is my command, Lady Oona."

"Leave a few ships here, Tallon, but we shall take the bulk of the fleet and return to all the places that you visited earlier this year. We shall see what we can do to repair the damage there, and to help those who can't help themselves. We'll take several supply ships with us as well. When we find those who have no place to go or no home we will be able to set them up again, or find places for them."

"Lady Oona, it's with great pleasure that I accept this task. There's just one small thing before I begin…"

"Get out," laughed Oona. "Tallon, I don't want to hear it. Go, go prepare the fleet." Laughing, he turned to leave the hall. "Tallon," called Oona as he reached the door. "What was it?"

"Take care of my sisters, Ladies," he laughed, as he ran through the doors and escaped into the sunshine of the day.

"What did he mean by that?" a voice asked softly, but Meera heard it.

"Good people; hear me now." The entire hall fell silent. "I have great news for the future of the empire. Both Lady Oona and I are carrying the next generation of the blood royal. The line will continue. To dispel any questions of line, be it known that the Chieftain of the House of Kellar has done his duty to the empire. All is well." There was a great round of cheering at that, much to Kellan's embarrassment.

A CYCLE LATER OONA lay cuddled in Meera's arms, nearly asleep. She could feel the new life within her as well as the rocking of the Raptor, and she smiled. In one short year she had lived a lifetime. It was her great hope that the next number of years would be years of peace in which she could teach her son or daughter the ways of a healer. Meera felt the restlessness in her and spoke softly.

"Lady Oona, is all well with you?"

"Yes, my beloved, all is well."

"Are you certain? I feel a restlessness in you. Perhaps I could..."

"Meera," laughed Oona. "Behave yourself."

"As you wish, my Oona, but if you have need..."

"Stop, for pity's sake stop. Go to sleep, Lady Badness."

"As you command, my Lady Healer," Meera smiled as she cuddled Oona closer. "But if..."

"Meera, hush."

"But,"

"Hush, that's an order." Oona sealed her lips with a kiss. Meera moaned with delight and pulled her closer.

The End

N ow take a peek into another lost world:

S.U.V.I

by

Prudence MacLeod

(second edition)

Forgotten World

On a far-off alien world, a near naked woman sat on a cold cell floor, her eyes closed, her posture serene, patiently waiting for that cell door to open for the last time. How did she get there? It began this way.

In the year of 2221, old Earth reckoning, the first of the five great ships set out. Each ship carried ten thousand settlers, all highly skilled, extremely intelligent, people who were anxious to extend mankind's reach into the galaxy.

They all believed they would be in constant contact with the rest of the colonies, but that's not what happened. Soon after the third ship was launched, a war devastated Earth. The last two ships barely made it into open space. There were few survivors left on the home planet, and they didn't last long.

The man whose vision the great ships were, had foreseen this, and hatched a plot in secret. Each colony was dropped off then abandoned forever with no way off the world on which they had landed. Mankind had been seeded into the galaxy, and the visionary's hope was, even if only a few of the colonies managed to survive, mankind would continue to exist.

He had no way to know if he had succeeded or not, but he had. The great ships, once they'd dropped off the colonists, returned to Earth for another group of settlers, but they found it devastated and uninhabitable.

They gathered at a single ship, chose one by lots, then robbed the other four for fuel and supplies. The idea was to find a new planet to start a colony of their own from the combined crews. Mankind had perished on the home world, but lived on, alone in forgotten places.

That is, until the one ship returned. The one ship had wandered for many years until the captain gave up the search and returned to where he'd dropped off his original colonists, hoping they would welcome more settlers. It didn't go as he'd planed.

Chapter #1

SUVI

Farouk Bladon sighed and stared at the display screen. "So, the great ship returns."

"Yes, First Prime," said Jonah Thornton, the small man beside him. "It draws closer as we speak. There's no doubt it's returning at last. Sir, what should we do?"

Farouk seemed lost in thought. "Hmm? Do? I think we should welcome them, don't you?"

"But, Sir, what if they've brought more colonists?"

"Then we welcome them as well, they can decide for themselves what to do once we've gone. Bring SUVI 5 to me. We'll hold a feast; she can provide the meat. Tell her to wear her hunting gear."

"At once, First Prime." The man hurried away.

Farouk returned his gaze to the screen. Yes, there was no doubt, the ship would reach a docking orbit within hours. He wondered what those people on the ship would think when they found the original colony deserted. It should prove interesting."

Smiling, he turned to the other man in the room, a man wearing only a loincloth and carrying a bladed weapon. "Nineteen, my friend, destiny has smiled upon us this day. Once SUVI 5 is on her way, prepare your troops, they will be needed soon." He returned his gaze to the screen, a cold smile playing at his lips.

THE LOCK CLICKED OPEN, and the cell door swung wide. The near naked woman sitting cross-legged on the bare floor didn't even look up. Her eyes were closed, and she was taking deep slow breaths. Jonah Thornton shuddered then squared his shoulders and spoke. "SUVI 5, by the command of the First Prime you will don hunting gear and return to the scanner room with me. He wishes to speak to you."

She opened those glowing amber eyes. He swallowed the lump of fear in his throat as he watched those eyes slowly return to their natural green. "If I'm to hunt I'll need weapons, Second Prime."

"You'll collect your weapons before you transport to the surface, as always. You know full well you can't carry weapons in the presence of the First Prime."

"As you command," she replied as she rose and dropped her loincloth to the floor. She reached for the folded leathers on the shelf beside her and pulled on the breeks, chaps, and jerkin that she wore when hunting. She pushed her feet into thick moccasins then followed him out of the cell.

Jonah led her back to the observation room, nervously fingering the controller in his hand. He was terrified of this woman and, even though he knew full well the pain collar fastened around her neck would make her compliant, allow him to control her, he was still soaked in sweat. "First Prime, SUVI 5."

Farouk turned to give her an oily smile. "Come closer, SUVI 5. See that blip on this screen? That's the great ship, it's finally returned. I wish to have a celebration, a feast for the ship's officers. You will go to the surface and acquire meat for the feast. No small rodents now, kill something big enough to feed a few dozen people. Go now, and hunt well."

She turned and started away, but his voice called her back. "SUVI 5, do not fail me."

"As you command," she replied, showing no emotion at all, and strode away.

The woman stepped into the corridor and from there into another room where she approached a glowing platform. SUVI 19 was waiting there with her weapons, two large daggers, nothing more. She was not trusted with more, yet she was still their most successful hunter. A look of understanding passed between them as she accepted the knives from his hand, then she stepped onto the platform. There was a flash of light and she was suddenly standing on a similar platform on the planet's surface.

Drawing a deep breath of fresh air for the first time in days, SUVI 5 stepped off the platform and smiled. For the moment she was free. They wouldn't call her back until she'd completed the hunt, and she was in no hurry. Knowing they couldn't see her, she grinned with delight as she pulled the two long sharp spears from their hiding place. Excited by the destiny she sensed nearing, and ready for a run in the open air, SUVI 5 set out for the hunt.

"WE'VE ACHIEVED STANDARD orbit, Captain Baris."

"Thank you, Helmsman. Maintain Orbit. Commander Volkov, how do things look down there?"

"Dead," was the curt reply.

"What???"

"Sir, there's nothing moving down there. Place looks like it's been deserted for a long time. The habitats are completely grown over, most have been broken open. There's not a single sign of human ... wait, I've got something. There's a woman, looks like a primitive human. Sir, that looks a lot like a T-Rex chasing her."

"What??? Good Christ, get her up here, now. I'll be in the transportation bay." The order was relayed as the captain hurried from the bridge and down the corridor to the transport room. He burst through the door. "Where is she?"

"She's moving too fast, Captain; I can't get a lock on her. Shit, that things's caught up to her."

The ten people in the room held their breath as they watched the screen. The monstrous beast reached for the fleeing woman. Just as the jaws were about to close on her she dropped to the ground and braced the butt of her spear. The animal impaled itself on that shaft and the woman scrambled away as it snapped in two.

The beast was bleeding profusely, but far from dead. "Got her!" exulted the man at the controls as he threw the switch to transport her to the ship. Unfortunately, at that moment the animal charged.

The woman arrived in the transport room, but so did the beast. It attacked instantly, biting one security man in half while ripping the arm off the other. It whipped around, its tail knocking down three more people, but the woman was on its back now, her knives slashing at its throat. The animal leaped and bucked, trying to dislodge the creature that clung to it, but to no avail.

Blood sprayed everywhere, people screamed and scrambled away as best they could, and the woman kept slashing with her knives. Slowly the beast began to tire, the blood loss was taking its toll. It stopped moving and just stood still but the woman didn't stop slashing until the animal collapsed to the floor. The warrior wiped her blades on the dead animal then sheathed those deadly knives.

"Should be out of reach now," she said as she grasped the strange collar at her neck, "if not I'll lay dead beside this garog, for I'll be a slave no longer."

With a primal scream her muscles lurched, the veins on her forehead and neck stood out, throbbing. She grunted with effort as those mighty muscles writhed and bunched, and then the metal parted with a sizzle and snap of electrical connections being torn and metal breaking.

With a wild shout of joy, she threw aside the broken collar and whipped out her daggers. She took a stride towards the captain who swallowed hard, his eyes wide with fear, but she dropped the knives to the floor and knelt before him.

"Captain Baris, it's good to see you again. I'm afraid I've lost my ball, so we'll have to wait for another time to resume our game."

Don't miss out!

Visit the website below and you can sign up to receive emails whenever Prudence MacLeod publishes a new book. There's no charge and no obligation.

https://books2read.com/r/B-A-ZKBBB-EEEAD

BOOKS 2 READ

Connecting independent readers to independent writers.

Also by Prudence MacLeod

Children of the Goddess
Lady Blue
Fallen Angel
Lady Justice
Lady Shadow
Lady Seeker
Watcher and Warrior
Shadow Ascending

Children of the Wild
Immortal Tigress
Children of the Wolf
Vampire's Lair
The Hawk and the Wolf
The Oregon Incident
Race the Wind
Heir to the Throne

Elvish Chronicles
Rise of the Queen

The Road Home
A Winter Seige

Forgotten Worlds
Suvi
Echo of the Past
Survivors
Ship
Fleet
Unite
IGEN
T.E.N.

Nova series
Novan Witch
Assassin of Nova
Beyond Nova
Claimstake
Red Nova

Standalone
The Second

Watch for more at https://www.prudencemacleod.com/.

Telling a story is like knitting a sweater. Start with a ball of possibilities, pull out one small thread and begin. With luck and patience you will create something quite wonderful.

About the Author

On a far off windswept island Jennifer Crandall sits with her dogs and cats creating fantastic stories for all to enjoy. She publishes as JL Crandall, Prudence MacLeod, and Jenni Leigh.

Read more at https://www.prudencemacleod.com/.

www.ingramcontent.com/pod-product-compliance
Lightning Source LLC
Chambersburg PA
CBHW020231260626
47156CB00002B/635